BLUE MOON

TESS THOMPSON

United States, 2016

This is a work of fiction. Names, characters, places, brands, media, and incidents are either the product of the author's imagination or are used fictitiously. Any resemblance to similarly named places or to persons living or deceased is unintentional.

For Maria Petrone Palmer (Petronie), a true and generous friend, for more years than either of us care to admit.

BLUE MOON

noun
1.
the second full moon occurring within a calendar month
2.
(informal) once in a blue moon, very rarely; almost never

CHAPTER 1

UNDER A CLOSE OREGON SKY the color of white marble, I clicked along the sidewalks of downtown Portland in my black high-heeled boots, pulling my ultrafine merino wool jacket tight against my chest. It was cold, instead of our customary mild rain. Not a drop shed for at least twenty-four hours. No umbrellas. No mist to curl my hair up on one side and down on the other. On a typical November morning, umbrellas float in the air above their owners, almost touching but just missing, like bubbles in a champagne glass. They hide and protect us from the rain and also from one another, making us distinguishable only by the pattern, width and color of our bumbershoots.

Temperatures had dropped the day before to below freezing, icing over highways, streets and sidewalks. This might have been an indication that something dramatic was about to shift in the trajectory of my life, but I couldn't see clearly back then. Like a racehorse with blinders, shiny and groomed, muscles primed for speed, mind focused and ready, I had no view other than what was right in front of me, striding without hesitation the five blocks from my condominium building to my office. With my figurative blinders on I paid little attention to the weather or anything around me except for the need and subsequent retrieval of my leather gloves that normally spooned happily with my business cards in the side pocket of a Kate Spade purse, both waiting for their usefulness.

After tugging the gloves over my manicured hands, I tucked the cards back into the side pocket. I'd need them later for a cocktail networking event where I would meet hundreds of people I didn't know and didn't especially want to know, dressed in various-hued business suits, all the while trying not to cringe when I said my name. *Bliss Heywood*. Bliss does not sound like the name of a CEO, a shark, a mover and shaker. Bliss is the name of an unfortunate soul born in the early seventies to a hippie mother and spineless father. Like Johnny Cash's *Boy Named Sue*, I've spent most of my life fighting to prove I am no Bliss.

A gust of cold wind stung my ears and travelled up my skirt, the warmth of the hot yoga class I'd taken before work a distant memory. The streets of downtown Portland were narrow and congested. Buildings made of brick and concrete hinted at a simpler era when this river town was the home of rugged longshoremen working the swift waters of the Willamette. Statues of Portland's own Beverly Cleary's characters peppered the sidewalks: Henry and Ramona and Beezuz— all friends from my youth, when I spent a majority of time with my nose in a book. Today, despite the cold, sidewalks bustled with business people in suits and shiny shoes; young adults with piercings, tattoos and unwashed hair waiting for public transit; and mothers pushing strollers while wearing those horribly ugly comfortable leather shoes the women in the Pacific Northwest are so fond of.

I reached my office building and stopped at the foot of the stairs, searching for Sam and Sweetheart. They weren't in their usual spot. My chest tightened as I scanned the street, suddenly feeling the cold. Had the weather driven them away? Where would they go? Were they hurt? But I needn't have worried. They were tucked under a blanket just inside the space between the buildings, seeking shelter from the wind, no doubt. I walked toward them, reaching into my purse and pulling out a five-dollar bill from the inner zipper pocket where I kept my "Sam money." At the beginning of every month I walked into my local bank and asked for enough cash for every business day of the month in five-dollar bills. Not knowing if it would be safe to give it to him all at once, I gave him only five dollars at a time, except for Friday when I gave him enough to carry him through the weekend.

Sam, bearded and dirty, dressed in layers and layers of clothes regardless of the season, lived on the streets with Sweetheart, his three-legged border collie. He carried a tin coffee can with a simple note attached to it: "Sam and Sweetheart." I wasn't sure where he went at night, but every morning he was at the steps of my office building with

Sweetheart and his can. I wanted to ask him where he slept and how he ate and so many other questions, but it was futile. Sam was mute.

I caught his gaze and smiled before leaning over to pet Sweetheart. And that dog! She never let me down. At the first sight of me, the little black and white furry love machine always ambled onto her three legs and wagged her tail so fiercely it might have knocked over a small child. Today was no different. I scratched behind her ears, taking off one of my gloves so she could lick my fingers, before reaching into my coat pocket for a doggie treat. I had no idea what Sam did with the money I gave him—booze or food. I hoped it was food, of course, for Sweetheart and himself. He certainly never appeared intoxicated or drugged. Sweetheart, when I felt the space near her ribs, seemed perfectly fit.

I know what people would say about this small and perhaps foolish gesture of kindness. I did it to assuage my guilt because I had so much and he had so little. I understand this sentiment, but it wasn't exactly true. I know some might say, too, that there are better ways to give back, through charity donations and foundations. I understood this to be true, of course, and having come from poverty I gave generously every year to several charities for underprivileged youth and battered women. But this was different. This was personal.

There was Sweetheart, of course. She was special. Anyone could see that. Animals, especially dogs, were much easier for me to be around than people. They seemed to understand what I needed without having to ask. It had been on my list for years to get a dog of my own, but I knew it wouldn't be fair to them because I traveled frequently. I couldn't bear thinking of a dog alone for half the month, or worse, stuck in a kennel.

And Sam? Well, the truth is, he reminded me of my late father. Mostly it was his eyes, faded blue and unfocused like he wasn't sure whether he knew you for a second or two, until several rapid blinks brought recognition.

I leaned over and dropped the money in his can. He put his hand over his heart; the corners of his mouth twitched. This was his way of expressing gratitude. I understood.

I met his eyes, watery today from the cold, and red-rimmed. Sad, defeated. They conjured the father that I knew mostly from photographs, as he'd died when I was nine years old. Blythe says he was kind but overwhelmed, that even his ordinary life proved too much for him. She'd recently told me she wondered if his car accident was really an accident. When she brought it up, I waved away the question and made an excuse to get off the phone. I prefer dogs and mute homeless men to hard questions from the sister I adore.

"Sam, I'm worried about the weather. It's supposed to get even colder. Do you have a warm place to sleep tonight?"

He nodded and pulled Sweetheart closer, as if to say, "The mutt will keep me warm."

"Okay, well, stay safe. I'll see you tomorrow."

Again, the hand over his heart.

* * *

After I left Sam and Sweetheart, I walked up the stairs to the lobby of my office building, thinking how fast my two years in Portland had passed. Throughout my career I'd lived in ten cities across the country. Because of its aesthetic and historical charms, Portland was one of my favorites, even though I sometimes felt conspicuously different than the general population. I'm a snob when it comes to fashion. I admit it. The number of granola types in Portland is enough to wake Coco Chanel from the dead. I blame the lack of vitamin D rather than a general disregard for beauty. How else do you explain the number of misguided souls who think Birkenstocks are an appropriate footwear for, well, anyone? Is there a more unattractive sandal? No! Followed shortly thereafter by those plastic "hiking" sandals, which have the added bonus of stinking like a boys' locker room after a football game. And the fleece vests that come in all colors and seemingly for all seasons for both men and women? I shudder just thinking of them.

Although the people of every city are as varied as the religious beliefs in America, it has surprised me that it's possible to buy a condo in any metropolitan area identical to the one from which you just moved. Despite my vow each time to try something different, I always ended up with the same white-walled, sparse condo with high ceilings and large windows that overlooked the city. During the first few mornings after moving, just for a moment, I didn't know in which city I was waking. But it didn't matter, because the closet that looked just like the last closet in the last city I lived in still held my designer shoes and dresses. There is comfort in the familiar.

I always arranged my furniture, which consisted of a couch and bed and a couple of tables, in the same configuration, telling myself that this time I would hire a decorator. But I never quite got around to it. Down the street, a salon and spa gave me the identical haircut and color to the one before: honey with straw-colored highlights, sleek, long bob. Nordstrom, strangely, no matter the city, was always just two, maybe four blocks over from my condo. When I walked into a new job every other year or so and started to categorize those who would remain and those who would be sent away, and that which would become streamlined and that which could be abandoned, I always felt at ease. Work was my spouse, my family, my purpose.

As I stepped into the elevator to go up to my offices on the twelfth floor, I felt good, almost giddy. I'd successfully taken CreateBiz public three days ago, and I anticipated a warm reception from my board, replete with accolades for the high valuation of the company that had subsequently made the stock worth almost twenty dollars a share on our first day out on the public market. While most games for girls are centered on fashion or beauty, our product created virtual businesses. For the most part, I think games are a ridiculous waste of time given how many wonderful books there are in the world, but being the entrepreneur and capitalist that I am, I was enamored with our product. It was fun, thought-provoking, creative and educational all at once. On my first day on the job I told my new staff it was the smart girls' answer to virtual gaming, a phrase which our marketing executive immediately seized upon and implemented into a full-fledged campaign that yielded huge numbers within its first month on the market. We were a sensation, the most sought-after product of last year's Christmas season, and similar sales were predicted for the upcoming holiday season.

The founder, Ralph Butters, was a young, male version of a crazy cat lady, designing genius games in the basement of his house with six cats at his feet. He sported a receding hairline and a greasy ponytail—yes, it is possible to have both. A nervous twitch made his right hand jerk about like Mick Jagger holding a microphone on the last night of the last tour of his life. All of which rendered him completely unable to interact in the real world. I secretly wondered if he created games as a way to cope with his loneliness.

Regardless of the reasons for Ralph's creation, his strangeness made it necessary to hire me. My goal, as it had been many times throughout my career, was to make it profitable and take it public. I did that, in two years, which no one thought we could do, including my board of directors. As was usually the case, we had an impressive board from the high-tech community to whom I was accountable. The board had not only invested substantial amounts of money into CreateBiz, it also advised me on certain aspects of the business. However, Ralph was still in charge, as he owned a majority of the shares, so ultimately I answered to him. So far that hadn't been an issue. The one and only time I'd met him, he sweated so profusely—I assume from nerves—that he hadn't ventured into the offices again. He left me alone for the most part, deferring to my experience and business acumen. For my part, I had the utmost respect for his mind and creativity, knowing he was certainly a genius, whilst I was merely good at business. There's a difference, and I'm humble enough to know it. Having worked with many creative geniuses over the years, I've noticed that the smarter they are, the less likely they are to be comfortable with people. On a certain level, I understood this frailty, as I also found human, emotional connection difficult. I presented a persona of well-dressed, polished businesswoman, charmed rooms full of people with ease, made networking connections that led to deals and steered large groups of employees in a common direction. But that was only on the surface. No one was allowed inside weakness. I made a conscious choice to remain uninvolved with anyone in any emotional capacity, with the lone exception of my sister. This quality was a blessing as an executive. I could make decisions from a place of logic rather than emotion. But in my personal life? Perhaps I was more like Ralph than I cared to admit, minus the cats.

After stepping off the elevator, I stood for a moment just inside the glass doors of our office. It was abuzz with productivity, with excitement, with people doing good work. Was there anything better? I'm sure there was, for people lucky enough to have families and lives outside of work. Here, I felt useful and grounded. It smelled of coffee, new carpet, various perfumes and colognes, burned popcorn from one of the absentminded software developers. The sounds of various printers, the buzz from the overhead lights, phones ringing, the receptionist putting calls through were a type of music to me.

I sighed happily as I waved a greeting to our receptionist and headed to my office. I had five minutes before my first meeting and wanted to check with Charlotte about the schedule for the rest of the day. Charlotte, my reliable assistant, had been with me since I started two years ago. A single woman in her thirties with an English degree and a dream of getting her mystery novels published, Charlotte made a living by working a day job for me. As was the case with all good assistants, I couldn't function without her. She sat at her desk, already typing at her computer, and looked up with a wan smile. Her eyes were bloodshot, and her usually perfect makeup had been either rubbed or cried off. Had she been out all night? It was not like her to be out late partying, but she might have been celebrating the Initial Public Offering. I had made sure she received a handsome stock grant to reward her for all her hard work, hoping that someday she would make enough on the stock that she could devote herself to writing full-time.

"Late night celebrating?" I asked, teasing. "I hope it was with a boy."

I expected her to laugh and confess all, as she sometimes told me tales of her online dating escapades, but instead her eyes filled with tears. She rose from her chair, murmuring a tearful apology, and ran toward the restroom. What could be wrong? Charlotte was solid, unflappable. Was there trouble with a boyfriend? I didn't think she had one, but she had mentioned she'd been on a string of first dates she met online. That's it, I thought, she must have gone out with a jerk from one of those sites. All online dating sites should have the tagline "Guaranteed to Make Grown Girls Cry."

I glanced at my calendar that Charlotte had up on her screen. All it said was "conference room," with no mention of whom I would be meeting with. Charlotte hadn't returned, so I decided to head there anyway. I was surprised to find the head of the board, Eli Winn, and our HR Director, Rachel Fallow, sitting at the end of the long, oval table. I stepped inside. "Hey, guys. Are you expecting me?"

"Yes, come on in. Close the door, please," said Rachel.

Eli nodded his head in greeting as I shut the door and took a seat.

"What's going on? Do we have trouble with an employee?"

Rachel wouldn't look at me. Something wasn't right. The hair on my arms stood up. Then it occurred to me: I was about to be fired. I'd been on the other side of this table with Rachel enough times to know what was about to happen. My heart started to pound. Scalp tingling. Damp palms.

Before they had the chance to say the words I knew were coming, I asked, "Why?"

Eli shook his head, almost shamefully. "Ralph wants to run things without your influence. He thinks you degrade his authority."

Rachel put a hand on his arm. He wasn't supposed to say anything revealing and truthful, and he'd already said too much. She spoke next, her voice devoid of any inflection. "Ralph believes he's the right leader to take the company forward. He wants to be more of a public presence both here at the office and with our consumers."

"He'll have to answer to shareholders and the board now. It's not just him in his basement. Does he realize that, Eli?"

Eli's usual olive complexion had a green tinge this morning. An image of the Grinch flashed through my mind. The bags under his eyes indicated he hadn't slept much. Strangely, I felt compassion for him, despite the fact that he was in the process of firing me. This was business, where at any given moment a decision could be made that obliterated any future success. He knew getting rid of me was a mistake, but there was nothing he could do. As if he knew my thoughts, Eli nodded. "He owns a majority of the stock, Bliss. He can still call the shots. And the board supports the decision."

That stung. "Right. I understand." No reason to act emotional. If Ralph wanted me out, there was nothing I could do. Never let them see you sweat, I told myself, borrowing the marketing phrase from the eighties deodorant commercial—my mantra through many stressful situations. I was cool on the outside while inside my stomach felt like I'd just taken a large and unexpected dip on a roller coaster. I've always hated roller coasters.

"We have a package for you," said Rachel. "It's generous, in exchange for your signature of release."

"Yeah, right. I know the drill."

She hadn't lied. The terms were generous. I kept all my stock, which if things continued to go well, could be worth millions, and a year's salary plus benefits. But it wasn't the money. It hadn't been about the money for at least three companies now. I'd set out to have enough money in savings and stocks by age fifty that I could retire if I wanted to. I'd made that goal by thirty-five, the result of equal parts living frugally and choosing several companies that did well on the public market. I always took stock over salary, and it had paid off several times. I was rich. Rich enough for me, anyway. But this hurt, regardless. Ejected without warning from something I felt I had built with eighty-hour workweeks for the last two years, not to mention the employees I'd had a hand in hiring and mentoring. As was the case with all my positions, this wasn't just a job for me. This was my life.

"You have seven days to decide," said Rachel.

I gave her what I hoped was a withering stare. "I'm quite aware of how this works." I flipped to the last page, where I was to agree they'd done nothing wrong and that I wouldn't turn around and sue them. I signed and slid it back across the table. "Well, now I know why Charlotte was crying."

"You'll be missed by the staff," said Eli.

"We'll pack up your things and have them sent to you via messenger," said Rachel.

The old "you can't even pack up your own things because you're a threat to the company" routine. What did they think? That I'd be foolish enough to harm my reputation by sending some kind of angry message out to the employees? Suddenly I was surprised they didn't have security waiting to walk me to my car. "My laptop is in my office." I slid my work phone across the table. "You'll want this too, I suppose." At least I'd been meticulous about keeping my personal business on my personal phone. Not that I had much personal business. Actually I had no personal business, except for emails from Blythe and my nieces. Blythe and the girls. What was I going to tell them? Aunt Bliss has been canned, given the old sack, fired. I stumbled toward the elevator, a ringing in my ears.

CHAPTER 2

I DON'T REMEMBER HOW I GOT THERE, but suddenly I was outside, the bright light blinding me momentarily as I fumbled for my sunglasses. Fired? Had I really just been let go three days before Thanksgiving? I had my stock and more than enough money, I told myself, pulling my jacket tighter. It was freezing. Had the wind picked up since I'd been inside, or was it the frigid air meeting my sweaty body that made it seem colder? Getting fired makes you sweat, even if no one sees it. Stopping at the bottom of the stairs, I took two big breaths, in and out. There's no reason I couldn't fully recover from this, I told myself. CEOs were asked to step down all the time after a public offering. Only that was usually when the stock wasn't performing well.

I started down the street toward home. Maybe I'd stop for a drink at the bar a block from my building. A drink sounded about right after you get the big ax. I never usually had time to stop because I had work waiting. But now I had no work. I could get a drink if I wanted. Maybe two. I glanced at my watch. Not yet nine a.m. Probably too early for a drink. The holiday was coming. I'd planned on working through it, but now? Tonight I could order Chinese takeout and binge watch old movies, but what about the rest of the long weekend? The days loomed before me with nothing but my empty condo and no more *Breaking Bad* episodes. Why couldn't they make decent movies or television for intelligent people who had no friends? Was that too much to ask?

No job? It didn't seem possible. I'd never been without one, not since I turned fifteen. Even in college I had a job as part of my scholarship package, working at the library. I'd loved that job, scanning books for checkout and shelving returns. Who was I without a job? That was my last thought as my feet slid out from under me and I fell backward like someone on a comedy show slipping on a banana. My head smashed onto the hard cement. Instantaneous, blinding pain shot through the right side of my head. I blinked as if that might lessen the throbbing, and looked up at the white sky. A small crowd gathered around me. A dog barked and then Sweetheart was next to me, her tongue licking my hand. Through black bubbles that floated in front of my eyes, Sam appeared, his face scrunched up in concern, the corners of his eyes wet. A young woman came to stand next to him. Dressed in pink scrubs, she held up three fingers. "How many fingers am I holding up?" I opened my mouth to answer, getting nothing but a weak moan came out for my efforts. Then everything went black.

*   *   *

I regained consciousness in the interior of an ambulance. Two EMTs, both of whom looked like soap opera actors, at least in my blurry vision, hovered about. I was vaguely aware of tubes and a needle poking my arm and the pain lessening slightly and then feeling sleepy. Before I closed my eyes again, succumbing to the blackness, I heard one of the EMTs say to other. "Did you see that? The homeless dude and his dog chased us for like six blocks."

I awakened next in a hospital room. Stark white and gleaming, it smelled of bleach and the chemical components of medicines. My eyes darted around the room—empty of people or even a hint that any living thing existed. I felt a surge of panic. What had happened? What hospital was I in? Had they called Charlotte? God forbid anyone had called Blythe and worried her and my nieces, Lola and Clementine Then I remembered. They wouldn't call Charlotte. No one would ever call Charlotte on my behalf again, because I had no assistant. I had no job. And now I was in the hospital. This day could not get any worse.

I tried to move to look for some kind of call button like I'd seen in the movies but the searing pain on the right side of my head stopped me. A small moan of pain escaped. I licked my dry and scaly lips. How long had I been here? Just then a nurse shuffled into the room and came to stand over my bed. Tall, with the body of a twelve-year-old boy—no breasts and shiny, pink skin that looked like a freshly scrubbed baby's bottom. She wore pink scrubs that matched the hue of her cheeks, and a touch of lip gloss. Her hair hung in two braids. Probably had organic yogurt and granola for breakfast. Her nametag read Kelly Smith. Suddenly I remembered the nurse who had hovered over me on the sidewalk. Had she called the ambulance? Was this her hospital?

Kelly smiled and arrived at my bedside in two strides of those twig-like legs. "How're you feeling?"

I glanced down at her feet. White Birkenstocks and socks to match. I knew it. "Like a truck ran over me."

She picked up my right arm and took my pulse, staring at the floor in that way nurses do when they're taking your vitals. With an unreadable expression, she let go of my arm, tucking the blanket between my side and arm. "Do you know what year it is?"

What was it with nurses asking obvious questions? "2015."

"Do you know who the president is?"

"Of the United States?" Had I heard her wrong?

"Yes." She nodded, her eyes focused on my face.

"Obama." I paused. "Unfortunately."

This caused a slight smile. "You sound like my father. Not a popular viewpoint here in Portland."

"I know. Liberals. They're everywhere. What happened to good old-fashioned free enterprise?"

I'm almost certain I caught her rolling her eyes before she walked to the end of the bed and picked up a clipboard.

"Do you remember what happened?"

"I slipped on ice. That's about it. What's wrong with me?" I felt afraid suddenly. Was it serious?

"You have a traumatic subarachnoid hemorrhage."

"What does that mean?"

"It means you bonked the you-know-what out of your head and have a small amount of bleeding on the brain. The doctor wants to keep you here overnight to monitor you. He always errs on the side of caution. But you should be fine."

I tried to keep up but it was nearly impossible for me to sort through this information, especially given my aching head. "How long was I unconscious?"

"Five minutes or so. Then you were conscious but somewhat incoherent. You don't remember anything?"

"Not much. No."

"The EMTs tried to keep you awake. That's important with a head injury."

"Right." What were the odds? Slipping on the ice right after I got canned?

Kelly bustled over to the sink and filled a pitcher with water. Despite her height, she moved like a cat, quiet and stealthy. At my side again, she poured some water into a cup. After plunging a straw into it, she set it aside and pushed a button that made the top part of the bed rise slightly. "How does that feel?" she asked.

I closed my eyes against the pain. "Awful but I'm dying for water."

She put her arm around my shoulders and helped me take a sip of the cold, cold water. Nothing had ever tasted as good.

"When can I go home?" I asked, almost cringing at how weak I sounded.

"Depends on what the doctor says. But I'd assume we'll just keep you overnight unless the bleeding gets worse. Only a precaution; nothing to worry about. But no driving for a while." She placed the cup of water back on the bedside table that moved in and out like a flat, plastic arm. "I think you're going to live, if that's what you're worried about." She smiled again, looking mischievous. Everyone's a comedian. "Do you feel up for a visitor?"

"A visitor?" Who would visit me?

"Charlotte. She says she's your assistant."

Charlotte. Good old faithful Charlotte. "Did you guys call her?"

"No, she arrived just as they brought you in."

"Sure, I feel fine. Would love to see her." To my disgust I felt like I might cry.

A few minutes later Charlotte came in, holding a small plant, and looking paler and puffier than when I'd last seen her at the office. On most days she was a beauty, dark-skinned with startling eyes just a shade darker than an amber-hued gemstone, and masses of tightly curled brown hair that fell attractively around her face. She started to cry as she put the plant on the bedside table. "Thank God you're all right. I was worried sick. I'm sorry about this awful plant. It's all they had. I think it's a begonia but I don't really know anything about plants."

"I do, unfortunately." My hippie mother and the relentless gardening. "It's not a begonia. It's a spider plant."

"Are you all right? I thought you might be dead." She shrugged out of her raincoat like she was hot, tossing it onto the chair next to the bed. Charlotte, although short and petite, had a curve to her hips and bottom, which she constantly complained about and dieted over, without any credence given to the fact that men drooled over her on a regular basis.

"I'm going to be fine." I handed her a box of tissue from the bedside table. The spider plant's leaves wilted over the sides of its plastic container. That plant was near death, I thought. It needed water, but I wasn't about to burden poor Charlotte with that information. "How did you know I fell?"

She blew her nose before answering. "I was in the coffee shop at the bottom of the building having a little cry when I saw you fall. I ran out there to help but I couldn't get to you because of the crowd. Say what you will about Oregonians but they always help their fellow man."

Charlotte. Always the philosopher.

"Anyway, I saw Sam and Sweetheart."

I interrupted her. "Wait, you know them?"

"Well, not personally. But I know you give money to them every day." I lifted my shoulders from the pillow in my best impression of a sit-up but thought better of it when my head started to throb.

"How do you know that?" I asked, weakly.

"I'm your assistant. I know everything."

I couldn't argue with that. I was quite aware of how efficient and all-seeing Charlotte was.

"He chased the ambulance for several blocks."

"Yeah, I heard the EMTs say something about that." I'd forgotten it until now. Was I truly fine? I felt like something on the bottom of one of nurse Kelly's Birkenstocks, and clearly I was suffering from short-term memory loss.

"Sam sent this." Charlotte handed me a piece of paper. I opened the note.

Miss Heywood, please be all right. I had a head injury once and now I can't speak. Sam.

Sam. To my surprise, tears came to my eyes. They must be contagious, I thought. I brushed them aside and turned gingerly to the window, body aches from head to foot. Apparently falling on concrete not only bruises your ego but also opens you up to emotions you didn't know you had. It was late afternoon, darkness closing in outside the window. Ice, like intricate decoration on a cake, crystalized at the corners of the glass. Where was Sam now? Was he warm enough? How would they eat without my money if I couldn't get to them tomorrow? I'd have to think about that later. I looked back at Charlotte.

"Charlotte, execs get kicked to the curb all the time. It's as brutal as dating. I'll land on my feet. I promise." I said the last part in a softer voice because she'd started to cry again.

"I, I don't like it. After everything you did to get them where you are and how you always look out for the employees, well, it's just not right." Her voice had the wobble you get after crying on and off for half the day. Unfortunately I was familiar with this too. Back when I used to cry, thanks to my mother. Charlotte continued. "I hate business. I have no heart for it. I hate it. The only thing that made it bearable was you."

"Charlotte, you'll have a different boss and I'm sure whoever it is, it will be just like working for me." But as I said it, I realized there were no openings for executive assistants in the company, which meant she'd have to work for Ralph. I hadn't even thought of that until now, so concerned with my own situation. Poor Charlotte. I would call some recruiters later to see if any of them knew of some executive assistant roles. I grimaced. "Did they say you have to work for Ralph?"

She nodded, crying harder. "Ye-ye-yes." Suddenly she took in a long, shaky breath and stopped crying, her pretty face determined and her small hands clenched into fists. "When they told me, I marched right into Rachel's office and quit on the spot."

"What about your stock?"

For the first time, her mouth turned up slightly into a half-smile. "I pretended for a minute I was you and I told them I wanted my stock fully vested."

"But they didn't agree to that, surely?" Of course they wouldn't. Companies didn't give resigning employees anything except the open door.

Now Charlotte smiled wide. "They did when I told them Ralph put his hand up my skirt at last year's company Christmas party."

"Is that true?" Ralph. Bloody Ralph.

She nodded. "I never told you because I knew you'd make me do something about it. And since he's never really in the office, it didn't matter."

"Did Rachel believe you?"

"I don't know. But I could tell she didn't want the hassle of an investigation and all that, so much so she offered me six months' severance on top of the stock."

I shook my head, amazed. "Well, Charlotte, welcome to the big league."

"You told me last week I needed to put my big girl panties on. Well, I did."

"Holy crap, I was talking about dating, not taking on corporate America."

"Oh, it was much easier than dating," she said.

"So, why were you crying just now? This is a happy day for you."

"Change always makes me cry. And I was worried about you. And, well, just everything. Putting big girl panties on is harder than it looks."

We started to laugh as nurse Kelly came in holding a needle. I cringed, knowing it was meant for me.

"Visitor hours are over." Kelly tapped the needle with one of her long, efficient fingers.

Charlotte gathered her jacket and purse. "I called Henry. He'll be here to pick you up in the morning."

I reached out my hand and Charlotte took it. "Thank you. You'll be in touch?"

"Of course. I'll call you after the holiday. Maybe we can have a drink or something." She blushed as she said this, perhaps unsure if it was appropriate now that we were no longer boss and assistant.

"I would love that, Charlotte."

"All right. I'm off now for a visit home to San Diego. My parents." She rolled her eyes and made a slashing motion on her neck. "I may or may not survive."

We said our good-byes and Charlotte left as Kelly prepared the needle. "This will just help you sleep," she said.

"What kind of head injury causes muteness?" I asked, thinking of Sam's note.

She looked at me quizzically. "If you injure the Broca area of your brain. Frontal lobe damage can cause impairments to your speech. But don't worry, you don't have that."

I didn't bother to reply, thinking instead of Sam. He must have damaged his Broca area and that's why he could no longer speak. No wonder he'd looked so frightened when I'd fallen.

Kelly took my arm, prepping it with rubbing alcohol before she slid the needle into my skin. It felt like nothing more than a slight prick. That was a relief. Needles, nasty little things, I thought, dreamily. Just then my eyes felt as if they could not remain open another second. Charlotte, loyal to the end, was my last thought before blackness came.

CHAPTER 3

I WOKE IN DARKNESS except for the ticking sound of machine in the corner that had a blinking red light. Was that the indication I was alive? I sat up and put my feet to the floor. Cold tile made my toes slightly numb as I walked toward the door, hoping to find a light switch. Just as I'd almost reached the door, it opened. A nurse, not Kelly, halted, her rubber-soled shoes squeaking on the tile. "No, no. We mustn't be up and about, honey." She flipped on the light and took a firm hold of my arm as she escorted me back to the hospital bed. "I'm Virginia," she said. "Your night nurse." I noted a more age-appropriate head of white hair for a nurse than twelve-year-old Kelly, and a rotund middle under her pink scrubs.

After she'd tucked the sheets around my shoulders, she went to the end of the bed and picked up my chart. "Well, Bliss Heywood, nothing for you to worry about. You'll be released in the morning. Best thing you can do for the rest of the night is sleep. I'll see you tomorrow." With that, shoes squeaking, she snapped off the light and was out the door.

Wait. Where was that nice little drug Kelly had given me? My head ached and I was wired like I'd had an ill-advised second espresso. I stared at the red light across the room that blinked on and off like a chant in my head, Bliss, Bliss, Bliss.

Bliss. What a name. As it always did, thinking about my name made me seethe with anger toward my mother. Almost forty years old and I still couldn't let her behavior go, which Blythe often reminds me hurts no one but me, to which I reply that she should stop watching *Oprah*.

The light continued to blink.

Now, mesmerized by the blinking light, I asked myself, what had I done with my life that was of any true value? With my talents, I'd made the lucky few rich. An argument could be made, also, that through my work I provided work for others, which stimulated the economy and enabled many to have fulfilling lives. All this was true but what about relationships? Who would miss me when I was gone? What if I'd died today? Other than Blythe and the girls, would it have mattered to anyone?

The truth is, no one else would miss me.

The light blinked, again and again. I was alive, I thought. I had the rest of my life to build a new kind of existence. Silently I said a little prayer. "God if you're there, could you send me some people to love? Show me my friends."

Friends. That might be a good first step. I needed some friends. I needed connections other than my network I used for business purposes. How did someone my age go about getting friends? It wasn't like in college when everyone s in a new environment and seeking friends. At my age people already had their group of friends. Especially women. I saw them sometimes when I ate dinner alone with my spreadsheets open on my laptop. They sat at the bar talking and laughing and drinking pink drinks, sometimes squealing with apparent delight. Until now I'd never felt the need for friends. I had Blythe. Even at college, I'd kept to myself, studying harder than anyone else because I had so much to prove. I didn't care that I was a loner. I liked it. Less chance to get hurt, I suppose, is what I thought.

But now? I wondered. What had I missed by being so driven, so sure of the desired outcome, so fearful of hurt? What would it feel like to have a friend other than Blythe?

Could I change? Could I become the type of woman who would be mourned once gone? My life spread before me like pages of an unread book. What had I done of importance? Who was I? To whom did I belong? Whom did I love? And then, *go home*. That was all. *Go home*—just those simple words, repeated in a silent, insistent chant in time with the blinking light. But I was a woman without a home, an ambitious wanderer chasing wealth and esteem. My home? The only home was my sister, Blythe. *Go home to Blythe then*, the voices in my head shouted like muses to an artist. *Go home and open the unread*

pages of your book. Find meaning in a soulless life that existed without purpose, without love. Do something different than the day before.
Go home. Go home to Blythe. I fell asleep.

*   *   *

I awoke in the morning to the sound of my cell phone ringing. It was Kevan Lanigan, my sister's boyfriend. My heart skipped a beat. Had something happened to Blythe or the girls?

I picked it up, not bothering to keep the panic from my voice. "What's the matter?"

"Nothing. Nothing at all." He sounded chipper, happy. Well, he should be happy—he had the three best girls in the world by his side. Blythe had fallen madly in love with Kevan last summer, just a year after her divorce was final. He was a multi-millionaire from the Lanigan family of Lanigan Trucks. Love at first sight was how Blythe explained it. "We fell in love in three days," she told me. Three days? I thought at the time. That's ridiculous. No one falls in love in three days. Lust maybe, but not love. Blythe dismissed my concern, uncharacteristically bold and bossy, attributes typically reserved for describing me. A month or so later when I visited them in Seattle, I had to admit I'd never seen Blythe as happy, or as much herself. Maybe this was love, I thought, observing the two of them in the kitchen washing dishes with their hips touching, giggling like teenagers. True love makes you more yourself. Or more your best self. I dismissed that idea as quickly as it came. Good Lord, I was starting to sound like Oprah.

"Blythe, you still there?" Kevan asked now.

"Yeah, sure. What's up?"

"I'm calling to ask your permission to marry your sister."

"My permission?"

"Yes. You're her family, and I want to make sure you'll give your blessing before I ask her."

Well, even my cold, dead heart couldn't resist that. "Of course you have my blessing." I stumbled on the last words, choking up in spite of my best efforts. "Be good to her, though. I swear to God if you cheat on her like her first husband, I will kill you myself."

He laughed. "Don't worry. I'm not the cheating kind."

"And the little girls? You'll love them too?"

"I already do."

"And what about your daughter? Does she approve?" Rori, Kevan's daughter, was eighteen and attending college at the University of Oregon. She'd had some troubles, according to Blythe, but was better now. Blythe was the best thing that ever happened to the girl, I was quite sure of that.

As if he read my thoughts, he said, "She knows the best thing to ever happen to either of us was the day Blythe entered our lives. I adore your sister, Bliss. I love her and those little girls, too. I'll make sure no harm ever comes to them."

"You can't really promise that, but I get your point."

"Bliss, you need a little more faith in humanity."

I chuckled. "You *have* been hanging out with Blythe."

"Listen, will you come out for Thanksgiving? We're going to my house in Idaho. Blythe wants to cook a big meal. Fortunately, my mother can't make it." This time he chuckled, but it didn't sound totally convincing that there was any humor associated with his mother. She was a wicked witch as far as I could tell, but at least she wasn't a flake like my mother. Riona Lanigan had a sharp tongue and a mean streak, but she wasn't stoned by ten in the morning. That was a good mother in my world. Kevan continued. "Anyway, I thought you could surprise her. She doesn't think you'll come. Said you usually work holidays."

Go home to Blythe. "I will. I'll come."

"Excellent. I'll email you directions and details."

"Great. See you soon."

It didn't occur to me until after we'd hung up the phone that I couldn't drive out to see them. No driving, the doctor had said. How was I supposed to get to Idaho without driving?

CHAPTER 4

THEY RELEASED ME FROM THE HOSPITAL the next morning, the doctor declaring me well enough to get back to regular life, with several warnings: no driving or flying. I dressed in the clothes I'd been admitted in, wishing I could have a shower and a fresh pair of panties to wear. I had decided, after some back and forth in my mind, not to tell my sister I'd been in the hospital. She was busy with the girls, and I was fine. No reason to worry her.

Charlotte called from her parents' in San Diego to tell me she'd arranged for Henry, my occasional driver, to pick me up outside the hospital. "You didn't have to do that," I said. "You're not technically my assistant any longer."

"True. But I'm still your friend."

Friend? Was this an answer to my prayer? *Show me my friends.* "Thank you, Charlotte. I appreciate it."

We talked for a few more minutes. Charlotte told me her parents had managed to offend her within an hour of her arrival by ridiculing her plan to finish her mystery novel.

"Don't listen to them," I said. "You can accomplish anything you want if you decide you want it bad enough."

"I don't know about that," she said.

"Give all the doubters the finger, even if they're your parents, and get to it."

She laughed. "Maybe I'll stay home for Christmas. Nothing like family to make you feel worthless."

Depends on your family, I thought. *Go home to Blythe.*

I told her of my plan to head to Idaho for the holiday before we hung up, promising to see one another when we were back in town.

The weather, according to the nurses, was bad enough that they were advising people to stay off the roads unless absolutely necessary. It was colder by five degrees than the day I'd entered, just twenty-four hours ago, but that seemed like a month. The cloud cover had disappeared and the bright burned my eyes. I put my sunglasses on, thankful they were in the pocket of my bag. I felt like I'd been at an after-hours nightclub only without the fun to show for it. I stood waiting in the cold, shivering. Something in the last twenty-four hours had diminished me, made me feel small and vulnerable. I didn't care for this feeling. Not one iota. I watched flecks of ice so miniscule they would be invisible except for the way they sparkled in the sun as they drifted sideways in the wind.

Henry arrived then, pulling into the patient loading area and leaping from the car. For a man in his early sixties, he was lean and agile. "Miss Heywood, how are you? I was quite alarmed to hear you were in the hospital." English, he possessed the loveliest accent, which only added to his charm and mystique. I often wondered about the details of this elegant man who drove a car for a living, but never asked, for fear he'd think it presumptuous, given his austere demeanor.

Now, he looked at me a few seconds longer than he normally would, usually the epitome of appropriateness—in his view, I am a client not a friend. With that thought, I looked at him closely. Could Henry be a friend? Probably not. He no doubt had a lot of proper gentlemen friends with which he did English activities like croquet and equestrian sports wearing those cropped riding pants. I glanced at his left hand. He didn't wear a ring. Was he single? Surely not. A handsome man in his sixties who still had his hair? He'd be snatched up in a second.

"Miss Thorne filled me in on the details of your injury. Nothing to take lightly."

"Charlotte worries too much."

He hesitated, as if he might like to add something, but instead opened the passenger door of the black town car without further comment.

"I'm fine, really. Nothing to worry about." I slid into the seat, cringing slightly. My tailbone must be bruised. Why hadn't anyone mentioned the rest of my body, now that I thought about it? Nothing a hot bath wouldn't cure, I thought, suddenly longing to be home. "Maybe the head thing will knock some sense into me, do you think?" I laughed, feeling awkward.

He stared at me for a moment, with humorless eyes. I looked away, pretending to look for something in my purse. Making jokes with anyone other than Blythe wasn't as easy as other people made it look. But I needed humor in order to attract friends. Funny people were always popular.

Henry shut the door and got into the front seat and pulled out of the hospital driveway and onto the street.

"I'm glad you're out and about despite the ice, Henry."

"I'm my own boss, Miss Heywood. It would take more than a bit of ice to keep me from my work."

Henry didn't work for a car service but instead owned his own car and worked for a select group of people, of which I was one. I was curious what his other clients were like, whether they were business people or little old ladies too feeble to drive. He always dressed in a black suit, crisp white shirt and a tie. One time he'd mentioned something about his former life as an actor, which would explain the smooth timbre and perfect articulation of his speaking voice, and also how someone obviously intelligent, conscientious and handsome drove rich people around town for a living. He reminded me of an old-fashioned movie star, maybe a cross between Fred Astaire and Frank Sinatra.

My head ached. I closed my eyes and tilted my head back to rest on the seat cushion.

"Miss Heywood. Are you sure you're quite all right?"

I opened my eyes, meeting his from where they watched me from the rearview mirror. What was it I saw there? Fear? Sadness? "Perfectly fine."

"I'll get you home right away."

"Can you make one stop for me on the way?" Sam. He needed money by now. And this cold. Where had they slept last night?

"Of course."

I directed him to my office building.

He raised an eyebrow but said nothing. We entered the freeway, headed downtown. Traffic was light. Despite this, Henry stayed in the slowest lane, going five below the speed limit. Was this typical for him? I wasn't sure. Normally my face was buried in my laptop when he drove me to the airport or to occasional business functions where I knew there would be alcohol. I did not drive, even if I'd had only one drink. Plus, I didn't care for driving. Last summer I bought my sister a new car and drove it to Seattle. It was the longest trip I'd driven for years. Someone as antsy as me doesn't do well with a long stretch of highway and nothing to keep me occupied. The only thing that saved me was an audiobook.

I watched the back of Henry's head as we moved along the freeway. It was nicely shaped, and his hair was really quite thick for an older man. I'd never noticed it before.

"Henry?"

"Yes, Miss Heywood."

"Do you have a family?"

He smiled slightly before sadness crept into his eyes. "My wife died five years ago. My son lives in New York."

"Will he come for Thanksgiving?"

"Oh, no. He has a big job that keeps him busy. Like you."

We were both quiet for a moment. Henry took the downtown exit and we stopped at a red light. The streets and sidewalks were nearly empty. "Is it supposed to get any colder?" I asked.

"In the teens tonight, according to the local news."

I sat with this for a moment. Sam and Sweetheart might freeze to death in this cold. Moving about on the seat, I sighed and tapped my fingers on the window. This trip seemed to be taking forever.

"Are you sure you're all right?" Henry's eyes watched me from the rearview mirror.

I removed my hand from the glass and let it rest in my lap. "Yes. Do you have a girlfriend?" I blurted the last part out, regretting it instantly, realizing too late that he might misinterpret my question. Would he think I was asking him out? I felt my face turn pink. This finding a friend thing is not for sissies, I thought.

"I do not have a girlfriend." He smiled and his voiced sounded softer than the moment before. "My son encourages me to try and find one." He shrugged. "But I'm not sure how one goes about that."

"Yeah. I understand."

We drove another block and then another before stopping at a red light.

"Henry?"

"Yes, Miss Heywood?"

"My sister's getting engaged."

"You have a sister?"

"Yeah. And two nieces."

"Oh, I see."

"Why do you say it like that?"

"Like what, Miss Heywood?"

"Like it's a surprise."

He shrugged. "I find it hard to imagine you outside of your professional persona."

My professional persona? Maybe this was the trouble. I was too buttoned up all the time. I should get a pair of jeans and tennis shoes. Oh, God, no. I can't be expected to change my entire personality just to find some friends. I didn't speak for a few moments, gazing out the window at a frozen mud puddle. "I'm supposed to go to Idaho for Thanksgiving to visit my sister and my nieces and Kevan, her betrothed. But I can't fly." I pointed to my head. "Or drive."

"Oh, well, that's a shame." He said this with a hint of concern in his voice, which was the most emotion I'd ever heard from him.

"I want to go. The thought of the long weekend alone..." My voice cracked as I trailed off, suddenly unsure what the last part of that sentence should be. What in the world was wrong with me? About to cry over something so trivial? People had real problems. Maybe my head injury had caused some kind of permanent damage? Had it turned me from a badass businesswoman to a simpering dame in a matter of twenty-four hours?

"I could take you, Miss Heywood."

My head snapped up. I looked into the rearview mirror for his eyes but they were focused on the road. "But it's all the way to Idaho. I mean, like, the-middle-of-nowhere Idaho. There's snow and stuff. Maybe snow monsters." This was another attempt at humor, but instead of an awkward laugh, I welled up. Oh, what the hell. Just let it out, I thought. "My sister's boyfriend called and asked my permission to marry her. Isn't that thoughtful? He said Blythe needed my blessing because I'm the only one she has. Our parents, well, you know, my dad's dead and my mother's a hippie. The two of us clung together growing up. She practically raised me. She taught me to read when I was four years old." I shook my head, feeling the pink flush of embarrassment on my cheeks. Why couldn't I stop talking? "Well, anyway, it's too far for you to drive me." I turned to look out the window once again. Ice had formed on the glass. I placed the palm of my hand against it, wondering, idly, if the heat from my skin could melt it.

"Miss Heywood." He cleared his throat. "It's certainly not my place to pry, but I think you need to go to Idaho." Had I flustered him? "I'm afraid to say I understand something about lonely holidays. I could take you, would like to take you. It would be no problem. You'd be doing me a favor, actually. I could use a little extra money. There's something I had in mind for my son. For Christmas, I mean. A surprise."

"There's a little inn. You could stay there and take me home after a few days. I'd pay for everything, of course." My sister had stayed in a bed and breakfast in the small town of Peregrine before a chance encounter had brought her to Kevan. She had told me all about it, along with its proprietor, Moonstone, a self-proclaimed psychic and enthusiastic antique collector.

As if this were the most ordinary request in the world, he answered without hesitation. "Of course, Miss Heywood." We passed the waterfront park. During summer months, children played in the giant water fountain. It was empty today, icicles hanging from benches. Columbia River sparkled in the sun. Overhead a gaggle of geese in the formation of a V headed south, late for their date with warmer climates.

"Thank you." We were near my office building now. He pulled up to the curb. I searched for Sam but didn't see him in his typical spot.

"Are you going up?" asked Henry, obviously meaning to my office.

"No. They fired me yesterday."

His voice went up an octave. "You were fired?"

"Yeah. It was a crappy day." I scooted to the other side of the car, hoping to get a clearer view of the alley between the buildings.

Sam was there, tucked away. "I'll just be a moment," I said to Henry as I stepped out of the car. The cold wind blasted my face. I started to move toward Sam but then fear overcame me. Ice. Would I slip again? These boots were not meant for walking, I thought. Wasn't that an old country song? Or the title of a book? I couldn't remember which. I turned back to the car and knocked on Henry's window. He slid it down.

"May I help you, Miss Heywood?"

"I'm afraid I might slip."

His face softened. Without a word he exited the car and offered his arm. For a moment I felt transformed to another time, expecting lights and a red carpet for the premier of some movie starring Jimmy Stewart. That's the way of Henry, I realized. Charisma. No wonder he'd been an actor. You can't fake that.

"It's just Sam here." I pointed toward the homeless man and his dog, both of whom appeared to be asleep. "I give him money every day, and with this weather I'm worried." I stopped, glancing up at Henry's face.

He met my gaze, scratching the side of his face with his index finger. "There's a shelter six or so blocks from here. Perhaps he goes there at night?"

"Maybe." I gripped his arm a little tighter. "But what about Sweetheart? His dog. Do they take dogs at shelters?"

He grimaced, as if searching for an answer, and looked down at me. "I'm not sure." Henry was tall; he must be well over six feet. I'd never noticed that before, having never really stood next to him. I'm almost six feet with my heels and he still had several inches on me. "Miss Heywood, what is it you want to do here?"

"Nothing, I guess. Just give him some money, like I do normally. That's all. The stupid holidays just have me thinking."

"Well, of course. And you suffered a bit of a shock, I imagine, with the hospital visit and all." His voice was low, almost soothing, and certainly sympathetic.

"Exactly, Henry. I woke up last night thinking about my life. What am I doing with it, really? How much more do I have to prove?"

"Prove, Miss Heywood?"

"Yes. You know, how much money do I have to make before I say, enough." I sighed, pulling on a lock of my hair. "I'm lonely, Henry. I didn't realize how much until last night staring into the light of some machine. I need to focus on relationships more than work. I need a life."

"While I understand the sentiment, I would be remiss if I didn't point out that Sam, well, you don't know what kind of troubles he might have. It's no accident that he lives on the streets."

"Right. Of course." I paused. "But he chased the ambulance. He sent a note." I lowered my voice. "He's mute. For some stupid reason I thought that made him illiterate too."

"I see."

I looked at up at him. His lids were at half-mast. What was he thinking? "Well, anyway, let's give him some cash to get him through the next couple of days," I said.

We headed toward Sam and Sweetheart. When we were a few feet away, Sweetheart jumped to her feet, wagging her tail harder than I'd ever seen her do. I knelt down and she licked the back of my hand. Sam opened his eyes, sleepily at first, before they flew open and he leaned forward, his mouth moving, distorted, as if he wanted to speak but no sound came.

"Sam, I'm fine. I wanted you to know," I said.

He nodded and smiled.

Realizing I'd forgotten my purse, I looked back at Henry. He had returned to the car, his arms folded over his chest like he was a guard on duty. I called out to him. "Henry, will you bring my purse, please?"

"Yes, Miss Heywood."

"Sam, I'm leaving you some money. I'm going away for the holiday and I want to make sure you're okay while I'm gone."

He made the gesture over his heart. Henry, behind me now, handed my purse over and I emptied my wallet of all the cash I had, about $140. I gave it to Sam. "Can you keep it safe from thieves?"

Shrugging, his gaze darted down the street.

"Put it inside your jacket."

He shook his head, no, before beckoning Sweetheart. She went to him and, as if she knew exactly what to do, bowed her head. I'd not noticed before but her collar was wider than most. He unbuckled it from her neck and turned it over, holding it up for me to see. It had a zipper. A secret compartment. Genius. I glanced at Henry. He appeared as surprised and impressed as me. Sam slipped the money inside.

"Well, get to a shelter tonight, okay? Or buy a room for the night. Just stay warm."

He nodded but I couldn't tell if he understood or not. I said good-bye and assured him I would see them when I returned after the holiday.

Once in the warmth of the car, I shivered. No one should have to be out in this weather tonight, I thought. I have the power to do something about it. So do it, I told myself. Man up. Henry started the vehicle and was about to pull into the street when I stopped him. "Wait. This isn't right. We need to get him a room for a week somewhere."

"We, Miss Heywood?"

"I mean me."

"What sort of room?"

"Like a motel room. That takes dogs."

Henry put the car in park and turned all the way around to look at me. "Miss Heywood. I don't think you're thinking all this through properly."

I hesitated. Had I lost my mind? No. I was fine. It was this cold front and the holidays and my vow to build relationships. Building friendships started with kindness. That was all. I wanted to make sure Sam and Sweetheart remained safe and warm. What was wrong with that? Nothing. It was the rest of the world that was crazy. Why were people like me around with more money than they knew what to do with when people like Sam were out on the street? That was the question. Not whether or not I should do something. Hadn't I made a pact with God last night in the middle of that dark hospital room? I needed to do something with my life besides just make money. This was the beginning of the new day I'd promised Him. "You know what?"

"What's that, Miss Heywood?"

"I'm going to take Sam and Sweetheart home with me tonight."

The look of horror on Henry's face almost made me laugh. I would have, but I didn't want to further alarm him. "Home. With you? Oh no, this is not a good idea."

"Why not?"

"You're not well. And you don't know if he's dangerous. What if he robs you? Or, God forbid, hurts you."

"He won't. He's harmless. Just lost. Henry, he needs me. We can't just let him freeze to death out here."

"Again with the *we*, Miss Heywood?"

I ignored him, letting the momentum of my righteousness fuel me. "Homeless people die in the cold all the time. I have the chance to do something." I stopped, thinking of Sam chasing the ambulance across town, somehow getting to the hospital miles away. He'd done that for me.

"Miss Heywood?"

"Yes, Henry?"

"Do you have a young man?"

I squinted at him, irritated and amused at the same time. "A young man?"

"A man in your life."

"I don't need a man."

He made a sweeping gesture with his hand, taking it off the steering wheel for a moment. "A man who would tell you this is a bad idea and to go home and get rested up before a long trip. Furthermore, it's obvious you need someone to look after you. This world is not meant for a woman alone. Dangers are everywhere."

"What're you talking about? This isn't 1950. I'm perfectly capable of taking care of myself."

He sighed. "They had some things right back then. Men knew how to treat women like ladies, and women knew how to accept it."

"I'm fine."

Henry raised his eyebrows in the rearview mirror. "Really?"

"I'm currently single, but I've had boyfriends. Or boyfriend-ish."

"What's this 'ish'? Is that code for—what do the young people call it?—bootie calls?"

I made a face and threw up my hands. "No." What was happening here? We'd gone from hardly speaking to Henry commenting on my sex life in the time it took to cross town. "'Ish' is the way I like it. No strings attached. Casual. Fun. I don't do the whole commitment thing well. I'm like Greta Garbo in this late night grand hotel."

"Greta Garbo?"

"Never mind. It's a song reference." Only Blythe would understand. Despite all the ways we differed, we shared an almost obsessive love of music, especially singer/songwriters. Our favorite was Nanci Griffith. I didn't bother to explain any of this to Henry.

I'd missed my opportunity to marry when I was younger because I was so focused on work. The men my age had married their sweethearts while I was in my twenties and thirties flying all over the world making deals. They were now all happily married—if not happy, at least married—and living in the suburbs with their perfect children and SUVs. The dating pool for women my age and older consisted of divorced men with baggage as long as the line at the Apple store on release day for the latest iPhone.

I may be successful and confident about my work, but when it comes to dating, I'm still the girl no one asked to high school prom. I was the smart girl, not the pretty girl, and somehow that little girl is still alive and kicking inside my toned body and perfect hair and designer clothes. Men want young women. According to statistics, the chance of meeting someone at my age is less likely than getting hit by lightning.

But I wasn't interested in a committed relationship. Would it be nice to have sex again? Yes. Was it worth the hassle? No. The combination of my couch, binge-watching *Breaking Bad* and a nice bottle of wine proved a much more attractive mate. There were good books to read, hot yoga, salted-caramel ice cream, and Nordstrom. I had my work, after all. What more did I need?

Focus, I thought. I needed to make my case about Sam. "Sam left me a note. That means something to me. It's almost like we're friends."

"You give him money, Miss Heywood. Do you think that might have something to do with it?"

"So what if it does?" I crossed my arms over my chest, feeling petulant. Henry's attitude made me feel like a child.

He didn't say anything for a moment, watching me. With one of his long fingers, he tapped the headrest of his seat. "Oh for goodness sake. If you insist on taking this, this, homeless man into your home, then I'm staying with you. Until it warms up."

Neither of us mentioned that it was not supposed to warm up for at least a week, or the fact that we were leaving the next day for Idaho. I would decide what to do about that tomorrow. One day at a time, I assured myself. This is how you become a friend, I thought. One day at a time until suddenly you love one another. Sam and Henry were going to be my friends whether they wanted to or not. I'd chosen them. The list was formulating in my mind.

Find love for Henry.

Save Sam.

I smiled to myself as we once again parked and headed for Sam and Sweetheart.

CHAPTER 5

WHEN I PROPOSED THE IDEA to Sam, he cocked his head to the side and stared at me with those watery blue eyes. Sweetheart, on the other hand, seemed to understand right away. She rose to her feet, tail wagging, and pointed her nose to Henry's car parked and waiting at the curb. Then she barked, loudly, as if to say, "Let's go. I'm cold and hungry." Sam got to his feet but remained glued to the side of the building. He shook his head, no, and then pulled at the front of his jacket. I looked at Henry, hoping for a translation, as if the English could decipher the gestures of a mute.

"He thinks he's too dirty." Henry turned to Sam. "Isn't that right?"

Sam nodded, yes.

"You can get washed up at my place," I said, like I was talking to a girlfriend before a night out. Washed up was the ultimate understatement. It would take a week's allotment of hot water and soap to cleanse Sam. But that was just fine, I told myself. I had two bathrooms and lots of towels.

Sam continued to shake his head, no. Sweetheart whined and looked up at him with sad, pleading eyes.

Henry, shifting his feet, glanced at me with one eyebrow raised. "He has a point, Miss Heywood."

I looked over at Henry. "After you drop us off, you can go out and get him some new things to wear."

Sam pulled off his wool cap. His white hair, long and matted, clung to his scalp. He tugged on a strand. What did he mean? I looked over at Henry. Maybe it was the acting training, but he seemed to understand Sam, regardless of words.

"He's worried what they'll think of him in your fancy building."

"Wait, you know where I live?"

Sam shook his head, no.

"He knows you live in a fancy building," said Henry. "Anyone can tell that by looking at you."

"Oh, right. How about a haircut?" I asked. "Henry, do you know how to cut hair?"

Henry sighed and rolled his eyes. "I'm a former actor. I know how to wait tables and drive rich people around in my car. That's it."

"After you get cleaned up, Sam, we can get you a haircut. If you want," I said. I'd ignore naysayer Henry for now. I was surprised someone like Henry wouldn't have more sympathy for the downtrodden. Weren't all actors a bevy of bleeding hearts?

"I'll order Chinese takeout, Sam. And we'll get dog food for Sweetheart. She'll like that, right?"

It was the promise of dog food that did it. Sam pushed his hat back on his head and walked toward the car. Sweetheart, after what I swear was a wink of her eye right at me, followed obediently. At the car, I told them to get into the back and closed the door behind them. "I'll sit up front with you, Henry."

"Right. Of course you will. The front." His voice was dry, and the look in his eyes? Distinctly disapproving.

"Henry, don't be such a buzzkill. We're doing something good here."

He squinted as he gazed at me. "Miss Heywood, I had you pegged completely wrong. I'm usually quite good at reading people, but you are a surprise." He said the last part almost to himself as he moved around the front of the car to open my door.

"What's that mean?"

"Never mind." He opened the door and waited for me duck inside.

I wasn't that easily dismissed. I wanted him to tell me how exactly how he'd had me pegged. "What surprised you? That I actually have a big heart under my designer suit?"

"Something like that."

"What else?"

"I thought you played it safer than this."

I nodded, thinking about that for a moment. "Well, that just shows you did have me pegged wrong. All my life I've done the unexpected.

It's a gift, actually. And, you know what, I built a career on it, too. I take huge risks every time I agree to come into a company and turn it around. I like projects, the harder the better." I paused, taking in a deep breath. "And last night, all alone in that awful hospital room, I decided my life was a little too sterile, despite the business risks I take. I need a life other than work, Henry. That's all there is to it."

"Might I suggest, again, a boyfriend? Maybe have a baby. Or just get a friend.

"Dammit, Henry, that's what I'm trying to do. I'm making friends."

"Taking in a homeless man and his three-legged dog? Well, Miss Heywood, that's not seeking friendship but rather just this side of crazy."

I laughed one of my deep belly laughs that usually only come out in the company of my sister. "Come on, Henry. You need a little crazy in your life. Let's shake it up a bit." I smiled and tapped my hands on the hood of the car. "How about you and me, Henry? You want to be friends? What do you say?"

"You're not going to make me take tequila shots, are you?"

I flashed him my best smile. "Great idea."

"Get into the car, Miss Heywood. Please." He actually looked pained when he said this, so I took pity on him and did as requested.

I settled into the car, fastening my seatbelt, and then put my gloved hand up to my nose. One thing was for certain. Sam needed a bath. I think he was about eight years late for his date with a bar of soap. And Sweetheart? She smelled like ten dogs instead of one, three-legged pooch.

It was going to be a long ride to my condominium.

*   *   *

I instructed Henry to park in the garage of my building, as I had a guest spot no one ever used next to my car I rarely drove. Sweetheart, sniffing, put her nose on the window and barked. She was ready for the next adventure even if her master, who looked decidedly apprehensive, was not. "Come on, gang," I said. "Let's go up. Sam, a shower will feel good."

He nodded and tugged on his cap. Henry was outside of the car by then, holding the door for Sam and Sweetheart. We all walked to my elevator in silence. For the first time since I'd hatched my plan, I felt apprehensive. Was this a terrible idea? Was Henry right? Had the bump on the head caused me to think crazy? I glanced at Sam. He was visibly shaking. "Sam, don't worry," I said. "You'll like my place. I have a guest room, and you'll have your own bathroom." Once inside the elevator, I pushed the button for the top floor. Sam gripped the railing as we travelled up. Sweetheart pressed into his legs. I was feeling relieved that we were alone on our ride up to my place, thinking we'd dodged questioning looks from judgmental people. Then, we stopped in the lobby. When the doors slid open, an older couple, carrying Gucci shopping bags, took a step forward to get on, spotted Sam and stopped dead in their tracks. Unfortunately, we'd managed to stink up the elevator as much as we had Henry's car. Not exactly the most inviting place in the world.

Being the nomad I am, I had no idea who this couple was or what unit they lived in, which in hindsight might be a reason to attend the twice yearly tenant parties, especially when sneaking homeless guys and their three-legged dogs into your residence. After a second or two, they stepped inside, both of them directing their gaze for a moment on Sam, then Sweetheart and then me. "Hi." I flashed my best dazzling business smile, known to make cranky businessmen lose some of their crank almost immediately. But no such luck today. They both looked at me like I was a demon in high-heeled boots. Henry, to my irritation, had hidden his mouth behind his hand. I couldn't decide if he was trying not to laugh or attempting to mask the odor of my new housemate. It doesn't matter what anyone thinks, I told myself. I don't need anyone's permission to invite someone into my home. It's not like he'll be roaming the building or anything. I just needed to get him up to my place and get him showered and cleaned up. The man punched floor 7 as the elevator doors slowly closed. The woman pulled several tissues from her purse and put them up to her nose.

There was silence as we ascended floor by floor. Why was this elevator so slow? About floor five, I glanced over at the woman. "Staying warm enough?"

Her only answer was a glower in my direction before moving even closer to the wall. The husband shifted his feet and held his packages closer to his chest.

They exited, and as the doors to the elevators closed, we heard the woman say to her husband, "Wait until I call Raymond about this."

Raymond, I was almost certain, was the president of the homeowners association for our building. No matter, I thought. Sam will be all cleaned up and presentable by the time anyone visits.

* * *

Three hours later, Sam and Sweetheart's makeovers were complete. With a few flicks of scissors, a slide of a razor and good old-fashioned soap and warm water, they had been transformed from grimy street dwellers into a respectable-looking man and his loyal companion. Well, and a trip to Nordstrom. No makeover is complete without a trip Nordys. Everyone knows that to be one of the basic tenants of attractiveness.

However, there was still the matter of his hair. I needed the big guns for that tangled web. No one but Aurora would do. Aurora was my Portland hair designer—that's what the fancy salon where she worked called them, as opposed to merely stylists or cutters or colorists. Aurora was a package of muscle dressed in stilettos and skinny jeans, with a tattoo of a purple rose from one shoulder blade to the other. As far as I could tell, she wasn't afraid of anything or anyone. I think that quality came with the Harley she rode. Or was it like the chicken and egg? I often wondered what came first, Aurora's attitude or the Harley? It didn't matter either way. I knew she'd help me out with Sam if I asked. Along with her badass attitude, she also possessed a soft heart. She'd have to come to my home, I thought, as I dialed her number. Sam could never handle the salon. I'd barely gotten Blythe into the salon in Seattle when I'd supervised her makeover last summer. Something about those places intimidates a person if they're not used to it. But look what my makeover had gotten Blythe: a multi-millionaire with a house in the foothills of Blue Mountain. I know it's not that simple. Obviously, there were other factors to their falling in love, not just the haircut and color I recommended. Good hair doesn't solve every problem. But it's a great place to start.

The first makeover I ever did was on myself. I'm not a great beauty. My face is slightly asymmetrical, for one, and studies have shown that the more symmetrical one's face, the more beautiful they appear to others. My nose is fine, of regular size, except one nostril is smaller than the other. My eyes are deep set and almost disappear when I smile. Also, there was the problem of my teeth. My mother refused to pay for braces, so I was lucky to have a wide mouth and small teeth. Unfortunately, my two front teeth were considerably longer than the others, giving me a rabbit-like countenance. All I needed was a carrot to pull off the entire look. No need for Halloween costumes, I always thought, just go as a bunny. As a child I did not smile in school photographs for that very reason, the outcome of which was twelve years' worth of stoic and somber poses that make me look a bit like a serial killer. Blythe says I exaggerate how bad the photographs are and how much I resembled a bunny. She should know, she always says, since she's a professional photographer, always adding that I most certainly did not look like a bunny. She says I was cute. But she loved me. Love makes one blind.

Regardless, years ago I put all that aside, this question of am I beautiful or not, knowing I am average, at best. However, it became clear from observing classmates in college, both male and female, that attractive students did better than unattractive ones. We all say, no matter our profession, that looks do not play into hiring decisions, grades, salaries and so on, but it's a lie. Attractive people are more successful. They get more opportunities, more mentoring, more everything.

With that understanding, I decided I would learn how to make the most of my appearance with the same dogged approach I used in my studies. I studied attractive women, both real ones and the ones in the media. I figured out a secret. Except for the truly beautiful, being attractive is a mirage, a trick. Anyone can do it if they have the tools and discipline to implement it. Anything you need to know is in books or periodicals, even those with anorexic fifteen-year-olds on their covers.

For most women, it's only vanity that prompts them to turn their attention to appearance, but for me it was deeper than that. I was outrunning my name, symbolic of my mother and my childhood. I would be successful no matter what. If appearance mattered, I would conquer it, just as I had the honor classes in high school and the stiff competition at Stanford and later, Harvard Business School.

So I made myself a project—a makeover project. I became a different kind of girl, one who should and would talk to any boy she pleased and would never be passed over for a career opportunity because of appearance. I studied current fashions and hair in the ridiculous women's magazines I abhorred. Those magazines instructed me on everything from what clothes looked good on a tall girl with long legs and small breasts to how one might choose the right hair color to flatter certain skin tones. For example, Blythe and I have dark blonde hair and butterscotch skin that tans easily, which is a great combination for straw-colored highlights that project the feeling of sun-kissed dewiness.

In addition to my study of clothes and hair, I took up daily exercise. I watched calories to remain slim, restricting my beloved peanut-butter sandwich to one a week. I had a dentist even out and whiten my teeth so that I flashed a toothpaste commercial smile. A professional makeup artist taught me how to make my deep-set eyes pop and advised me on the right shade of lipstick. I remade myself so that by the time I entered the business world, the geeky bookworm persona was dead and Bliss Heywood, executive, emerged. Most of the time I didn't even think of the old Bliss, remembering only when Blythe or I happened to look through the very few photographs from our childhood. The girl I see there I feel sorry for, mostly, for how lost and lonely she was, especially after Blythe left home. I love her, this girl with the bunny teeth. I want to tell her, *hang in there, you have the last laugh.*

I wanted Sam to have the last laugh, too. When he was in the shower, I called to ask if Aurora would consider coming to my house to give him a haircut. Once she heard of his plight, she agreed without hesitation. By the time he was out of the shower and dressed in my pink fluffy bathrobe, a gift from my nieces last Christmas, she was already set up in my kitchen with scissors in hand. Aurora has white-blonde hair she wears in long waves and makeup that looks like she just came off a movie set. She told me once that Aurora wasn't her real name; the salon she works for has them choose 'stage' names, which I find amusing. I think we should all get to choose our own names. That way I could get rid of Bliss, which, let's be honest, sounds like a name chosen by one of Aurora's hipster salon colleagues rather than a successful business woman.

Scissors flying as white hair cascaded to the floor, Aurora snipped away. Sam sat still as a statue, his hands clasped on his lap, the pink collar of the bathrobe pulled tightly around his neck. While she continued, I left the room to talk to Henry about heading to Nordstrom to buy Sam a new wardrobe. I felt like a child at Christmas, giddy and excited. My headache was long forgotten. I hadn't had this much fun since, well, I couldn't remember. Fun? I didn't really have much of that, I thought. But things were about to change, I promised myself. More joy, less work.

Henry was in the front room talking on the phone. When he saw me, he told the person on the other end of the line that he had to go and turned to me. "I'll need to run home and get some things for the trip tomorrow." He indicated the couch. "I suppose you'll want me on the couch tonight?"

"You really think it's necessary you stay here?" I asked. "Sam's totally harmless; even you can see that, right?"

As if she understood what I'd just said, Sweetheart let out a bark from where she was having a lie-in by the front door. "See? Sweetheart agrees."

"I do think it's necessary I stay here. Furthermore, what do you plan to do about your trip? Please tell me you're not bringing them both along?"

I hadn't really thought it all the way through. My sister would be even more appalled than Henry at this latest project. But I couldn't leave them here alone. Even I wasn't that crazy. "We are most definitely taking them with us. I'll book them a room right next to yours at the bed and breakfast." I snapped my fingers. "Don't let me forget to call them." I smiled. "Anyway, yes, you need to go home and pack, and on your way back here, you can stop at Nordstrom."

"Nordstrom? For Sam? Have you heard of Marshalls, Miss Heywood?"

"Oh, God no. I wouldn't wish that on you. It would take forever. I'll just call my girl over at Nordys. She'll get everything we need and all you have to do is pick it up." The problem was, I didn't know what size Sam was. He was skinny; I could see that from how my robe fit him, and I figured he was about the same height at me, around five feet nine if I guessed correctly. "What size is he, do you think?" I asked Henry.

"Thirty waist, thirty-six length, medium-size shirts. Size eleven shoes." He rattled it off without pause.

"Henry! Are you a clothes horse in disguise?"

He rolled his eyes. "No. I worked in the costume shop during my MFA program. I used to make a little extra money working with the seamstresses."

"So you lied."

"Pardon me?"

"You do have other talents besides waiting tables and driving me around."

He raised an eyebrow. "I was an actor, Miss Heywood. A fine one, but I am not good at much else, unfortunately."

"I disagree. So far you're a great wingman in my quest for friendship."

"I am not, and will never be, your wingman." He said it like he'd just taken a bite of something sour.

"I know you don't mean that. Isn't this fun?" I grinned at him as I dialed the number for my personal shopper, Marjory, over at Nordstrom. I asked her first to pick out a scandalous piece of lingerie for Blythe, winking at Henry as I did so, which made the tips of his ears glow pink before he shoved his hands in his pants pockets and turned away.

"Northwest casual," I told Marjory. "Jeans and some nice sweaters. Maybe a khaki pant for special occasions. Socks, of course. A nice pair of flannel pajamas and some shoes and boots. And boxers. None of the tighty-whitey stuff for Sam," I said into the phone before hanging up.

I looked over at Henry, expecting enthusiasm for this latest venture, but instead he met my gaze with an expression of horror on his elegant face.

"What? Everyone needs underwear, Henry. What you wear underneath says a lot about a man."

He whispered through gritted teeth. "May I remind you that this man is currently homeless? I don't imagine he's going on Match.com anytime soon, Miss Heywood."

"Henry, you're absolutely no fun at all. I thought actors were supposed to be wild and crazy."

"That's celebrities, not actors. We're often introverts and most certainly can't hone our craft by acting wild and crazy."

I laughed. "You know, Henry, you and I are more alike than you realize."

He shook his head in a gesture of either disgust or disdain, took my Nordstrom card and left without another word. Ah, but Henry was not fooling me. Behind his attitude of scorn I could see he was as engaged in this as I. We were doing something. Something that made us both feel alive. My instincts told me the reason for Henry quitting acting were complex and had rendered him diminished, unable to fully leap into life. I understood this for the first time, having been so very humbled just the day before. When your identity is suddenly robbed from you, everything that once glimmered is now like a black shoe in need of polishing. Or, sometimes, you just needed to throw the old pair out and buy a new one. The shiniest pair you could find. I made up my mind then and there to find out why Henry had quit acting. Maybe he could return to it, I thought, depending on why he'd left it in the first place.

Just then Aurora called to me from the kitchen. "Come see Sam's new look." Eager to see the results, I rushed into the kitchen and almost tripped when I saw him. I stared, opening my mouth to speak but unable to utter anything for at least ten seconds. "My God, Sam," I said, finally. "You're so handsome." Regardless of my commitment and full belief in makeovers, I couldn't believe the difference a good haircut made. He didn't even look like the same person. What had been a scraggly mess was now a gorgeous splay of silver hair somewhere between George Clooney and the Seahawks coach Pete Carroll.

Aurora reached into her bag and pulled out a good-sized hand mirror. "What do you think?" she asked Sam. He peered at himself, with darting, nervous eyes, as if he didn't really want to see. "Silver fox, am I right, Bliss?" asked Aurora.

"Completely right." I clapped my hands together.

Sam, still looking in the mirror, seemed to be in shock. When had he last looked at himself, I wondered. Then he smiled, wide and toothy. His teeth. I'd forgotten about his teeth. He must have cavities. And his gums? I didn't even want to think about those gums, probably riddled with disease. What were we going to about his teeth?

Aurora seemed to know what I was thinking, gesturing for me to follow her into the other room. She spoke in a low voice. "My dentist's accepting new patients. Want to see if I can get him in this afternoon? I know he works late several days a week and this is one of them, I'm fairly certain."

"Great idea," I said. This makeover was going to cost me a fortune. He probably had about a thousand cavities, not to mention his gums. Better order a twelve-pack of floss, I thought.

Aurora got on the phone, making the appointment for Sam while I went back to the kitchen. Sam was still staring at himself. "Listen, Sam. How would you feel about going to the dentist?"

He nodded in the affirmative.

"And, here's the other thing. Henry's driving me to Idaho tomorrow for Thanksgiving. You want to come with us? I'll put you and Sweetheart up at the local bed and breakfast, then we can all have turkey together at my sister's." I paused, trying to think what else to say to convince him to come with us. My instincts were telling me he wouldn't want to go. Sure enough, he shook his head, no.

"Sam, you can't stay here without me and I don't want you back on the streets. Give me a chance to help you."

He got up from the chair and went to the counter, where he grabbed a notepad and pen I kept near the phone. He wrote for a moment before handing it to me. His handwriting, as I'd noted at the hospital, was neat and angular.

Why are you doing this?

I shrugged, trying to think of how to answer. "I don't know exactly. I just want to do something good for someone else. That's all. It's totally selfish, I guess. A way to make me feel like it would matter if I weren't here."

He tilted his head, watching me for a moment before writing something else on the pad.

It would matter.

"Sam, will you tell me your story?"

My story?

"How did you get to this place? Living on the streets?"

He looked at me helplessly; his faded blue eyes watery.

"It's a long story, right?"

He shook his head, no, before writing something on the pad.

I fell at a job site. Lost my speech and most of my memories. Sometimes I'm dizzy and unbalanced. Sometimes confused. Lost my job.

"What was your work?"

They tell me construction.

"So you can't remember anything before the accident?"

He nodded, yes, and then slumped into the chair before writing another note on the pad.

I remember my mother. I remember she died when I was eight. Nothing after that.

Let it go for now, I told myself. He's had enough. "Sam, let's get some food in you." I went to the refrigerator, hoping to find something for him to eat but there was nothing but a half-empty bottle of chardonnay and a jar of pickles. As one might expect from the contents of my kitchen, I don't really cook. And that bottle of wine had been in there for at least a month. "You like Chinese food, Sam?"

He nodded yes, again. His eyes brightened.

"I wonder what Henry likes?" I looked over at Sam. "Write down what you like and I'll order takeout. Anything you want."

Eggrolls. Sweet and Sour Chicken. Fried Rice.

"Done." I picked up my phone. "I'll just have to guess what Henry likes. Between you and me, I bet he's picky."

Sam smiled, writing on the pad.

He thinks you're crazy.

"I know, but I don't care."

He smiled again before turning back to the pad.

I like my hair.

"Yeah, you look like a million bucks. Seriously."

I called my favorite Chinese takeout establishment and placed our order. They promised to deliver in under an hour. As I hung up, Aurora came back into the kitchen.

"All set for the morning, first thing," said Aurora. "Couldn't get him in until then."

"The dentist," I said to Sam.

I hate the dentist.

"Everyone hates the dentist," said Aurora. "Highest suicide rate in the world, dentists."

"That's awful," I said. "Think of all the good they do."

Aurora picked up her bag. "I gotta run. Hot date tonight with a fireman."

"I thought you'd given up on men," I said, remembering our last conversation.

"Yeah, well, my hiatus was short-lived. Damn Match.com. They're like the freaking mob the way they pull you back in."

I wouldn't know, I thought, shuddering. Nothing sounded worse than perpetual blind dates.

After Aurora left, I changed into yoga pants and a sweatshirt and plunged into the mighty task of giving Sweetheart a bath. I put her in my big tub and soaked her with warm water using the hand-held shower. Since I didn't have dog soap, I scrubbed her with my expensive shampoo that smelled of citrus, since I didn't have dog shampoo, soaping her up until she resembled a man's shaving brush on Monday morning. I'd closed the bathroom door, anticipating an attempt at escape, but to my surprise she not only cooperated but seemed to enjoy the scrub, looking up at me every so often and wagging her tail twice in each direction before bowing her head and sighing. Sweetheart was a girl after my own heart. Nothing like a little grooming to cheer you up in times of trouble.

After rinsing her, I dried her with one of my fluffy towels and then dug an old brush out of my drawer to finish her grooming. I sat cross-legged and patted the soft bathmat. "Sit, Sweetheart." She obeyed, sitting on her haunches with her eyes half-closed like a socialite getting a manicure, although tilting slightly to the left because of her missing right leg. This pooch was the best. "Who knew you were a hidden glamour girl, Sweetheart?" I murmured.

Thump, thump went her tail before she rested her head on my knee and looked up at me with eyes of an old soul. "So many troubles you've seen with Sam, huh, old girl? What can we do to help Sam start over?"

But as talented as she was, Sweetheart couldn't speak human and neither could her master. The details of their journey and the solution to move forward remained a mystery for the time being. For now I felt satisfied I'd gotten him this far.

CHAPTER 6

THE NEXT MORNING, after the teeth cleaning of all teeth cleanings for Sam, we set out on our adventure. I hadn't yet told Blythe I was bringing a guest or that Henry was driving me. It seemed too difficult to explain over the phone, and, like the little sister I am, I knew it was better to ask forgiveness later. With her soft heart, there was no way she'd turn the two men from her dinner table when presented with them face-to-face.

So this is how, on the day before Thanksgiving, an uptight former actor, a lonely and jobless executive, a mute homeless man, and a three-legged dog headed out together on the road bound for Idaho. We made a motley crew to say the least, what with my head injury, Sweetheart's missing leg, Sam's muteness, and Henry's decidedly bad attitude. We were like a twisted version of Dorothy and the rest of her gang on their way to see the Wizard, all of us looking for something others took for granted. I didn't know then what exactly we were searching for. It would become clear later in a way I never expected.

What a picture we made—the four of us in Henry's town car. Henry had insisted on wearing his usual black suit, even when I asked him to consider this more of a vacation. I, on the other hand, was dressed in stunning black high-heeled boots, skinny jeans, and an angora sweater the color of cranberries, covered by a white faux fur coat and matching Russian-style hat the texture of chick down. Henry had made some crack about Anastasia being found at last when he first saw me in it. But I knew I looked fabulous and completely ready for cold Idaho.

We headed east on Highway 84. The roads were dry. Mount Hood loomed in the distance. Sam and Sweetheart were in the back seat. Sweetheart sat upright with her nose against the glass as if she were trying to memorize the sights. Sam, wearing a new pair of jeans and an ice-blue wool sweater, held an icepack to his jaw after his lengthy visit to the dentist, and stared at his new black and shiny boots. I remembered the feeling, suddenly, of having a new pair of shoes as a child. I couldn't take my eyes off them, walking everywhere with my gaze directed at my feet. On the first day of second grade I'd run into a pole while staring at my new Hush Puppies. My grandmother had sent them, I remembered suddenly. She'd always sent them at the end of the summer with a short note to do well in school, until her death when I was in eighth grade. My mother's mother, Isabella. We never met her because she and Sally were estranged after her decision to live in the counterculture. Occasionally, an envelope arrived with an address from Marin County, California, written in old-fashioned curvy handwriting. The envelope contained a check, Blythe told me, cashed almost immediately by our mother despite her wish to "live off the land." Every September, two pairs of shoes arrived—one for Blythe and one for me. I'd forgotten those shoes until just now.

I shifted in the seat to look at Sam. "How's your mouth feeling, Sam?"

I'd put a pad of paper in the seat pocket. He pulled it out now and wrote quickly before holding it up for me to see.

Sore. Grateful.

"I'm grateful you're here, too, Sam." Sweetheart took her nose from the window to look over at me, wagging her tail. "You too, Sweetheart." I reached in my pocket and pulled out a treat, which she delicately took from hand. This dog was perfection. I wanted to know how long they'd been together, Sam and Sweetheart, but I felt it was best not to overwhelm him with questions.

The dentist visit had been less calamitous than I expected. There were several cavities, but nothing serious, the dentist had informed us. After they filled the cavities and cleaned his teeth, the dentist told me he suspected Sam had somehow been brushing his teeth on a somewhat regular basis, although his gums needed a diligent regimen of flossing in order to recover. I felt immense relief, like I was his mother or something. Was this what it felt like to be Blythe?

Always worried over the well-being of her children and soon-to-be stepdaughter, not to mention me? This mothering gig was exhausting, I thought, settling into the seat. I crossed my legs at the ankle and let out a happy sigh. It was good to leave work behind and see something new. "I may not go back, Henry."

"Back, Miss Heywood?"

"To work. For a while anyway. Maybe I'll hunker down in Idaho for the winter. What do you think?" I turned again to look at Sam. "What do you think, Sam? Want to spend the winter in Idaho?"

He didn't answer, giving me a quizzical look instead.

"The future doesn't matter for the time being, boys. We're on holiday." I slid a glance over to Henry. "Isn't that what they say in England, Henry? Holiday?"

"That's correct." Henry shifted slightly in the driver's seat next to me.

"Don't worry, I was just kidding about the tequila shots."

My being so close to him in the front seat made him uncomfortable, but I wasn't sure why. Was it the proximity to a woman or the fact that I'd broken some kind of old-school rule? *Clients sit in the back, Miss Heywood.* I could almost hear him speaking in his clipped British accent. The English were so much more class-conscious than Americans, I thought, stealing another glance at Henry, who drove with his eyes glued to the road and his back ramrod straight. We might be ugly over here in the States, but we know we can sit anywhere on the bus without apology. May you rest in peace, Rosa Parks, I said silently.

"How you doing, Henry?" I asked. "Excited for our adventure?"

"Practically shaking from excitement, Miss Heywood."

I laughed. "That's the right attitude."

"Quite."

In silence we continued to drive, eating up miles one at a time until we could no longer see Mt. Hood and the terrain became flat and arid. Henry turned on music, a pop station from satellite radio. I relaxed into the seat, watching the scenery. In the back, Sam and Sweetheart had both fallen asleep.

"Henry, can I ask you a question. Kind of personal?"

"You can ask. I'll decide then if I'll answer or not," he said.

"Fair enough." I smiled and shifted in the seat to get a better view of him. "Why are you no longer an actor?"

He kept his eyes on the road. "After my wife died, I no longer had the heart for it."

"Why?" Weren't artists supposed to gather comfort from self-expression, releasing emotion through their work?

"My wife was an actress. We worked together in repertory companies all over the country during our thirty years together. When she died, quite unexpectedly, the thought of doing it without her seemed untenable."

"I'm sorry, Henry."

"Well, there aren't many roles for a man my age. It was time to stop, settle into a more steady life, I suppose."

"There's King Lear."

"Ah, yes. I played him several times during my last years as an actor. One of the hardest roles ever written, especially for a man with no daughters."

"Just one son, right?" I asked. "The one in New York."

"That's right."

"Do you miss it? Acting, I mean."

"Yes, I miss all of it. My wife. The theatre. The work itself."

"How did you have a son and still work in the repertory companies?" I asked. "Was it hard for him, always moving around?"

"Apparently it was, Miss Heywood. He feels a lot of resentment toward us for what he calls a lonely childhood. We hired tutors instead of sending him to school, so he had little interaction with other children. Given our lifestyle, it was the most logical choice." He fiddled with the radio, changing the station to classic rock. "My son and I aren't close. When he left us at eighteen to attend college, we didn't see him much after that. It was hard on Mary—my wife— to be shut out like that. We were both under the illusion that our nomadic, artistic life was interesting and adventurous, and that he was better for it. Mary and I grew up in staid environments—both of us from working-class people who spent most of their life in a five-block radius. To us, our life seemed exciting and enriching. All he wanted, I understand in hindsight, was to be ordinary. Unfortunately, he was born to the wrong parents." Throughout this exchange, watching the emotions pass over his face, I saw a hint of the actor he must have been.

"When was the last time you saw him?"

"At his mother's funeral. Five years ago now." His words tapered off at the end, like hands squeezed around his neck, choking him. I felt the pang one gets in their chest when in the presence of suffering—helpless and inadequate to alleviate another's pain, yet wanting so very much to do so.

Poor Henry, I thought. All alone, mourning his wife, his career, the son who abandoned him. Then, a series of judgments crowded my thoughts. The son should forgive and forget. He was missing out on a wonderful father. I'd give anything for a father like Henry. "That's a shame." I felt lame the moment I said it. What a stupid phrase to utter when someone's just confessed a loss such as this. There seemed no adequate words to convey how truly sorry I was for him.

"Never mind all that, Miss Heywood. It's all in the past. Nothing to be done now." His voice had returned to its usual clip. Like a door slammed in my face, the intimacy between us was gone.

I turned away, looking out the window, and thought of my mother. Like Henry's son, I left home and cut ties. Did she miss me? Did she have regrets? Would she have done things differently if that had assured a relationship after I became an adult? I doubted it. She didn't have it in her to suffer the remorse and sorrow I heard in Henry's voice.

My phoned chimed. I reached into my bag on the floor near my feet to grab my phone. It was a text from Kevan saying how excited he was that I was going to join them for the long weekend. I returned it with the same sentiment, adding some exclamation points for good measure. When I put the phone back in my purse, Henry looked over at me. "It's actually alarming how fast you text on that thing."

I smiled saucily. "Oh, Henry, you say the nicest things." Yawning, I settled into the seat and promptly fell asleep.

CHAPTER 7

WE ARRIVED IN THE TOWN of Peregrine, Idaho, as it was getting dark, which this time of year was a little after four in the afternoon. I'd called ahead to make reservations with Moonstone, owner and proprietor of the Peregrine Bed and Breakfast, before we left Portland. Yes, she had two rooms available, she assured me, adding that it was slow this time of year because of the weather. That made me smile. Their lack of customers probably had less to do with the weather and more to do with the fact that Peregrine had a population of five hundred people and the resort and skiing community of Sun Valley was thirty miles away. If you travelled to Idaho for Thanksgiving, you went there, not to her little town of Peregrine nestled in the foothills of Blue Mountain. I kept that opinion to myself, not wanting to offend Moonstone and her little town. Having grown up in River Valley in southern Oregon, I knew small town people were protective of their communities and immediately defensive if they sensed any hint of criticism, in the same way people are about their families. You can criticize crazy Uncle Jesse, but if anyone outside the family chimes in, be prepared to see the hounds of hell unleashed.

I knew all about Moonstone and Peregrine from talking with Blythe on the phone over the last six months. My sister had fallen as hard for Idaho and Blue Mountain as she had for Kevan. She'd told me every detail of her experiences, including her budding friendship with Moonstone, a self-proclaimed psychic with unfortunate hair choices who owned the one and only bed and breakfast in Peregrine.

The bed and breakfast was in a converted Victorian home in the middle of town; we found it with no trouble. There was only a scattering of other businesses, including the bar and grill where Blythe had met Kevan, a hardware store, a library, and a grocery store. I knew from Blythe's description that Kevan and his brothers' houses, all built on a massive piece of property, were further up the highway to the north. I'd get Sam settled in first before I asked Henry to take me out to see them. I needed a chance to tell Blythe that we had two extra guests for dinner tomorrow.

Henry grabbed the bags from the back of the car while Sweetheart took a bathroom break. Then, walking in a line like school children, my crew of distorted Oz characters traipsed up the stairs and into the lobby. Muted light from old-fashioned table lamps, the smell of cinnamon, and a roaring wood fire in the hearth greeted us. A woman with eighties-style large, flaming orange hair and a bosom the size of a small country sat at the desk, typing into a computer. Moonstone. Blythe had described her perfectly.

"Welcome, weary travellers." She leapt to her feet, almost shouting, with her hand over her heart. "Oh thank the goddesses of the universe. I had a terrible feeling you might run into trouble, but I'm glad my psychic powers seem to have taken a vacation for the holiday. That happens sometimes. Strangest thing." She came around the desk and drew me into a tight hug, filling my nose with a strong aroma of patchouli. She smelled like my mother. Was this really Blythe's friend? "Bliss, I'm so happy to meet you. Blythe talks about you so much I feel like I know you." She drew back slightly, taking me in. "You're as pretty as she said you were." Making a clicking sound with her tongue she rested her long, purple nails lightly on my face for a split second. "Has something happened? There's a shift in you. I can feel it."

I smiled, feeling uneasy. "I fell a couple of days ago. Doc told me to take it easy."

Nodding as if she already knew this information, she let her hands fall to her sides. "That's it. Something's changed in you. For the better, I must say." She turned, then, to my companions. "Gentlemen, welcome to my humble inn."

Henry said something polite and stiff, holding out his hand for her to shake. Sam, conversely, seemed either shy or suddenly tired, because he refused to make eye contact, staring at the floor with Sweetheart at his feet.

Moonstone gestured toward a sitting area we could see through the door. "Are you hungry? I have a fresh batch of snickerdoodle cookies waiting for you in the kitchen. Made them myself."

"We should probably get checked in," I said. "I want to go out and see my sister and the girls in a few minutes. Henry's going to take me."

"Of course. Those girls of hers are the sweetest. And so pretty. Like their mother and aunt."

"Thank you, Moonstone." Really, trying to say her name with a straight face was an exercise in great restraint. "I can't wait to see them."

Moonstone went behind the desk and punched something into the computer. "You want to be there in time for the proposal."

"Yes, we do. Plus, I have a little gift I brought Blythe from the lingerie department at Nordstrom."

Moonstone winked at me. "Right on. Kevan will enjoy your gift, I'm sure."

I glanced at Henry. He was examining his nails, as if he hadn't heard me. This greatly amused me and made me want to torture him further, but I didn't have time because just then we heard footsteps coming down the stairs. I looked up to see a woman with white hair expertly cut into a short style that framed her face. I guessed her to be in her late fifties. With her fingertips brushing the rail, she descended as if on air, wearing a light blue sweater dress and low-heeled calfskin boots. She held a book in her hand and when she saw us standing in the lobby, she stopped three steps from the bottom, taking us in.

"Mrs. Pennington, is everything all right?" asked Moonstone.

"Oh, yes, just fine. I wanted a cup of tea is all." Mrs. Pennington was fair-skinned and had dark blue eyes above high cheekbones. She didn't seem to be trying to look younger by dressing a certain way or not, I thought. A woman comfortable in her own skin.

"I'll make it for you, Mrs. Pennington. And I made cookies, too. Snickerdoodles." Moonstone gestured toward the sitting room.

"Snickerdoodles are my absolute favorite, Moonstone. How did you know?"

"I know things," said Moonstone, like a shy little girl might speak to her favorite teacher after receiving a compliment.

Mrs. Pennington smiled at me as she came all the way down the stairs and into the lobby. "But don't make a fuss over me. I can see you have other guests here. I can make a cup on my own just fine." She had arrived next to me by now. I caught a whiff of her fragrance, something spicy. Gucci, if I wasn't mistaken. "My mother was British, and she taught me to expect tea at four in the afternoon."

She was lovely, I thought, trying not to stare. No makeover required.

"I'm Bliss Heywood." I held out my hand.

"Lauren Pennington. So pleased to meet you." She took my hand in both of hers, not the handshake of a man but of an elegant lady, with perfectly manicured round, short pink nails. She's exquisite, I thought. Even her hands were warm. Why hadn't I had a mother like this woman? Maybe then I wouldn't have turned out so mean and pointy.

And her voice? It was soft and sophisticated, aspirating her t's and long vowels positioned in the front of her mouth like a television broadcaster or an actress. Was she an actress? Would Henry notice her voice like I had? He'd be able to tell me if he thought she was a trained actress. I looked over at Henry. His eyes were glued to this lovely Lauren Pennington until he saw me watching him, at which time he quickly moved his gaze to a painting of the ocean on the wall. To my utter amusement he seemed to take sudden and great interest in this piece of mediocre art, leaning in as if to examine the brush strokes. The unflappable Henry taken down in an instant by the transcendent Lauren Pennington? Life was certainly full of surprises.

Moonstone, catching my eye, winked at me. "Mrs. Pennington, this is Henry and Sam and his pooch, Sweetheart." Sam shuffled backwards, toward the fire. Mrs. Pennington seemed to understand right away that Sam was different and made no move toward him, saying instead, "Hi Sam." Sweetheart, conversely, had risen to her feet and wagged her tail, looking completely as if she were smiling at Mrs. Pennington, like they were old friends. Mrs. Pennington leaned down and stroked Sweetheart's ears. "Oh, what a beautiful dog. I love it when they smile like this."

"I was just thinking the exact same thing," I said. Mrs. Pennington and I had a lot in common, I thought. We both love dogs and dressing well. We're practically the same person.

Henry came forward, holding out his hand. Without an introduction of any kind and in a very informal American-type way, I might add, he blurted out, "I'm British and quite fond of tea."

It took everything in me not to burst out laughing. Perhaps I wasn't the only one instantly in love with Mrs. Pennington.

Another woman was coming down the stairs carrying a portable masseuse table. She couldn't have been taller than five feet and was terribly underweight. Jutting collarbones and the loose skin on her gaunt face made her appear older than she really was, as instinct told me she was around my age. She wore a long-sleeved sweater that did nothing to hide how skinny her arms were or that the distance between her shoulder blades seemed no larger than Clementine's. The table must be light, I thought, as this frail thing didn't look strong enough to stand upright in an ocean breeze. She needed a hamburger with extra mayonnaise, pronto.

Moonstone greeted her and then introduced her to the rest of us as Ida Smart, local masseuse. Ida nodded in our direction with a wan smile and then scuttled out of the room carrying her table like a hermit crab with a new shell. "She's the shy kind," whispered Moonstone, after she was gone. "But a wonderful masseuse if any of you want me to arrange a session for you. She'll come here."

"I had one yesterday," said Mrs. Pennington. "It was divine. I know you wouldn't think so, but her hands are quite strong."

Moonstone agreed with Mrs. Pennington's assessment, as she pulled keys from hooks behind her desk. Real keys, I thought, instead of the plastic cards all the hotels used now. Had our trip to Oz carried us back in time?

Sam had settled into the chair by the sofa, his face directed toward the fire. I moved over to him and put my hand on his shoulder. "How you doing, Sam?"

Moonstone came from behind the desk to stand by his chair. "He's tired and wants to rest in his room. Isn't that right?" She directed the question at Sam.

He nodded, yes. How had she known that? Was mind reading a part of her psychic abilities? I suppose it could be true. The stories Blythe had told me about Moonstone's abilities were a little spooky and, honestly, fascinating.

As if she heard my thoughts, she turned to me. "We don't always need words to communicate." She pointed toward the stairs. "Come along, Sam. I have a very nice room all ready for you."

He got to his feet and patted the side of his thigh for Sweetheart to follow. The three of them headed up the stairs, with Moonstone chattering away about the various antiques on display. Blythe had warned me about the clutter, saying there wasn't a space unfilled in Moonstone's place of business. From where I stood in the lobby I spotted an antique typewriter, stacks of books with dusty, tattered covers, Depression-era glass of various sizes and shapes, and one of those old wash basins and pitchers.

When they were out of sight, I turned toward Mrs. Pennington. "You know, I don't have to rush off. Let's have tea and some of those cookies before we head out. What do you say, Henry?"

"Yes. Sure. Quite all right. Yes." Henry shoved his hands into his pants pockets and resumed his careful observation of the painting.

"Won't you join us, Mrs. Pennington?"

"I'd like nothing better," she said.

One thing was clear. Henry and I were smitten and we needed to get to know Mrs. Pennington a little better. But, clearly, he was hopeless. He needed my help. I would be Henry's wingman, or in my case, his winggirl, whether he wanted me or not. Lucky Henry. Once I have an idea, I'm like a dog with his favorite toy. Nothing will keep me from it.

CHAPTER 8

"SO WHAT BRINGS YOU to Peregrine, Mrs. Pennington?" I nibbled on the edges of a cookie, trying to figure out how to subtly explain that Henry and I were not some kind of Harrison Ford-Calista Flockhart romance, in case she'd gotten the wrong impression.

She sipped her tea daintily, like a character from an old movie, before answering. "I don't know, really. I've been travelling the last several months in my car, just wandering until I find a place I'd like to stop for a day or two. I was in Sun Valley for several days, and of course it's wonderful, but this last week, because of the holiday, it became a bit congested for my taste. I had no place to be for Thanksgiving, and all the crowds there somehow made me feel lonelier. So I drove a while and found myself here."

"Travelling with no destination? Sounds great to me," I said. No other place to go? What did she mean? Surely she had a family. Why didn't she have a job? Travelling alone? Why was this? I had to practically sew my mouth together to keep from prying into her in full force. *Bull in a china shop.* Once during an argument Blythe had accused me of acting this way. Go easy, I cautioned myself. Nice and polite. Gentle, like Mrs. Pennington. Before anything slipped out, I stuffed the rest of the cookie in my mouth. That should shut me up for a moment, I thought hopefully.

Mrs. Pennington reached for a cookie and brought it to her nose, taking a quick sniff before breaking it in half and setting in on the saucer without taking a bite. "I shouldn't start with a bite, or one cookie will turn into five." She lowered her voice, glancing toward the lobby. "But Moonstone is quite adamant about trying the cookies. I only arrived here yesterday, and so far there have been three varieties."

Mrs. Pennington was a cookie sniffer, not a cookie eater. This was an interesting fact that hinted at a disciplined and moderate personality. Both perfect qualities for Henry. I glanced at Henry to see if he'd noticed her obvious self-discipline and ladylike behavior, which he would no doubt approve of, but I couldn't figure out what was going on in that crazy English head, for now he was staring into his teacup like he had the painting in the lobby. His behavior could easily be translated as boredom. But I knew better. His neck was flushed red just above the collar of his white button-down shirt. His clothes were all wrong. The black suit and white shirt screamed driver or host at an expensive restaurant. Why had he insisted on wearing his work uniform, for lack of a better term? I made a mental note to talk to him again about dressing like a normal person for the rest of the weekend. He might be more willing to listen if he wanted to impress Mrs. Pennington.

We didn't want Mrs. Pennington to see him as a driver. She must know about his long career as an actor, a stage actor no less. He'd played King Lear and Hamlet, for pity's sake. He was the real thing, which was impressive and must be conveyed. How could I work it into the conversation, I wondered. She must understand he was an actor—intelligent and cultured, not to mention a successful business owner. But back to his flushed neck. I'd never seen that, even as flustered as I'd made him yesterday with my whole "Save Sam" campaign. If we kept on like this, she would never get to see Henry's true personality. What did winggirls do in situations like these?

Right then it came to me. She must come to Thanksgiving dinner. Henry and Mrs. Pennington must have a chance to know one another, and what better way than over one of Blythe's meals in Kevan's beautiful home? It was the perfect setting for love, obviously, given that Blythe and Kevan had fallen in love in three days right in that very house. Yes, I thought, warming to the idea. The two of them seated next to one another, eating turkey and sipping white wine. With the assistance of tryptophan and effects of alcohol, there would surely be a love connection. My mind fast-forwarded to this time next year. Their initial courtship would lead to a small, intimate wedding right here at the Peregrine Bed and Breakfast. And then a life together, replete with teatime at four and walks on the beach and holding hands on the couch while watching miniseries on BBC. I don't know where I got the beach image, but surely Mrs. Pennington was a walk-on-the-beach type of woman. I bet she even had one of those feminine sun hats, given how pretty her skin was.

Yes, I saw it as clearly as the tips of my black boots. This could turn into something—a something that would mean an end to Thanksgivings alone for both of them.

"What brings you two here?" Mrs. Pennington adjusted the bottom of her dress.

I explained about Blythe and my head injury. "Henry was kind enough to drive me out here from Portland so I wouldn't miss the engagement and Thanksgiving."

Henry pulled on the collar of his shirt like he was warm. "I often drive Miss Heywood to business functions and the like. I couldn't let her miss such an important event. As it turns out, I had no place to be for Thanksgiving either. Since my wife died, my son has little interest in spending holidays with me."

"I'm sorry to hear that." Mrs. Pennington smiled at him gently. "No one has any use for us at our age, I suppose."

He smiled back. "I suppose not."

I kept my excitement to myself, but this was playing out before my eyes just as I'd hoped. These two were meant for one another.

"Do you have children, Mrs. Pennington?" I asked.

"Unfortunately not. My late husband and I wanted them very much but we weren't able to conceive. He was opposed to adoption, so we had to be happy without."

Late husband. She was a widow. Henry a widower. Perfect. I had to restrain my hands from clapping in glee by clasping them together.

"May I ask how long your wife's been gone, Henry?" she asked.

"Five years now. You?"

"Just over six years. The first two were the hardest. After a while you adjust. I retired last year and have been travelling, as I mentioned. It was something we'd planned to do together, but then he was diagnosed with lung cancer, even though he'd never smoked a day in his life. I lost him after only six months."

"That's terrible," I murmured.

"It was a shock." She set her teacup into its saucer. "We'd been together since we were twenty years old. My foot still reaches for him in the middle of the night. Isn't that silly?"

"Not at all," said Henry. "I'm still surprised to wake in the morning and find her side of the bed empty."

They'd forgotten I was even in the room. Not that I minded.

"I understand completely." Mrs. Pennington turned to me, her brows furrowed. "Who's the other gentleman with you?"

"You wouldn't believe me if I told you," I said.

"She won't want to believe you," said Henry.

"Ah, well, now I'm intrigued," said Mrs. Pennington.

"It all started when I saw them outside my office building," I began. She listened intently without comment but nodded her head on occasion as I told her how we'd come to have Sam and Sweetheart as travelling companions. When I finished speaking, she shook her head as if amazed.

"Miss Heywood, this is a remarkable."

I grinned at Henry. "See, Mrs. Pennington thinks it's remarkable."

Henry rolled his eyes. "She didn't say it was a good idea, simply remarkable."

Mrs. Pennington laughed. "Well, it is unusual, no doubt about that. It's also extremely kind."

I smiled, elated. Mrs. Pennington understood. I'd done something good. Something important.

"But what do you plan to do next? You'll need a strategy to make him independent at some point, isn't that right?" Mrs. Pennington sipped her tea. "This could prove challenging, I'm afraid."

"He needs a job and a place to live," I said. "The problem is, I don't know anything about his past except that he had a head injury that caused loss of speech."

"Well, all in good time, I suspect," said Mrs. Pennington. "I have a feeling you of all people will figure out a way to help him."

I surged with delight at the compliment. "Mrs. Pennington, would you consider joining us for Thanksgiving dinner tomorrow? My sister's a wonderful cook. Sam and Henry are joining us as well."

Henry stared at me. "We are?"

"Yes. You didn't think I'd leave you here alone on the holiday, did you?" I turned to Mrs. Pennington. "My nieces will be there. They're adorable. Anyway, please say yes."

She smiled. "How can I refuse? I'm always interested in meeting new people." She looked over at Henry. "And you *will* be joining us, right?" She put the emphasis on the word will. Mrs. Pennington might look gentle, but I had a feeling a tiger lurked within.

"Yes, yes, of course," he stammered.

"You know, Mrs. Pennington." I stood. "Henry's going to drop me off in a few minutes at my sister's, which means he's free for dinner."

Henry had turned white by the time I glanced over at him. Mrs. Pennington stood also, smoothing her sweater dress over her slender frame. "Well, that's a coincidence, because so am I. There's only one place to eat in town, Henry, and it's only mediocre, but food's always better in the right company. Shall we dine together at the Peregrine Bar and Grill? Around seven?"

"Yes. Yes. Splendid."

The Peregrine Bar and Grill? Kevan and Blythe had first met in that very bar just six months ago. "Blythe says to sit at the bar," I said, casually. "No kids. Less distractions."

"Sounds perfectly perfect," said Mrs. Pennington.

I stifled a self-satisfied smile. My work for the day was done. Perhaps I was getting this friendship thing after all.

CHAPTER 9

"YOU'RE SITTING IN THE BACK, Miss Heywood." Henry opened the door to the sedan, pointing to the seat.

"Fine." I pulled my coat tighter around my middle.

The minute he got into the car, Henry glared at me from the rearview mirror. "What, Miss Heywood, was that?"

"I assume you're referring to Mrs. Pennington. You're welcome."

"I'm not thanking you. On the contrary. I'm quite irritated with you."

"You like her. I was just helping you out. I'm kind of a modern-day cupid, now that I think about it." I grinned at him and twirled a bit of the soft fluff of my hat with my index finger.

"There's a name for you, and it's not cupid." He pulled the car out of the parking lot onto the side street and then turned left onto the main street in town, which according to Moonstone would take us to the entrance to Kevan's long, dirt road.

"Matchmaker?"

"Busybody. Haven't you ever read *Emma*?"

"Jane Austen's *Emma*?"

"Yes. She gets herself into loads of trouble interfering in other's business. You should keep that in mind."

"It's too late, Henry." I scooted forward on the seat and poked him on the shoulder. "You're thanking me on the inside. You would never have had the courage to ask her out if I hadn't interfered."

"Nothing will come of it. I'm leaving to go home after the weekend. She's travelling about, which I haven't the income to do. The whole thing's futile." He turned up the music on the radio, as if to indicate to me the discussion was over.

I settled back into the seat to watch the scenery. Evening now, it had begun to snow. Big, soft flakes. Moonstone had told us the first snowfall had come just that morning and that more was expected over the weekend. "Isn't the snow lovely?" I asked.

"Let's just hope we can get home on Sunday."

Henry was nothing but a pessimist, I thought, watching the flakes fall outside the window. It wasn't like either of them had anything to hold them down or keep them apart, should they fall in love. Anyway, it only takes a moment for your whole life to change, for better or worse. They could be one another's future. One never knew when a miracle might happen. I kept all this to myself, knowing that Henry was hopeful beyond what his words might convey. The way he tapped his finger on the steering wheel in time to the music betrayed him.

CHAPTER 10

HENRY INSISTED HE WOULD NOT STAY to meet my family, reminding me that they didn't yet know that I'd brought a gaggle of misfit toys, one of which was homeless and the other a mangy dog, all said in his British accent, making it that much more humorous.

"Henry, just have fun tonight. I'll ask Kevan to fetch the bags in a moment."

"Tonight will be an utter disaster, I'm sure. I haven't had a date in forty years."

"It's about time you did, then."

"Get out."

Laughing as I stepped out of the car and into the falling snow, I lifted my face to the sky, letting the flakes settle on my cheeks. How wonderful it felt, as if they might wash clean all the sins of the past. And then my nieces were shrieking and running toward me. I held open my arms and hugged them as tightly as possible. They'd grown since I'd last seen them, and I felt that same pang I often had when first seeing them after a time away. *I should be with them more. It all goes too fast.* They let go of me just as my sister arrived. She wore only jeans and a sweater and had her arms crossed over her chest against the cold. Flakes of snow stuck to her hair as she grabbed me into a hug.

"Surprise," I whispered in her ear.

"How did this happen?"

"Blame your boyfriend. He's very persuasive." I withdrew, and looked into her eyes. "Suffice to say, I didn't want to miss this weekend. Enough so that I quit my job."

"What?" she said, peering at me.

"The IPO was very lucrative. So I'm taking some time off. Maybe I'll move to Idaho."

I'd meant to tell her I'd "left" my job, figuring I would explain the details to her later, after the excitement of the engagement passed, but instead the word "quit" came out of my mouth. I know it's a fine distinction, but the minute I said it I felt guilty, knowing the truth was neither *left* nor *quit*, but *fired*. Obviously I wasn't yet ready to admit that I'd failed at something. It was important to me that she saw me as she always had—the successful professional.

We linked arms and walked toward the house with Blythe chattering away about this and that: plans for the weekend, what was for dinner, how happy she was to see me, how much I was going to love Rori and Cole, who were out now but to return soon, how perfect that the snow had come in time for my visit. We went around the front of the house to the side door, instead of going inside through the sliding glass door that opened to a snow-covered patio. Blythe explained that the main entrance to the house was really here at the side, as it was the location of the necessary Idaho mudroom where shoes and coats were left. We entered through two massive cherry wood doors to a room with a tile floor, shelves and hangers for coats, and bins that I assumed held various outdoor necessities like gloves and hats.

Blythe assured me that it was only children who had to take their shoes off before entering, so I merely slipped out of my hat and coat, hanging them on the hook nearest the door. They were not labeled with names. This was not Blythe's house yet, I thought. As soon as they're married, she'll insist on labeling everything. Just one of the ways Blythe tried to control chaos, which, again, could be blamed on our mother. Rather than hooks for jackets, my mother employed the strategy of piling it all in the damp corner near the door. I shuddered just thinking of the spiders that so often had hid underneath.

"Do you have spiders in Idaho?" I asked.

"I've seen one," said Clementine. "But it was outside. Don't worry, Aunt Bliss. Kevan has a housekeeper and she keeps everything really nice."

I made a funny face to make her laugh. "Oh good. I hate spiders."

"Who doesn't?" said Clementine.

"I'll give you a tour of the house later," said Blythe. "But for now let's say hi to Kevan and get you settled in the guesthouse." She indicated for me to follow. As we walked down a hallway into the front room, I snuck a peek behind me. There were several doors, presumably to bedrooms and perhaps a bathroom. When I entered the front room, Kevan was kneeling by the wood-burning fireplace, a stack of magazines near his feet. Shakespeare, his yellow lab, was asleep in a dog bed to the right of the fire. Kevan grabbed the top magazine and threw it into the fire.

Clementine grabbed my hand. Lola mouthed something to me I couldn't understand.

"Kevan, what did you do, buy every copy in Idaho?" asked Blythe.

Kevan stood but did not turn around, his head bent toward the fire. "Yes, and I plan to burn them all."

Blythe gave me a look that I couldn't interpret. I had no idea what was in the magazines, but apparently it was something Kevan didn't want anyone to see.

"Honey, Bliss is here," said Blythe.

Kevan stood and turned toward us, arranging his face into a smile, leaning on the poker like a cane. "Bliss, I'm so glad you could make it."

"Me too. Thanks for inviting me." I gave him a quick but enthusiastic hug, which he returned with his free hand. I kneeled to pet Shakespeare, greeting him with a soft murmur. He looked up at me with his dog smile on a wizened face replete with gray whiskers, wagged his tail twice, then put his head down and closed his eyes.

"Shakespeare's slowing down. Sleeps most of the day away." Kevan turned away, but not before I saw the shine of tears in his blue eyes.

Just then, Kevan's daughter, Rori, and a young man, presumably her boyfriend, Cole, came into the room from the kitchen. They were both wearing their Oregon Ducks sweatshirts and were holding hands. Blythe introduced them to me, explaining that they'd arrived the day before from Eugene, where they both attended the University of Oregon. They looked like a photo in a college recruitment catalogue, although a study in contrasts. Rori was a petite blonde with striking blue eyes and fair skin, like her Irish descendants, whereas Cole was dark-haired, at least six feet, and muscular. I knew from Blythe that they'd loved each other since they were kids. We made the usual pleasantries. I complimented Kevan's home. Lola commented on my boots and with a not-so-subtle glance at her mother said she couldn't wait to be old enough to wear high heels. Blythe ignored Lola's comment, asking instead if we'd had any trouble with the weather on the drive. Clementine bounced next to me, tugging on my hand as I replied that, no, the weather had been fine.

"Obviously we're all happy you're here safe. A few of us have been counting down the hours." Blythe gave her youngest an indulgent smile.

"That was me, Aunt Bliss." Clementine hugged my leg with her cheek pressed against my thigh.

I put my hands on the sides of her face. "Guess what? I was counting down the hours until I could see you."

"I missed you. A lot." Her eyes, so like my sister's at that age, hazel with unusually thick eyelashes for a blonde and the same sweetness, smiled at me.

Releasing her face, I pulled her into a hug. "I missed you too, sweet girl. More than you know."

Behind us, Kevan threw another magazine into the fire and dusted his hands by wiping them against one another. I looked around the room, trying to be polite when all I really wanted to do was to see why he felt compelled to burn this particular magazine. The room's decor, a study in contrast—warm furniture, a free-form wood coffee table, cozy black leather lounge chairs, a rosewood and leather sofa, and a Navajo-inspired rug—was in juxtaposition to the concrete walls and steel fireplace. Blythe had described it as a true reflection of Kevan, and I understood now what she meant. Like him, it was understated, with a mixture of modern and rustic in a way that made it feel comfortable. Yet, although cozy, one still had the feeling of being outdoors, gloriously celebrated through the oversized windows that looked upon Blue Mountain.

Blythe put a hand on Kevan's shoulder just as he threw another magazine onto the fire. "Sweetheart, will you go out and get Bliss's bags and put them in the guesthouse? Her driver's outside waiting."

Clementine dropped my hand and ran to window, pressing her nose against the glass. "Wow, a driver."

"Of course. I turned the heat on this morning, Bliss, so it should be warm by now. Also, I need to feed the horses." Kevan nodded at us and left the room.

"Did you know Kevan has three horses?" Clementine turned from the window to look over at me. "Boo, Peep and Buttercup. They're old and no one wanted them."

"Headed straight to the old glue factory," said Lola. She sounded so old and almost sassy. How had this happened since I last saw her?

"Lola! Where did you hear such a thing?" asked Blythe.

"Isn't that where they go?" asked Lola. She widened her eyes. "I read it in a book."

"Not anymore," said Blythe. "At least I don't think so." She turned to me. "Kevan couldn't bear to see them destroyed and rescued them from their previous owners."

"They were going to get killed," said Clementine. Her eyes filled with tears. "Can you believe anyone would do that?" This question was directed at me. I knew enough to answer quickly.

"No. It's awful. Isn't it wonderful that Kevan rescued them?" I asked.

"He told me once that he prefers animals to people. Except for me and Lola and Rori and Mom." Clementine smiled. "We're his family now. He told me so when he tucked me in last night."

I glanced at Blythe. There were tears in her eyes too. Kevan needn't have worried about asking my sister to marry him. They were all devoted to one another, marriage certificate or not.

"Well, Kevan and I have that in common," I said to Clementine. "Animals are better than people, present company excluded."

Clementine's forehead wrinkled as she turned back to the window. "Why do you have a driver, Aunt Bliss?"

"She's afraid to drive in the snow," said my sister.

"She hates driving," Lola joined Clementine by the window. "She was really old when she got her license."

Blythe chuckled and shot me an apologetic gaze. "I wasn't there to teach her how, Lola."

Outside, Kevan took my suitcases from Henry and they stood chatting, breath like clouds in the cold air. I held out my arms to both girls. "Come, give me another hug, both of you." I squeezed Lola and kissed the top of her head. She smelled differently than the last time I saw her. It was an almost infinitesimal difference than the little-girl smell of Clementine, but there it was just the same—the smell of a preteen, slightly musky, a hint of oil in her hair. Again, the pang of time tapped my heart as I let them both go and moved over to warm my legs by the fireplace. "I do hate driving, but actually I had a little accident on the ice earlier in the week. I fell coming out of my office and had to go the hospital. So Henry drove me."

"What? Are you all right?" Immediately Blythe rushed to me and placed her hands on my upper arms, scrutinizing my face, as if to determine whether or not I had a concussion.

"I'm fine, Sister Sue." I slipped into our childhood nickname for one another. "It's no big deal, really." Facing the fireplace once again, I held my hands up under the guise of warming them but really wanting to avoid Blythe's scrutiny. She could read anything on my face within a second. I glanced down, remembering the magazines. It was a celebrity gossip type of magazine, like *People*, only less reputable. The actress, Hope Manning, dressed in an extremely scant bikini, sat on the lap of a shirtless man. The photo was grainy, obviously taken from a distance, so his face wasn't entirely clear. I made out brown hair and that he was tall and muscular—the waif Hope Manning looked about the size of Clementine on his lap. They appeared to be on a boat of some kind. The title said, "Hope Manning's New Man."

"Why is Kevan burning these?" I asked.

"Because Uncle Ciaran's picture is on the cover," said Clementine. "Kevan doesn't want anyone to see."

I looked at Blythe for confirmation but she was gesturing toward the outside. "You girls should help Kevan feed the horses. I want to talk to Aunt Bliss alone."

They left, mumbling to one another about how unfair it was to be a kid, how you always miss the good stuff, and why did Mom always hog Aunt Bliss to herself.

Blythe moved to the fireplace and picked up one of the magazines. She handed it to me, smiling. "This is Kevan's brother, Ciaran, with

Hope Manning. I don't know why Kevan thinks burning them will do
any good. The photos are everywhere, not just this magazine. He must
have bought every copy in the entire town of Peregrine."

"This is the youngest brother, right? Ciaran?" Ciaran, rhymes
with beer-on, I thought. Best way to remember how to pronounce his
name, Blythe had told me several months ago over the phone.

"Yes. That's him. Hope Manning's an old friend of his from high
school. I had no idea they were romantically involved. But, who
knows with Ciaran. He's involved with a lot of women."

Ciaran, according to Blythe, was charming and intelligent but an
unapologetic "player." He spent a lot of time in Idaho, but also kept
busy sunning himself on the deck of friends' yachts or at film
festivals seducing actresses—somewhere between James Bond and
Warren Beatty, back before he was domesticated.

I flipped through pages of the magazine until I found the article.
There were further photos from the yacht, obviously taken in a
sequence, starting with her on his lap and ending with him carrying
her in his arms to someplace out of reach of the cameras. In an
additional photo, the two of them were arm in arm on the red carpet
at one of her movie openings. Another showed them smiling at one
another at a charity function.

I scanned the article.

Hope Manning (35) and Ciaran Lanigan (37), heir to the Lanigan
Trucks fortune, appear to have reignited an old flame. The former high
school sweethearts, according to close friends, have carried torches for
each other for many years but have remained only friends up until
recently. After Hope's sex tape scandal with rapper T. Katz last year, she
reached out to the youngest Lanigan brother for comfort. One thing led
to another. "She's finally happy," said a friend close to the couple. "He's
the steady influence she's needed to remain grounded."

A close associate to the trucking heir says, "Hope Manning has
managed to tame one of American's most eligible bachelors. We've
never seen Ciaran so in love."

This all leaves Hope's fans with many questions. Will she leave
Hollywood for good like Grace Kelly to marry her prince? Is this the
end of her party girl ways? Will playboy Ciaran Lanigan finally
settle down?

The article went on to describe Hope Manning's childhood in Idaho, the daughter of a steel parts manufacturer, and her subsequent rise to fame in her early twenties after an Oscar-nominated supporting actress part in an independent film that managed to hit box office gold. Since then, she'd been a tabloid darling for her escapades both on and off the screen, including topless sunbathing, an unapologetic potty mouth, a propensity for dating rock stars—sometimes married—a fight with a paparazzo where she'd punched him so hard in the face he had to get stitches, a drunken appearance on one of the late, late shows where she danced on the host's desk in a skin-tight blouse, red cowgirl boots and a skirt short enough that it was quite obvious she wasn't wearing any panties, followed up shortly thereafter with a sex tape with famed rapper T. Katz. All of this interwoven with stunning talent—she had two Oscars and a bevy of other awards to prove it—and a distinctly anti-Hollywood attitude. "Girls from Idaho don't do Hollywood," she'd been famously quoted when she bought a home outside of Sun Valley.

Although I'm not one for popular culture—I couldn't tell you the names of most of the reality stars who populated the entertainment magazines—my passion for film had caused me to follow Hope Manning's career for years. Not only was she talented and skilled, her unrepentant attitude toward conformity made her one of my favorite actresses.

"Why is it bothering Kevan so much?" I asked. "It's not like Hope is some thoughtless reality star or something."

"I honestly don't know." She shook her head. "I've learned with Kevan that it's best not to push for answers if he's not ready to talk. He's a complicated person."

"Aren't we all?" I said.

"True enough." She glanced outside, as if nervous Kevan might hear her, but he and Henry were still chatting by the car. "Ciaran's coming for Thanksgiving. Maybe he'll tell us the scoop."

"Coming here? Does Kevan know?"

"Not yet." She grimaced and made a hopeless gesture with her hands. "But they have to sort out their disagreements at some point. Why not start now?"

"What about the other one. Ardan?" I asked.

"He's in Europe for the year. He took a sabbatical from teaching to finish his novel. He rented a villa in Italy and won't be back until next September. That's why I'm starting with Ciaran, even though Ardan would be easier."

From what Blythe had told me of the conflict between the Lanigan brothers, I knew it was not something simply solved over drinks by the fireplace. But I kept that thought to myself, not wanting to crush Blythe for her good intentions.

"Is Ciaran bringing Hope Manning?" I asked, already thinking through all the experiences in her various movies I wanted to ask her about. Starstruck—I admit it.

"No. He didn't say one word about her when I talked to him several days ago," she answered. "Which makes me doubt the whole story."

"Probably for the best. I'd go all fangirl on her and act like an idiot."

Blythe laughed. "I'd love to see that. I wish she were joining us. She might distract Kevan and Ciaran from fighting with one another."

The fifty acres of land that had been the site of their summer home had been left to the five children. In the good times, before the conflict, but just after their father's death, the five siblings had agreed to keep the Idaho acreage and divide it amongst themselves, each planning to build a residence of their own, so that they might remain connected in the place that held the happiest memories of their childhood. Riona, their mother, had been only too happy to relinquish the land to them, happily settling in San Francisco and content to visit without the responsibility of ownership. The siblings amicably agreed about which acres they wanted, giving Kevan, as the oldest and the brother who had taken on the burden of running the family business throughout his adulthood, first choice. He'd chosen the section nearest the highway, although still a mile down a dirt road, because it was the site of the original summer home, which had been torn down several years before. The house was near a small lake, fed by a creek that curled and gurgled throughout the acreage. Not far from the house, a horse barn was home to the horses.

Blythe, during the summer she'd spent here, discovered a path that ran along the creek, made from years of little boys' feet running and playing. It was the path that connected the houses, well used until four or so years ago when Kevan's wife and the second brother, Finn, were murdered. Suspicions and false accusations between the remaining brothers caused a deep and hurtful riff. Despite the truth exonerating them all, they would not reconcile.

Instead of walking to one another's homes alongside the gurgling creek, the Lanigan brothers knew of one another's presence only by the wisps of gray smoke from their chimneys on winter days. Their vehicles passed by Kevan's property without stopping. Birthdays went unrecognized. Kevan no longer knew when they would arrive, how long they would stay or many of the other details of his brothers' lives. They knew only that they were all innocent in the deaths of their brother and Kevan's wife, which had been in doubt for some time until the true murderer was discovered. It was a starting point, Blythe assured me. The road back could begin. She intended that healing to begin this very weekend.

"Being consciously thankful is the first step in forgiveness," she said now, interrupting my thoughts.

Where had she come up with that? It didn't even really make sense, although I kept that to myself. I pointed to the window. "Henry's off, looks like."

Outside, Henry's car was doing a slow turn in the driveway. Kevan stood watching and then gave a quick wave before setting out across the yard toward a shed.

"I hate the thought of Henry being all alone for Thanksgiving." I paused, waiting for Blythe's inevitable reaction.

She blinked. "Alone? No, that's absolutely unacceptable. He must join us. Would he accept an invitation, do you think?"

"Well, I'm sure we could talk him into it, although he's all about propriety and all that English stuff."

"I've invited Moonstone as well. The more the merrier. After the work of making all the food, it's wonderful to have a big crowd around to eat."

I wanted to tell her about Mrs. Pennington but I figured that would have to wait until I confessed about Sam and Sweetheart. The table was large, I told myself. Three more surely wouldn't be a problem.

Blythe inspected me for a moment, then took my hand and pulled me over to the couch. "Here, sit. With this head injury, are you allowed to have wine?"

"They didn't say anything against wine. Just driving. And not hitting it again for several weeks. Not that I make a habit of hitting my head on a regular basis."

"Well, thank goodness for that." She walked to the bar at the other end of the room and disappeared under the counter for a moment before coming up with a bottle of sauvignon blanc. Coming toward me with a glass of wine in each hand, Blythe stared at me with her laser-beam mother's eyes. There's no way to escape them—one just has to surrender and give her the information she wants. "What's happened? You're acting strangely. Skittish. Like a hungry cat."

I took the glass from her outstretched hand and took a generous sip before answering. "I was fired."

"Fired?"

"Sacked. Let go. Kicked to the curb."

"Why on earth?"

"Ralph wants to run things."

"Ralph? Run things? After you made him so much money taking it public? She plopped on the chair across from me, putting her feet on the ottoman and kicking off her boots. Her boots. I hadn't noticed before but they were brown with thick soles, like something a lumberjack would wear. Her socks were wool, not to mention the color of canned peas. Choosing discomfort was something one only did in exchange for fashion, not practicality. Was this her Idaho attire or had she lost all sense of my direction from the makeover I'd given her last summer? I inspected her hair. It looked good, actually. She wore it shoulder-length with a few layers around her face—very flattering—and had kept the honey highlights I'd insisted she add to her dark blonde hair during our makeover session before what turned out to be her epic road trip to Idaho. And she was wearing makeup, as I'd suggested. That was a good sign. Idaho hadn't fully ruined her yet. In all honesty, I had never seen her look better. Slim from her daily runs and looking well rested, along with that glow a woman gets when she's in love. I'd seen it many times over the years and it always made me slightly envious. What would it feel like to love someone that much? And to have it returned? I couldn't imagine.

"The ego on that guy. What a fink." Blythe drank from her glass.

"Fink? I haven't heard that word for awhile."

"Rat fink." For whatever reason, this made us both laugh, the silent way we'd developed as children in our shared bed at night, not wanting to be heard by our mother and one of her multitude of boyfriends. This silent laughter, like two children trying not to giggle in class, only made us laugh harder. Finally we composed ourselves, wiping tears from the corners of our eyes. After another sip of wine, I explained my theory of why I'd been let go, all the while fighting against this feeling that I'd failed her. An embarrassed, apologetic tone slipped into my voice, as much as it made me inwardly cringe. "Apparently he felt threatened by me and wanted me out. They gave me all my stock and a year's salary to get rid of me." I gazed into my glass, feeling like I might start to cry. Why is it when you tell something hard to the people you love most, it always makes you want to weep, when only moments before you were fine?

Sensing my emotion, as she always does, Blythe slid from her chair, set her wine aside and pulled me into an embrace. "I think you should seriously consider taking some time off. You really could stay the winter here. Watch your movies. Read. When was the last time you took any time off?"

"1983?"

She laughed. "I don't think you've ever taken time off. Not once since I can remember."

Before I could reply, Kevan appeared, carrying several pieces of firewood, bits of snow shaking from his boots making a trail of water behind him. "He's so manly," I whispered to Blythe, which set us off on our silent giggles once again.

Kevan set the wood in the iron holder by the fire and turned to us. "What are you girls up to in here?"

At Blythe's insistence I told them in detail the story of my firing while Kevan stacked the firewood, tossed two more magazines into the fire, and swept the hearth. He nodded sympathetically, threw in several supportive comments, one of which was emphasized with a swear word before Ralph's name, making me laugh but getting a disapproving look coupled with a dart of her eyes to the back of the house from Blythe. "The girls," she said.

"Sorry, sweetheart." Apparently finished with his chores, Kevan went to the bar and poured a glass of wine for himself, then sat across from us in the chair Blythe had previously occupied. As we sipped our wine, they filled me in on the latest with the girls, including how well they'd adjusted to their father's new wife and the presence of Kevan in their lives, at which point he raised his eyebrows and grinned at me like a kid with a secret. In spite of my cold, dead heart, seeing them together melted me until I felt like warm chocolate coursed through my veins. They were like teenagers in love, only better because they were actually adults who had earned the right to be together.

The half glass of wine had gone to my head. It must have been the mountain altitude or something, because suddenly my tongue was as loose as Clementine's. I started telling them about my fall and how as I'd lain in the hospital bed that night a transformation of sorts had come over me. "I thought about the course of my life, as trite as that sounds, and decided I need to rethink my priorities."

Neither interrupted as I told them that my driven life was lonely and how I wanted this next chapter to be about family and friends. I explained the situation with Sam and Sweetheart—how it had come to be that they were here in Idaho—and concluded by confessing to my plot of uniting Henry and Mrs. Pennington. They both sat in what I can only describe as stunned silence for a moment after I stopped talking. I gulped some wine and focused on Kevan, afraid to see what my sister would say and do next.

Kevan spoke first. "So let me get this straight. You brought a homeless guy and his dog to Idaho, along with an out-of-work actor who you now want to set up with a woman you met this afternoon." At the word dog, Shakespeare raised his head and wagged his tail before sighing and resting his face between his paws.

I grimaced, feeling my neck flush. "Yeah, it sounds crazy when you say it like that."

Apprehensive, I turned to my sister, expecting horror and swift admonishment. To my surprise, she smiled and clapped her hands together. "I think it's wonderful you're trying to help Sam and Henry. Don't take this the wrong way, but it's sort of unlike you. Well, completely unlike you."

"Exactly," I said, still feeling sheepish. "Being good is not as easy as you make it look."

"But is it safe? This Sam could be dangerous," Kevan stood, threw another magazine in the fire and sat back down.

"I feel he is," I said.

Kevan didn't say anything further but I could tell he was either worried or disapproving by the way his brow wrinkled. I couldn't blame him. It really did sound insane when I said it all out loud. Henry's reaction had been the same. Any sane person's reaction would be, I supposed.

"They're all coming for Thanksgiving dinner," said Blythe.

I glanced at Kevan. He was looking at my sister with a bemused expression. He thinks she's crazy but loves her anyway. That's as good as it gets for a Heywood sister, I thought, stifling a smile. "Well, I would like to get a look at this Sam for myself, and I know you two can't be talked out of anything once you've launched a plan." Kevan put another magazine on the fire and then gestured outside. "I shoveled a path to the guesthouse and out to the lake." He stood. "Now I'm going to take a shower. Blythe, do you want to take a little walk down to the lake after I'm done? The edges are frozen over."

"Sure, honey. That sounds great." But I could tell from her tone of voice she was distracted by my news. Not for long, I thought. Soon she would be gazing at a fat diamond on her finger and forget all about my escapades.

"No funny business in the snow, you two," I said, teasing but barely containing my excitement. I dared not look at Kevan for fear of giving away the secret. After he left, Blythe hugged me again. "Come on, let's get you settled into the guesthouse before dinner."

After we layered up into our coats and hats, Blythe and I set out, following the newly shoveled walk. I linked my arm with hers, holding tighter than I usually would. No need to fall again, although the snow felt more cumbersome than slick as we trudged along.

About a hundred yards or so from the main house, we reached the guesthouse, a lovely thousand-square-foot space that mimicked the big house in design and architecture, with the same steeply slanted roof, windows spanning the front, and similar mixture of modern and rustic design. Blythe opened the door and we went inside, where it was warm but dark. She flicked on several lamps, filling the room with an orange glow. One large room encompassing both the kitchen and sitting area, decorated in black and tans, gave me the immediate feeling of serenity, like a visit to a high-end spa without the smell of eucalyptus and ginger. Through an open door, I spotted the bedroom, where my luggage waited beside a high four-poster bed covered in a white duvet with bunches of pillows in various shades of grass.

"The housekeeper stocked the fridge and liquor cabinet before she left for her vacation." Blythe pointed toward the kitchen area, which was more substantial than one in a family-friendly hotel room but similar in that it took up one corner of the main room with only one bit of counter space next to the sink. A refrigerator and stove a third smaller than standard sizes mimicked the big house kitchen, like a skinny spinster sister to her wide-berthed older sibling. Blythe flicked on the gas fireplace, further adding to the warm glow in the room. "Make yourself at home." She opened the refrigerator. Various cheeses, cold cuts and apples were stacked neatly on the shelves, along with several bottles of white wine.

It felt like a home. I'm ashamed to say it was better put together than any of my recent homes, and without question there was more food in the refrigerator.

Blythe sat in the brown leather chair near the fire. "Were you serious when you said you might spend some time here?"

I glanced outside. Icicles glistened like fine glassware from the awnings. Maybe I should stay through the holidays. It would be nice to stay in this little house and spend a month or two reading by the fire and watching the snow fall. For the first time in my life, idle time sounded appealing.

Blythe gestured toward the window. "Something about Idaho and Blue Mountain can put things into perspective. Look what it's done for me."

I smiled. "Well, yes. Coming here was the best decision you ever made."

She laughed. "You only say that because it was your idea."

"Well, that's true enough." I joined her in the sitting area, plopping on the couch and unzipping my boots. Rubbing my feet between my hands, I thought about Sam and Sweetheart. I turned to my sister. "What should I do about Sam?"

She twisted a lock of her hair between her fingers, like she did when we were children and I asked her a difficult question. "I've been thinking about that. What if he came to work here on the property? There's maintenance and upkeep for all the houses. He could be a caretaker of sorts."

My mouth dropped open. How had my sister, in the time it took to hear my story and walk to the guesthouse, decided my hopes for restoring Sam's life were not only valid but something she wanted to aid? Blythe—generosity, friendship, it all came like breathing to her. I, on the other hand, had to work at it. "Do you think Kevan would agree?"

"Let's see how Thanksgiving dinner goes. If Kevan can see he's harmless—if he is indeed harmless—we will make a way for him to stay." She raised one eyebrow, scrutinizing me. "As luck would have it, the caretaker the Lanigans have had for years and years, a local man, just retired. He was ninety years old if he was a day and decided to finally accept his daughter's offer to live with them. His duties were to keep an eye on things but mainly to take care of the horses while we're away. Anyway, Kevan would certainly consider it, I'm sure, if tomorrow went okay. There's a little cottage out by Ciaran's where he would live. It's not much, but it has heating and plumbing and a small kitchen."

We talked through a few more details before she left so I could unpack and get settled. A plan, I thought. We had a plan.

CHAPTER 11

AN HOUR LATER I sat on the covered patio of Kevan's house with my nieces, wrapped in blankets and sipping hot chocolate in fat, cobalt blue mugs. Blythe and Kevan had left for their walk. Kevan had told us they would stop to sit on Blythe's favorite bench by the small lake, where he would present the ring and ask for her hand. He would give us the thumbs-up if she said yes—our cue to prepare the champagne and sparkling cider. Blythe was oblivious, which made it all the more fun. Not to mention the ring, an enormous diamond in an old-fashioned setting, which screamed Blythe. It was perfect, I'd told him earlier. He knew her, I thought.

Just then, we saw Kevan and Blythe sit on the bench near the lake. Snow fell all around us. They kissed for a moment and then gazed toward the lake.

"Gross," said Clementine.

"Don't you like kissing?" I pulled her close and kissed the top of her blonde head. Her soft hair smelled freshly washed and sweet.

"I'm eight, Aunt Bliss. Kissing isn't allowed."

"But that doesn't mean it's gross."

"It's gross to kids."

"She doesn't always make sense," said Lola. My Lola—eleven going on thirty-five. They both sounded exponentially more grown-up since the last time I'd seen them. Their changes and growth were like measurements on the Richter scale, multiplying at a rate times ten with each year that passed. Children marked the passage of time like nothing else. From the vantage point of adulthood, my nieces were chubby babies only minutes ago. My heart ached thinking of them as babies, wishing to hold onto time.

"So you guys think Kevan's a good guy?" I asked.

"Yeah. He's nice," said Clementine. "He takes care of a lot of things for us now. And he's really good at helping us with our math. Mom's not the best on math. Sometimes she doesn't even know the answers. Can you believe that, Aunt Bliss?"

"Which part?" I chuckled.

"The part about Mom."

"Math isn't really her thing," I said. "But she's good at many other things."

"Yeah, like hugs." Clementine's hand slipped in mine.

"She's an expert hugger," I said. "Did I ever tell you guys how she took care of me when I was a kid?"

"Only a thousand times," said Clementine.

I chuckled. "Old people tend to repeat themselves."

Clementine nodded knowingly. "I've noticed that."

"Mom doesn't cry on the bathroom floor anymore," said Lola. "That's why I like Kevan."

"You knew about that?" I asked.

"She went in there to hide from us but we knew anyway," said Lola.

"We could hear her sniffs. It made us sad." Clementine snuggled closer, her cheek pressed against my shoulder.

"No crying since Kevan, though," said Lola.

"Which means he's doing his job," added Clementine.

"His job?" I asked.

"He asked us if it was okay with us to marry Mommy so that his job could be to make her happy for the rest of his life," said Clementine.

His job was to make her happy? My eyes stung, and tears turned the white, shiny world before me blurry. I dabbed at the corners of my eyes with a cocktail napkin. My sister was taken care of now. Finally, someone had come who loved her as much as the girls and I, which meant I no longer needed to worry.

The night Michael had left her, she'd called me from the bathroom floor, crying. After all these months later, it all seemed like a distant but terrible dream. *He's left me. For someone else. She's thirty years old.* For weeks she called sobbing, and we spent hours on the phone. I listened, mostly, and offered advice about the financial side of things, along with referring her to an attorney I knew from business contacts. Although it troubled me that she was hurt, I felt she was better off without the cad. I'd always found him immature, controlling, and self-centered. I only started worrying when, after a few months, she stopped calling me. When I called her, there was a quality to her voice that conveyed acceptance but also that she had given up the good fight. She was depressed. The cheating, lying bastard had broken her. I wasn't sure she'd ever come back all the way. I wondered if she went through the motions only for the children. If they hadn't been around, I shudder to think how low she might have gotten.

But now here we were under the spell of the silent snow and the scent of fir trees and Kevan. There is light after darkness. Second chances at love. Another run at happy. "Thank you, Kevan Lanigan, for being ours," I whispered out loud.

"Our what?" asked Lola.

"Our second chance at happy," I said.

"You know it's all because of you, Aunt Bliss?" said Lola.

"What do you mean?"

"You're the one who convinced her to come to Idaho. She never would've come if you hadn't been so bossy about it."

I thought about that for a moment. It was true. I had pushed her into taking a trip. "Well, bossy is my specialty."

"Me too." Lola sighed. "I try to hold it in but then my inner boss just comes out."

I laughed. "I understand, Lola. Don't worry. Someday you can use it for good."

Cole and Rori joined us. "We finished the dishes. What's happening," asked Rori. "Is it time yet? How long is this walk anyway?" They sat together in one of the big chairs, holding hands.

"I think he just pulled out the ring," whispered Lola. "Be quiet so it doesn't ruin the moment."

Rori giggled and whispered back. "Good call, Lola."

My niece looked at her soon to be stepsister with adoration. Was I being replaced as the coolest person they knew? I dismissed this selfish thought and focused on my sister and Kevan.

The lovers sat on the bench. From where we were we couldn't hear their voices, but we knew Blythe's answer was yes by the way they fell together in an embrace, then kissed. My little nieces pressed their small bodies against me as Blythe and Kevan turned to us. Kevan gave the thumbs-up, and we all began to cheer and clap. I reached for the bottle of champagne I'd placed at my feet and popped the cork into the yard. I turned back to the girls.

Clementine was jumping up and down. "Let the happy begin, right Aunt Bliss?"

"That's right, baby. Let the happy begin."

*   *   *

We retired to the front room. Kevan put additional logs on the fire and poured champagne for the adults and apple cider for the children. I noticed the stack of magazines was gone, either burned or recycled, I supposed. I had just snuggled up with the girls and was enjoying the beauty of the front room when the doorbell rang. Clementine leapt to her feet. "I'll get it." She skipped out of the room, headed toward the front door.

Kevan looked over at Blythe. "Who could that be?"

"It might be Ciaran. I invited him." She spoke as if it were of no importance. I stole a glance at Kevan. He was scowling.

"Ciaran?" Kevan crossed to the bar, where he proceeded to pour himself a scotch. "I thought he was sailing around the Mediterranean with Hope."

"That photo was taken days ago. He called this morning to tell me he's home through the holidays. I invited him over for drinks tonight. He sounded kind of lonesome."

"Ciaran has never been lonesome a day in his life," said Kevan.

"He says there's more to the story than the photo portrays."

"Why did you invite him tonight, of all nights?" asked Kevan. "I wanted it to be just our family."

"Kevan, he is our family. Anyway, that was before I knew about what a night this would be." She waved her finger in the air; the diamond sparkled in the light. "I want him to be part of our family, and Ardan too. You know how fond I am of both of them. Please don't be mad."

"I'm not mad, but you have too much faith in us. We're not as nice as your family. You and Bliss talk about things like grown-ups. We seem to resort to the same bear cub-like behavior we had as children." Kevan kneeled at the hearth, watching the flames. "You know what always happens when we're together."

"It's time to move forward. I want to have the whole family together for Christmas." Blythe spoke in a soft voice, with a glance at me as if I should back her up.

From the hall we heard Clementine's high voice chattering away and a man's low-pitched one in answer as they moved toward us. Ciaran's charms were not lost on girls of the little variety either, I suspected, if my niece's birdlike happy chirps were any indication. Would I need a force field around me as a way of protection?

Ciaran Lanigan came into the room, holding Clementine's hand, his face turned to her as she spoke excitedly about the engagement. I took this opportunity to inspect the playboy brother, as my curiosity was certainly piqued. There was no doubt why women flocked to him. He moved with the grace of an athlete, despite his height of well over six feet, his long limbs evoking the image of an elk, large yet graceful. Bronzed skin, probably from his latest exotic vacation, and hair the color of a walnut desk, he wore perfect-fitting designer jeans and a flannel shirt over a white T-shirt. Of course he dressed well, I thought, stifling a sigh. No makeover required. I moved my gaze to his feet, expecting to see leather ankle boots handmade by a Tuscan cobbler. But no, his feet were encased in high, black boots with leather uppers, rubber bottoms and thick soles, almost military in appearance except for the fleece lining poking out of the top. Idaho boots. And yet they looked stylish on him, despite the fact that his jeans, which as a side note, hugged his muscular thighs to the degree that I had to look away, were tucked into the boots circa 1980's Madonna. I moved my gaze up to his torso—wide shoulders and tapered middle—I swallowed, hard, and tried to focus on his shirt. Flannel, or more likely wool, in a pattern of blue and black squares gave the impression of a rugged outdoor man who could fell a tree, cut it up with a chainsaw, and chop it into kindling before breakfast, all without breaking a sweat. He should be on the cover of a fishing magazine, the epitome of a man's man, instead of a tabloid with a skinny actress in his arms. Men probably liked him as much as women, I thought. Gorgeous or not, I would not like him, I decided. Not one bit. I would be the only person in the world uncharmed by the charming Ciaran Lanigan.

I went back to staring at his boots. He tapped a toe, as if in greeting. I jerked my head up and there was his face. Right there. Staring at me with those dark eyes fringed in black lashes. What was the exact color of his eyes? Not exactly brown, but not green and not amber—somewhere in between. He smiled widely, with these dazzling white teeth that rivaled any movie star. Holding out his hand, he introduced himself. "I'm Ciaran."

"It rhymes with 'beer on'," said Clementine. "That's how he tells people to remember it."

He laughed and pulled Clementine's braid. "Good memory, Cinnamon Toast."

Clementine grinned and did this movement with her feet like a *kick-ball-change* in a jazz dance. "He calls me Cinnamon Toast because of my freckles. I'm a piece of white bread sprinkled with cinnamon, right Uncle Ciaran?"

"That's right," he said, his eyes twinkling at me.

"Uncle Ciaran gives everyone nicknames," said Clementine.

"Oh, well, that's very clever," I said.

Nicknames for everyone? How utterly enchanting, or not, depending on whether you were moved by such obvious gestures of manipulation. I knew about this kind of man, had seen him in business occasionally. Self-assured, completely comfortable in any environment, he could talk to anyone on any level and moved from an entry job to the boardroom in half the time it took others of the same intelligence and business acumen.

"Well, clearly, beauty was bestowed upon all the Heywood women." His eyes skirted down the length of my body. I became instantly hot, feeling naked under those elusive hued eyes, and stifled a shiver. Please, no, I told myself. Do not let yourself be attracted to this man who will soon be your brother-in-law, which is dangerously close to a brother.

I mumbled a thank-you and retreated to the couch, taking several quick sips of my champagne. Watching as Ciaran made his rounds, shaking Kevan's hand, kissing Lola on both cheeks like they were in Europe (she blushed scarlet from the attention—obviously she was my niece) and lastly giving hugs to Rori and Cole. "Rori-girl, you're stunning. I love that you're a blonde again." He glanced at me with a teasing smile. "They do have more fun, don't they?"

"Of course they don't." I gestured for Clementine to come sit next to me. "A ridiculous stereotype developed by the hair dye industry."

Ciaran's eyebrows went up. He looked like he was about to burst out laughing when Blythe handed him a glass of champagne and smacked his shoulder with the back of her hand. "Stop flirting with my sister. It's completely inappropriate."

He raised his glass toward me and winked, running the other hand through his thick brown hair, worn a smidge too long so that he looked exotic and almost dangerous. "I don't know what you mean. I was merely asking if it were true what they say about blondes."

My sister rolled her eyes. "Why don't you use your charm to make a toast to our engagement?" She held up her left hand for him to see. The ring caught the light.

"What? Engagement? Kevan, you're smarter than you look," said Ciaran. He gave my sister a hug. "Congratulations. I hope you know what you're getting into."

"I do." Blythe stepped from his hug but held onto both his hands. "And I'm so happy."

"You have met our mother, right?" asked Ciaran, grinning.

Ciaran strolled over to stand before the fire. Kevan was still at the bar, staring at the floor with a stony expression, his scotch glass empty. If they were to repair this relationship before Christmas, they had some work to do, I thought, regardless of Blythe's interference.

Ciaran raised his glass. "To my brother and his lovely fiancé. May the feelings you have for one another tonight remain for the rest of your lives." He looked around the room at each of us. "And to new family. How lucky we are to be together at last."

We all cheered and clinked glasses. I kept my eyes purposefully away from the handsome brother.

CHAPTER 12

LATER, AFTER OUR GLASSES WERE EMPTY and my nieces were attempting to stifle covert yawns behind fists, Blythe announced their bedtime. A few minutes passed while the girls hugged us all in turn, throwing out "I love you's" like confetti on New Year's Eve. It astonished me how affectionate and loving my nieces were, given how Blythe and I had been raised. Apparently my sister was able to give what had not been given to her. Somehow, she had broken the chain of dysfunction. A great mother, I thought, for probably the twelfth time that day, as I watched the three of them leave the room with Clementine nestled by Blythe's side and Lola several steps ahead, protesting that surely she was old enough to stay up a few minutes longer.

Cole and Rori, bundled up to go outside so they might say good night in private, I assumed, bade us all farewell and disappeared out the front door, with Rori promising her dad she would return shortly. Kevan, at the bar mixing a martini, presumably for Blythe, as she loves dirty martinis, caught my eye and shook his head. "I'm pretending I don't know they're going to sit in his truck and make out."

I didn't want to mention that it was almost certain they did a lot more at college in the narrow bed in one of their dorm rooms.

Ciaran laughed. "Reminds me of Dad and Teagan." He looked over at me as if to explain some private joke. "He was overprotective of his only daughter, whereas we could have been out all night and he'd have given us a high five in the morning."

"Rori's lucky to have a dad who wants to protect her," I said, without thinking.

Ciaran looked at me, his face softening. "You didn't have that?"

"Oh, it's fine. I don't need protection. Never did. But I'm just glad my nieces will have Kevan to protect them now."

"I'll do my best, Bliss. Either of you want another drink?" Kevan asked.

Ciaran rose from where he'd been sitting in one of the armchairs near the fire and went to stand at the bar. "I wouldn't turn down a scotch."

Without responding, Kevan reached under the bar and pulled out Glenlivet, which I knew to be high-end from some of my business colleagues over the years. I never touched scotch, finding it too strong with a nasty edge to it. Truth be told, I wasn't much of a drinker. I often poured a glass of wine at night with the intention of curling up in bed and watching a movie, but would quickly become distracted with work and forget to turn on the television or finish the wine. I'd find the half-empty glass the next morning, abandoned on the nightstand, along with the remote, both pushed to the far edges of the table by my laptop. It gave me pause, some mornings, to see that glass and the remote tossed aside in deference to my work. It said a lot about my life, of course. But, no more, I thought now. This was the new me, no longer concerned with work or being the best. No, I was good friend, doting aunt, and fully present sister. I was going to be well-balanced if it killed me.

"A small glass of white wine might be nice," I said to Kevan, interrupting my own thoughts. Regardless of my intention toward fun, acceptance of another drink was probably unwise. The champagne had already made me feel spongy, like my skin had become suddenly porous and vulnerable. Being here, in this house where love lived, my other life of meetings and statistics and sales numbers seemed far away, perhaps even fictional. I felt like a girl here, no older than Rori, and was suddenly wondering what it would feel like to have a man to wrap his arms around me as we walked under falling snow. Was this urge to love and be loved ingrained in all of us no matter our past experiences? Did we always have this hope that someone existed out there in the wide world that might see us and accept us—warts and all? Idaho, with its snow blanket and twinkling stars and diamond engagement rings as big as the moon, was turning me soft.

"Bliss, your wine." I blinked and looked up to see Ciaran next to me. I took the glass from his outstretched hand, feeling as if he'd read my thoughts. *Make your face bland, unreadable*, I advised myself. *Not a good idea to let your guard down around the brother.* He was the type to seep into porous spots and temporarily fill them with a warm, succulent liquid the color of scotch until you woke to nothing but the cold reality of morning upon your exposed skin.

Ciaran sat with his drink in his perch by the fire, the light flickering in his eyes. I settled back into the couch, watching the fire, hyperaware of Ciaran in the chair opposite the couch, doing the same thing. The walls seemed close, the fire too warm. I took a sip of wine. It was divine, of course. These Lanigan brothers knew how to live, that was for certain.

My stomach growled. I remembered the leftover enchiladas. I'd been so excited at dinner, like a kid at Christmas, that I hadn't eaten much. Was anyone else hungry?

"Did I just hear your stomach growl?" asked Ciaran.

I gasped, feeling heat travel the entire length of my body. Shrugging and using my flippant voice, I answered, "It's impolite to comment on a lady's bodily noises." Bodily noises? Where had I come up with that saying?

He laughed. It sounded like it started from his tailbone and moved up his body until it came out through his mouth, low and loud. To my horror, I found it quite infectious. I had to consciously keep my mouth tightly closed so as not join him. And, he laughed with his head thrown back. I love that quality in a person. It means they're not afraid to go all in. When something's funny, it's worth laughing hard. Although, it wasn't really that funny, given that he was teasing me.

With the laugh still in his voice, he made his face look apologetic and humble. "I didn't mean to sound impolite. It was just really loud."

I smirked and tried to think of a witty comeback. This man flustered me. Ten minutes in and I felt the need to run outside and cool off by making a snow angel. Where was Henry when I needed him? He brought out the sassy in me. "I'm a little hungry," I finally managed to utter, sounding like a complete fool. "It always happens after I eat Blythe's enchiladas. I can't stop thinking about the leftovers."

Kevan approached with Blythe's drink, setting it on the coffee table for my sister's return. Slivers of ice floated on the top, just like she liked it. "I agree completely." He patted his lean belly as he sat into the other armchair. "The married life could make me fat in no time."

Ciaran raised a glass in his direction, like a teacher with a pointer stick. "I don't think so, brother. You're way too tightly wound to allow that to happen." This was said in a light tone that I assumed was supposed to be funny, but wasn't.

Kevan's face went dark. It did sound like an insult, no matter the tone of voice. "You wouldn't know much about that, now, would you, little brother? Never having worked a day in your life, it's not something you can really comment on."

"You know that's not true, right?" asked Ciaran.

Blythe came into the room then and chuckled when she spotted the martini. She plopped onto Kevan's lap and turned her attention first to Ciaran and then to me.

"What's so funny," asked Kevan, way too innocently.

"He's teasing me, Ciaran," she said.

"How's that?" asked Ciaran.

"The very first night I ever met him I had three martinis at the Peregrine Bar and Grill, and he had to practically carry me back to Moonstone's. Oh, the sweaty, guilty hangover I woke to. One for the record books." She wrapped her arms around Kevan's neck. "You're terrible to tease me about it the night we get engaged."

Blythe seemed to have shaken Kevan's hostility toward his brother for the moment, as he laughed and kissed her neck. "No, it's not a tease. I just wanted to make you your favorite drink on the night of our engagement."

"Well, I didn't say I wouldn't drink it." Then, my sister leaned down and kissed him full on the mouth. I assumed they'd stop, remembering they had an audience, but the kissing continued. Looking away, embarrassed, determined not to catch Ciaran's eyes, I stared into my drink like the Holy Grail was written at the bottom of the glass, just as my stomach let out another growl, this one louder than the first. The lovebirds paid no attention, continuing to make out like teenagers for a few seconds.

My sister rose to her feet, dragging Kevan with her. "We should probably head to bed. It's getting late." She pointed at the untouched martini. "One of you can have that."

They said hasty good nights and left before I realized that I would now be alone with Ciaran.

"Well, we know what they're headed to do," he said. "Lucky bastards."

"Yeah, I guess so," I mumbled. "Could they be more obvious?"

Ciaran scooted forward on his chair and winked at me as he leaned across the coffee table. "Come on, Blissful, let's eat something. I'm starving too."

"Blissful?"

"You like it?"

"I do not." I glared at him with my best boardroom glare but it did nothing to shake his self-confidence.

He smiled in that way that showed all those perfect teeth and made his eyes twinkle. Inside, my stomach felt like a free-falling elevator had taken residence. On the top floor one second and dropping fifteen floors the next. It started in my stomach and landed between my legs. I had forgotten about the free-falling elevator. I'd felt it last in high school. Greg Mercer.

Greg Mercer. Damn Greg Mercer. When I spotted him coming down the hall, all that careless strength that young men possess and take for granted, with legs that seemed to dance instead of walk and draped in those 501 jeans boys wore in those days, my stomach did the free-falling elevator every time. Girls couldn't resist a nice butt in those jeans. I knew this from eavesdropping on the popular girls in the locker room after PE. Unfortunately, neither Greg nor his 501s knew I was alive. We had no classes together, and while he was at football practice I was at the library studying. But nonetheless, what a crush I had on him, choosing certain hallways to make sure I'd catch a glimpse of him between classes and attending football games just to see him play, as I could have cared less for the game, which seemed to consist of nothing but a huddle followed by a chaotic scampering and ending with a pile of boys.

Greg was number 11. I can still see the way his shoulders filled out his red and white jersey. Even now, I flush with embarrassment, knowing what an utterly hopeless case of unrequited love it truly was. Not once did he talk to me, until graduation, when I gave the class speech about the power of taking risks in a life where everything and everyone screams, *"Be safe, be safe, be safe!"* Courage, I insisted, was the key to a happy and successful life. After the ceremony ended and we had our diplomas in hand, the clear southern Oregon sky June blue, and the football field impossibly green in that way that makes the world seem brand new, I made my way through the sea of graduates toward a flushed, proud Blythe and my mother with that stupid, placid smile she had when she was stoned, which was most of the time. As I passed Greg, he put his hand on the sleeve of my gown, just a slight tug. I halted and looked up at him, surprised and sweaty with a sudden force and more nervous than when I'd began my speech. His straw-colored hair fell over blue eyes just slightly paler than the sky. He pushed his hair back with his hand in a way that seemed impatient, angry even, so that when his words came out, I felt a little ping of shock in my chest. "Nice job. You're really smart. And you're right, you know, about what you said in your speech. But I won't be able to do it." We were so close I could see a patch of whiskers, blond under the sunlight, near his upper lip, that he'd missed with his razor.

"Do what?"

"Be that brave. I'll just look back on high school and think, *"That was the best time of our life"*—just like my dad does. And you won't even remember it."

That was it—the entirety of our communication. Just then some of his friends called to him, making a gesture like they were swigging a beer. A party waited, one I hadn't been invited to. But I didn't care. Greg Mercer had not only acknowledged me but said something profound and truthful. I felt seen. Whether it was from my speech or observation, I would never know. Irrespective, it gave me a barely contained zeal for weeks into that hot summer as I prepared to leave for Stanford. I wondered sometimes, while I swam in the river outside of town, if I should have been braver when it came to him. Should I have approached him, told him of my feelings? I knew the answer, of course. If you were a girl like me, it was better to have a crush on someone with no possibility of interaction. I could admire from afar, enjoy that elevator dip in my stomach and the liquid feeling in my limbs without fear of rejection or embarrassment.

Now, here was Ciaran Lanigan, giving me the free-falling elevator feeling in my stomach and taking me right back to before-she-blossomed Bliss. Bookworm Bliss. Stay-in-the-dorm-Friday-night-and-read Bliss. Smart-girl Bliss. Not since Greg Mercer had a boy, or man, made my stomach do the elevator plunge. In fact, I'd forgotten that feeling even existed until this very moment. Damn Ciaran Lanigan.

The fire reflected in his dark eyes, he stood and held out his large hand, tanned like the rest of him, and long fingers with just a sprinkling of brown hair above the knuckles. What would it feel like to have that hand on my hot skin? Were there calluses on the palms from workouts, or were they soft like the men's hands I shook at work functions? I took in a long, silent breath, willing myself to remain steady and strong. This man and his beauty were dangerous. This man had the power to hurt me, to take me back to a time when I had no power.

I'm lonely, that's all it is, I said to myself five or six times, like a mantra. Loneliness leads to bad decisions. That sounded like Blythe. She was always right on these matters, unlike me, whose intelligence clearly covered only academics and business. Men? I was as stupid as they come.

Setting my glass aside, I rose to my feet but ignored his outstretched hand. What could I say to distract him from bestowing me with that wolfish stare that made me feel unclothed and way too vulnerable? "Blythe's cooking *is* to die for," I mumbled. Food and weather were always good diversions when one couldn't think of anything else to say.

He grinned and shrugged, picking up my wine glass. "I think you'll want this." I took it as he leaned close and whispered in my ear. "Anyway, no one's dying tonight, unless you want a Shakespearean sonnet 'little death,' which I'm only too happy to provide."

I shivered as my stomach did the elevator nosedive thing again. Yes, I actually shivered, not with disgust as one might think, but desire. This is not good, not good at all, I thought. If most men had whispered a reference to an orgasm (I knew my Shakespeare; a little death was a reference to orgasms), I would have been repulsed. While an utterance of this sort should have been offensive, when whispered by the ruthless Ciaran Lanigan, it did nothing but excite me. I hated myself for it. Trust me. I wanted to remain unmoved by this man more than almost anything I'd ever wanted before. But, alas, the unscrupulous flesh wants what it wants.

As if on cue, Shakespeare lumbered to his feet, wagged his tail a couple of times and looked at us expectantly. Ciaran knelt and scratched him behind the ears. "I'm worried about this old boy."

"Do you have dogs?" I asked. Dogs. Safe subject.

"No, no. I can't stand the thought of having to say good-bye to them. I don't love animals as much as Kevan, but I'm a close second. It broke my heart as a kid when we lost Choochoo."

"Choochoo?" I asked, smiling.

"Our lab. I named him when I was three years old."

An image of this gorgeous man as a child was not hard to imagine. The dark eyes, those thick lashes splayed upon a plump, pink child's cheek.

"Dogs are so much better than people," I said.

He looked at me for a moment. "Depends on the person. And the dog, I suppose."

We ambled to the kitchen, Shakespeare behind us. Modern, with black counters, a high industrial ceiling, and gleaming stainless steel appliances, it faced Blue Mountain. From earlier I knew the large windows gave a spectacular view during the day, but now it was dark. No city lights like I was used to, and it was quiet, a stillness I was finding strangely comforting considering I had been a city girl for over twenty years now. An island divided the room, complete with a high counter where one could eat, in addition to the table near the window. Earlier, we'd eaten in the formal dining room, but I preferred this more casual space. Blythe had mentioned how much she appreciated the kitchen, as it was designed for someone who actually cooked, with double ovens, an oversized refrigerator, and a large double sink.

I went around the kitchen island to the sink. To hide my nervousness, I took a large gulp of wine and almost choked as it burned my chest. My eyes watered. I coughed and flushed.

"Hey, you all right?"

I nodded, wiping under my eyes. "I'm not much of a drinker." This came out apologetically, which irritated me. Who was this man to make me feel like a nervous teenager?

Setting aside the wine, I opened the refrigerator. The enchilada leftovers were stored neatly in glass containers. Behind me, Ciaran moved about as if it were his kitchen. Apparently he was quite familiar with the locations of things, as he went to the silverware drawer without hesitation and pulled out two sets of cutlery and set them side by side on the counter that overlooked the stove. Then, he went to the other cabinet and grabbed two small plates, setting them near the casserole dish.

"Hot or cold?" I asked.

"There's a choice?"

"Some people like it cold. Leftovers, I mean."

"Not me. Definitely hot." He grinned and raised one eyebrow. "You?"

Why did everything out of his mouth sound like a sexual innuendo? My mind was in the rotting gutter, that's why. I pretended not to notice. "I prefer mine warm, but Blythe always eats hers cold. Pizza, too." Here I was, blabbering on like a fool.

"I'll do what you do, except I'll chase mine with a beer." He went to the refrigerator and found an IPA made in Oregon. Leaning against the counter, he twisted off the top before tossing it with perfect precision into the recycle bin.

His hands. I couldn't stop imagining them on my skin. I tossed my head, as if this ineffective movement would banish those thoughts while I scooped piles of the casserole onto the plates. I placed one plate into the microwave, and then lingered over the buttons, confused.

"You need help?" Ciaran asked, standing behind me.

I jumped. How had he gotten across the room without me hearing him? There were so many buttons. I scooted to the side. "Will you just start this for me? Ninety seconds should do it."

"Don't microwave much, I take it?"

"I don't do much in the kitchen."

"I see. Well, I've got you covered." Grinning, he pushed several of the numbered buttons. "Just put in how many seconds you want and push this green one to start."

Green for go, I thought. "Right. It seems obvious now." I flushed, again.

The microwave let out a low steady hum. I moved to the sink, picked up my drink where I'd left it and sipped, careful this time not to gulp. Running my finger across the backsplash, intricate tiles in a green that matched the firs of Blue Mountain, I thought about my sister, what her life was like here with Kevan and the girls. The counter was a foot or so higher than the sink, designed for the cook to talk to the diners, I supposed. Blythe probably fed the little girls breakfast here, as she used to in her old house before her husband decided to leave her for a thirty-year-old. The thought of her ex-husband still caused angry heat to travel through my body. It doesn't matter now, I thought. Joke's on you, jerk. Since Michael had announced his decision to end their marriage, I refused to call him by his name. "Jerk" was just fine. Not in front of the girls, of course. Blythe had made sure of that. She was a better person than me in every way. I don't know if I would have been able to pretend he was Mr. Wonderful in front of their children like Blythe did. But I guess that's the difference between a mother and someone like me.

"So, you don't cook?" He crossed to the counter and picked up his beer before sitting on a stool, watching me.

I shrugged and took another sip of wine. "I'm more of the various-takeout-restaurants-on-speed-dial type of girl."

"Well, you're a working girl. No time to cook."

"Right." I would have added a smart comment about some of us having to work for a living as opposed to jet-setting all over the world, but the reverent tone in his voice stopped me. He'd meant it as a compliment. "Do you cook?"

"I do. One of my favorite pastimes. Bit of a passion for me."

The microwave beeped. I brought the plate over to Ciaran. "Go ahead. Start." I didn't want him waiting for me like we were on a date or something, and there was no way I was sitting next to him. Way too close.

"No, a gentleman always waits for a lady."

"Are you a gentleman?" I raised my eyebrows, before putting the second plate in the microwave. As I turned back to look at him, I saw a hint of something, a possible kink in the armor of self-assured, party boy Ciaran. Had my comment bothered him? I'd seen a hesitation, a flash of something across his face that could be interpreted as pain. But just as soon as it had appeared, it vanished.

"Don't believe everything you read in the papers." Grinning that infectious grin, he toasted me with his beer before putting a napkin on his lap.

"How long are you here for?" I asked, trying to think of something to say. Why did this feel like one of those awkward interviews I'd had with potential employees?

"Extended stay, I think. I flew into Hailey yesterday afternoon." He spoke conversationally, as if we were old friends. Apparently I was the only one who felt awkward. "Took a few runs on Baldy today. Felt great. I'm staying through the holidays, at least, maybe longer. Haven't spent as much time here as I'd like to."

"Baldy?"

"Bald Mountain. That's what the locals call it." He took a swig of beer. "What about you?"

I pointed at my chest with my thumb. "Me what?"

"How long are you staying?"

"Oh, I don't know exactly. I planned on just the weekend, but Blythe's trying to talk me into staying longer."

"Why's that?"

"I'm between jobs. And I have some things to figure out." The microwave beeped again. I took the plate out, careful not to touch the hot, melted cheese that threatened to run over the side, and set it on the counter near the sink. Steam rose as I poked it with my fork, smelling the red chilies and fresh tomatoes Blythe used for the sauce.

Ciaran sliced his casserole into small bites. He indicated the seat next to him by pointing at it with his fork. "You want to sit?"

"No, I'll just eat it here. Standing up," I added, as if that weren't obvious.

"Suit yourself." Taking a bite, he closed his eyes and made an appreciative grunt. "Delicious. How is it one sister can cook and the other can't?"

I brought a forkful of food near my mouth, blowing on it. "Blythe took care of things when we were little because our mother wasn't exactly the domestic kind." My voice threatened to crack.

This is why I didn't speak of my mother. Just thinking of her brought back all the old resentments and memories.

For as long as I could remember, Blythe had been the one to cook meals, pack my lunch for school, clean the house. There was a list, near the telephone, where Blythe would write what we needed from the store, never more than a few items because she had to ride into town on her bicycle and could only bring back what she could fit in the basket. I could see that basket, now, without even closing my eyes—white with red, plastic flowers, two of them—*like eyes* Blythe always said. She saw things like that, with eyes of an artist, elephants in the clouds, the president's face in the way the last of her breakfast cereal happened to float in the milk. I saw nothing but the truth—no symbols or shades of gray, or glimpses of the extraordinary in the ordinary. My eyes were those of a realist, ruthless with my judgments, unyielding to our mother's manipulation. When one views the world around them without sentimentality, without emotions, as an analyst, an observer, rather than a participant, the truth is obvious. Blythe, with her kind and sensitive artist heart could be influenced by our mother's half-truths and passive-aggressive behavior. It made her soften. Not me. I was hard, unyielding. It had served me well in many ways.

He poked another bite of casserole with his fork before looking over at me with a quizzical expression, as if he'd been able to read the language of the past on my face. "What do you have to figure out?"

I sighed, reaching over the sink to the counter, where I grabbed the napkin, bringing it to my mouth to stall for time. What didn't I have to figure out? "Just the rest of my life." I stabbed the fork's tines lightly into the palm of my hand. I'd lost my appetite. I pushed the plate a few inches away, set the fork aside, and rested my elbows on the counter, catching a glimpse of my distorted reflection in the sink's faucet. "As I mentioned, I'm between jobs at the moment." This came out sounding bitter and I felt the acid rise in my stomach. I purposefully softened my tone. "I was fired, very unexpectedly."

"I see."

"I've had a job every day since I was fifteen."

"Are you scared?" he asked.

"Scared?"

"To not work? Of all the time that opens up to think?" He looked at me, with his head cocked to the side and unflinching eyes upon me, listening with what I came to think of later as his whole body, as if every cell of his being had stopped to lean toward me. It was intoxicating.

Without meaning to, I began to tell him the truth of my life. How focused I'd been on work and that I'd neglected my personal life. "I'm hoping to make some new friends. Maybe travel. Take up a hobby."

"Not cooking, I suppose?"

I laughed. "Not likely, no."

He smiled, no teeth this time, with a soft expression in his eyes. "Your laugh makes me think of jingle bells.

I ducked my head, studying the floor.

"What then, if not cooking?" he asked.

"I have no idea."

"What do you like to for fun?"

"Fun?" I picked up the fork and prodded at the enchiladas before taking a bite.

He took another bite, chewing and watching me. "You don't have fun, do you?"

"Not really."

"Well, since we're practically family, I'd be happy to aid you in this pursuit. Fun happens to be my specialty."

"So I've heard."

He shrugged, smiling, but his eyes were flatter than the moment before. "My reputation is somewhat exaggerated."

I thought of the photo of Ciaran and Hope Manning. She wore a pink bikini, hardly larger than a hanky, which showed half of her tiny bottom, while the top covered her nipples and not much else. A girl that skinny with D-cup breasts? I didn't buy it. They had to be fake. Which surprised me. I would have thought Hope Manning above the Hollywood pressure to have giant breasts. I supposed she had to make some compromises in order to remain on the A-list.

I found it somewhat disconcerting that I'd thought the whole thing funny when I'd seen it this afternoon. But now, mere hours later, it irritated me. I decided to change the subject back to me. "I do have this little project, though, that's proving to be interesting."

He raised an eyebrow. "A project? That sounds like work."

"Not exactly." I launched into the story of Henry, Sam, and Sweetheart, along with Blythe's suggestion earlier, surprising myself once again by how easy it was to share the details of my thoughts with this man I barely knew. "I'm out of my comfort zone. I don't know anything about homeless people or muteness or how to help someone like that get back on their feet. I certainly don't know if Sam and Sweetheart staying here is a good idea or not."

"I've been involved with a charity that helps homeless people work back into mainstream society. I'd be glad to help, if you'd like," he said, casually.

I stared at him, unable to think of anything to say. Blythe hadn't mentioned anything about his charitable work. Maybe she didn't know?

He was smiling at me, his eyes twinkling. "What? Didn't think a spoiled rich kid like me had done anything worthwhile?"

"Kind of."

"Acts of charity shouldn't be done to advertise what a great guy you are." He took another bite of food. "If you're looking for recognition then your heart's in the wrong place."

I nibbled from my plate, thinking. Had I misjudged him? Just because he was a womanizer didn't mean he couldn't do good work. And it wasn't like he was hurting anyone. If the women knew what they were getting into, they had no one to blame but themselves.

"Like this thing you did for Sam. You didn't do it to get credit, right?"

"Of course not."

"Same with me. Plus, my real friends know what kind of guy I am, regardless of the tabloids."

"So, your escapades with women? Widely exaggerated?"

He grinned. "Well, I'm not a virgin."

I laughed. How could such a scoundrel be so utterly charming?

"This jingle bell laugh of yours. It's enough to win a man over." His eyes sparkled at me as he took another sip of his beer. "Speaking of which, where is your man? Surely you have one?"

"No. Not at the moment." I said this as if it were just a temporary hiatus but then thought better of my outright lie and spoke the truth. "Not ever, really."

"I find that hard to believe. You're single on purpose, then?"

"Something like that."

"Bliss Heywood. Bliss—so aptly named," he said.

My eyes opened wide with horror. "I am not anything like my name. As a matter of fact, I've spent my life proving I'm not the hippie name my mother gave me."

This time he laughed, with his head thrown back, like he'd done in the other room. "Like the boy named Sue."

I stared at him. How had he known that's how I thought of it? "Exactly like the boy named Sue. Did Blythe tell you that?"

He put up his fork, as if in self-defense. "No. It just popped in my head."

"Have you ever heard a respected businesswoman with the name 'Bliss'?"

"If it's so bad, why didn't you change it?"

That question gave me pause. Why hadn't I just changed it? I could have been Ruth or Mary or Elizabeth. Maybe Ella—that was the name of a sophisticated woman, not some hippie kid who had to be smarter and scrappier than everyone else. Suddenly, I knew why I hadn't changed it. "It's spurred me on over the years. Reminded me of where I came from so I never got complacent. I've worked harder than anyone else I know, and I have my flaky mother and my ridiculous name to thank for it."

He didn't speak for a moment, simply looking at me with soft brown eyes. "Do you ever grow tired of being so angry?"

"I'm not angry."

He raised his eyebrows but remained silent.

"Well, anyway, anger's good. It fuels you. Plus, if you'd been raised by my mother you'd be angry, too."

He laughed. "Have you met my mother yet?"

"No, just stories from Blythe, who always makes people sound better than they are, by the way."

"What did she tell you about me?" He took the last bite of his food and pushed his plate away.

"That you're a party waiting to happen."

He laughed and toasted me with his beer. "That's one way to put it."

"Translation: party boy, womanizer, jet-setter."

He put his beer on the counter. "You know what's funny?"

"What's that?"

"My brothers and sister should know me best out of anyone in the world, and yet they know the least. They have no idea who I really am, how I spend my time, what I care about."

"So none of those things are true?"

"Not really." He finished his beer and took the empty bottle and his plate to the sink, so close to me now I could smell the spiciness of his cologne. I stifled a shiver and I moved away, putting a couple feet of distance between us. He placed both hands on the counter and looked down, taking in a deep breath. His back muscles expanded and then contracted as he let out the breath before turning to look at me. "There are stories in every family that are told over and over until we become the stories. These roles we all play in a family, I guess you could say. Labels. My mother and father did a great job of comparing us to each other, classifying us early. Kevan was the achiever, the business mind, the one who followed what Father wanted without question. Finn was the peacemaker, the heart of our family, who could do no wrong in any of our eyes. Ardan was the spiritual one. My mother assumed he would join the priesthood and always treated him with a certain reverence. Teagan was Father's little princess. Ours, too. Mother said she was surprised she learned to walk because my older brothers carried her around so much. She had these red curls no one could resist."

"What about you? What was your role in the family?"

"Me? That's easy. To my siblings, the goofball who could make them laugh so hard they peed their pants. The party. To my parents I was the screw-up. My father hated me and my mother never took me seriously. No one bothered to look any little deeper, so I stopped trying." He pushed away from the counter and went to the refrigerator, coming out with another bottle of beer.

"Did your father hate you, really?" I couldn't imagine that was true. Ciaran was decidedly lovable.

He took a long pull from his beer. When he looked back at me, I spotted the wounded look I thought I'd seen earlier. This time he didn't try to hide it. "I was the scapegoat. That was my role. I did everything to get my father to view me differently. But he never did." He peeled the label from his beer and set it on the counter. "The question is like the chicken or the egg. What came first? The reputation or the screwing up?"

"My mother wasn't actually the nurturing type, either."

"Why do you say that?"

"She should never have had children." I didn't elaborate further. No need to go down the memory lane of her drug use and all the idiots she brought home or the sounds that came from her bedroom, one thin wall apart. Blythe bought headphones and one of those cheap Walkmans and cassettes to drown out the noises. "We were invisible to her."

"And you've spent a lifetime trying to prove you're not invisible?" asked Ciaran.

"Something like that." I lifted my eyes to his. And there, right then, something shifted between us. I saw his humanity beyond his gorgeous face and that hair that curled above the collar of his sweater. This was a man with a hurt little boy just beneath the surface. Two hurt children in adult bodies, I thought, staring into one another's souls. "I'm different than you, though."

"How's that?" he asked.

"She doesn't hurt me any longer."

"That right?"

"Yes. Blythe cares, or cared, anyway. I do not. I learned early on how to turn my feelings off. It's been a great asset in business."

His mouth went up in a slight smile; the corners of his eyes crinkled. "But maybe why you don't have any friends?"

I smiled and raised my glass to him. "Touché."

"You simply disconnect. Isn't that right?"

I sipped the last of my wine, mourning its disappearance suddenly.

"You don't want another?" he asked, as if he'd read my mind.

"No, thanks." I looked up, into his eyes. The color of his eyes, this particular brown that bordered on hazel—how would one describe it? Blythe would know. She always had the names of crayons to describe colors. It was surprising how many crayons there were. These were things you learned after becoming an aunt.

I yawned.

"Tired?"

"Suddenly, yes. It's been a long day." I hesitated. Was it appropriate to ask him to walk me to the guesthouse? I didn't want to admit I was afraid to walk alone. What if there were bears? Or cougars? As cold as it was, surely the blanket of snow had turned icy.

He smiled, setting aside his beer. "Come along, Bliss Heywood. I'll walk you home."

CHAPTER 13

WE PASSED THROUGH THE FRONT ROOM to gather our jackets and hats—the fire, only embers now, the only light in the dark room. At the door, Ciaran helped me into my coat, his hand just brushing mine as I slipped my arms into the jacket. I caught a whiff of his cologne and had the urge to stop exactly there, pull his arms around me and lean my head back on his broad shoulder. Just the right height for me, even in my heeled boots, I thought. But as quickly as the thought came, he moved away, snatching a down black jacket and wool hat that fit neatly over his head.

"Sorry if I look like a cat burglar." He grinned and raised his eyebrows. "I promise I'm harmless."

This man was anything but harmless.

I put on my hat, cringing in anticipation of his teasing. "Don't laugh. Henry said I looked like Anastasia."

He smiled and tugged my hat over my ears, brushing my skin with his thumbs. "He's right. You look like a beautiful princess."

I swallowed and turned toward the door.

Outside, the stars were bright and sparkling, the moon peeking between the bare branches of an elm. I stopped just outside the door, waiting for him to join me. The thermometer hanging by the light to the left of the door read seventeen degrees.

He must have noticed my gaze because he commented that the temperature had dropped ten degrees since he'd arrived earlier. "Always happens when the cloud cover moves away."

I shivered, and looked up to the sky. "My God."

"What is it?" he asked.

"The stars."

"They never get dimmer, no matter how old I get," he said. "I find that remarkable."

We began to walk along the shoveled walkway toward the guesthouse. My breath came out in clouds, illuminated in the light from the lampposts that peppered the driveway. We were about halfway when one foot slipped. I let out a squeal. As quickly as I began to slip, Ciaran reached out and steadied me, his hands tight around my waist. I instinctively wrapped my arms around his neck.

"You all right?" He spoke into my ear, husky, his breath warm against my skin. "You're shaking."

"I fell last week."

"Fell?"

"On the ice outside my office. The same day I got canned. An embarrassing trip to the hospital in the ambulance and everything."

"Hell, that's about as crappy a day as I can think of." He tucked a lock of hair stuck to the warm skin of my cheek, back into my hat. "I can't think of another woman worthy of this hat and coat." His eyes moved about my face, like a person memorizing a set of numbers.

I almost laughed, despite the fact that I was enormously pleased. "Is that one of your lines you use on the little actresses they film you with?"

He rolled his eyes. "You saw the photos."

"Nice abs, I have to say."

He threw back his head, laughing, the sound echoing in the quiet night. "That might be the first nice thing you've said to me." His face turned serious as he touched the tip of his gloved finger to my nose. "You're getting cold. Come along. I won't let you fall." He took one of my arms and tucked it firmly against his side. "Hold on, now." We headed across the icy path once again. It was truly slick, and I was hopeless in my high heels. Several times I started to slip but he righted me quickly. Neither of us spoke until we reached the doorway of the guesthouse, where we paused under the light that hung over the front door.

"See? All safe." He threw open the door and ushered me inside.

I could not feel my feet, a result of my unsuitable boots and the frigid temperatures. He strode to the gas fireplace and flipped the switch. The fire sputtered to life as I turned on a lamp. Then, shrugging out of his jacket, he plopped into the armchair closest to the fire and started unlacing his boots.

"What're you doing?" I asked. Prickles of alarm ran up my arms.

He grinned. "Don't worry, purely innocent. I came over on the snow mobile and have to take it home, so I'm going to warm up my feet a little before I go, if it's okay with you?"

"Sure. Fine." I avoided his gaze, making a fuss of shrugging out of my jacket.

"I blame you, of course."

"For what?" I asked.

"This is the best evening I've had in longer than I can remember, and I lost track of time." He stood in his stocking feet now. Dark blue and thick, over nicely shaped feet.

"More fun than Hope Manning in a bikini?" I sounded like a woman with jealous stalker tendencies.

"God, I hate the tabloids." He stretched his legs out, looking into the fire.

I needed to get off this subject before I embarrassed myself. Sitting across from him, I tried to think of what to say. I wanted desperately to take off my boots but didn't want to admit how badly my feet hurt. "I'm sorry. It's none of my business. I'm just teasing you." I wasn't just teasing him, of course, and my tight voice betrayed the truth.

"Hope Manning's a good friend of mine, that's all." He sounded resigned and fatigued, like he was tired of telling the same story over and over.

"Do all your friends sit on your lap in their bikinis?" This time my teasing tone came through. Back on track. Ciaran and Bliss, buddies, almost siblings, exchanging jabs.

"Of course. Don't yours?" Deadpan, then a wink.

I laughed. "I certainly do not have any bikini-wearing friends who sit on my lap, no."

"Hope and I go way back."

"I don't have any friends from high school who sit on my lap, either."

He smiled, looking at me. "Would you like to hear the truth?"

I acted like I didn't care with a shrug of my shoulders. "Like I said, your love life is really none of my business."

"Hope and I are good friends. We share some things from when we were kids that bonded us for life. Kind of like siblings, actually."

I didn't say anything, thinking again of the photographs, which seemed decidedly un-sibling like.

He continued. "She recently met a man she wanted me to meet. If you've followed her much, you know she doesn't always have the best taste in men, and we made a pact last year that I'd meet anyone she got serious with."

I nodded, reluctant to tell him what a fan I was of Hope Manning and that I followed her career closely. "After the sex tape with D. Dog or whatever his name is."

Ciaran laughed. "If you mean T. Katz, then yes. She didn't even know he took that. Just using her for publicity. I've never wanted to hurt a person more than I did him. So, yeah, I agreed to be more a part of her life after that. The paparazzi started filming us together and now apparently we're a couple."

"So that part's made up?"

"Exactly."

I sat with this for a minute. Were they truly just friends? Why did this make me feel like dancing? Never mind, I thought. Stay focused on his story.

"Anyway, I was a guest on the latest boyfriend's yacht. A music producer, very successful but way too old for Hope." The house creaked. Ciaran tugged at the toe of one of his socks.

"And?"

"Couldn't stand him the minute I met him. My gut instinct was substantiated a day or two later when Hope found him having sex with one of the kitchen helpers, who is sixteen if she's a day."

"Underage? Really?"

Ciaran looked green for a moment. "Makes me feel sick. Anyway, we're out in the middle of the Mediterranean, making it impossible to get to shore for a few hours. On our way back, Hope drank an entire bottle of champagne, maybe more. I found her drunk, where she rambled out the whole story to me, then cried on my shoulder."

"On your lap?"

"She passed out and I was in the process of scooping her up and taking her inside when those photos were taken. That must be some kind of lens, because we were still a ways from shore."

"Maybe pictures aren't worth a thousand words, after all?"

He smiled but his eyes were sad. "Exactly."

"Does it bother you that everyone has the wrong impression of your relationship?"

"I learned a long time ago not to care what people think." He leaned back, looking into the fire. "As a matter of fact, my notoriety actually helps in my charity work. Everyone wants to come meet me after they hear of my reputation."

"Well, we have that in common then. I don't care what people think either." I sank further into the cushions of the couch, unzipping my boots. "My feet are numb. I'm never wearing these again."

He smiled, watching me. "Too bad. You look hot in them."

"That was the idea, but I'm starting to see the flaw in my plan." I placed my boots neatly by the couch and then pulled a foot into my lap like I'd seen him do and rubbed it with my hands. Before I knew what was happening, he'd scooted from his chair and knelt on the floor near me. "Can I look?" He held up his hands and wriggled his fingers. "All very brotherly, of course."

"I guess."

He tugged off my socks. "Your feet are blue. We need to get you some decent boots."

I didn't answer, trying hard not to make any embarrassing noises of pleasure as he began to rub one foot and then the other with his warm hands. In a few minutes, feeling had returned to both feet, along with awakening several other parts of my body. I took in a long, silent breath, trying to control my thoughts, as I imagined his fingers finding their way up my legs. I shifted, tapping his shoulder with my fingertips. "It's good now. Thank you."

He rose and sat on the other end of the couch. The fire gave the room an orange glow and cast shadows under his eyes. "So, if we're to be siblings now, you have to let me show you around this weekend. We could go down to Sun Valley. Do you ski?"

There was nothing sisterly about the way I felt about this man. I shook my head no to the question regarding skiing.

"There are a couple of fun bars and restaurants in Hailey. Maybe we could go Friday night. The day after Thanksgiving's always a blast."

"I don't really hang out at bars."

He grinned. "That's because you never have any fun. Remember you're supposed to be having fun?"

"Right. I forgot." I smiled, feeling warm and happy at the prospect of spending an evening with Ciaran, despite my better judgment.

Patting his chest with his hand, he raised one eyebrow. "You are beautiful, especially when you smile like that. I think you need to smile more often. I'm going to take it upon myself to get you to smile more than you frown. That begins with letting me plan some fun. Deal?"

"Sure," I mumbled, standing and wishing I had something to do, something to fetch, and thought to offer him a drink. "Do you want another drink? I saw wine in the fridge earlier."

"Maybe some water before I head out?"

"Sure."

He followed me over to the kitchen area as I yanked open the refrigerator, remembering some bottles of water and appreciating once again the fully stocked kitchen. The person who had arranged for my stay needed to move in with me permanently and save me from the fate of endless takeout food. With that thought, I felt Ciaran behind me. I knew from his scent that he was close. I held my breath. If he moved another inch toward me, our bodies would touch. "I'll let you choose—either bubbles or regular." I moved aside so he might grab the water, feeling as if I was now barreling down tumultuous river rapids after a storm with the way my body felt magnetized to his. If we touched, it would be all over. I knew this, even then, on that first night.

Instead of leaning down to choose a drink, he shut the refrigerator door and inched closer to me. I instinctively backed up, my gaze on the left side belt loop of his jeans, until the counter stopped me. A knob on a drawer jabbed into the spot just above my tailbone. "Did you change your mind about the water?" I looked up into his eyes. They seemed almost black in the dim light and somber, all hint of the teasing way he'd looked at me all night having vanished. Every nerve ending up and down my body tingled.

With his knuckles, he brushed my left cheek. "You don't think you're beautiful? Why?"

"You have no idea what you're talking about." I tried my confident, smirking smile and cold tone that had become a savior when flirtatious men in the workplace made inappropriate comments. Usually it came easily and shut down a man's advances in less than a second, conveying an assurance that I thought myself too good for them. In my experience, men were cowardly creatures and despite bravado, deeply insecure. A confident woman made them want to run home to their mothers. However, tonight it did not work. My smile trembled instead of smirked, and my speech turned bashful instead of cold.

"I do, though. Most women have no idea of their true beauty," he said.

I knew this was true, thus the need for makeovers to reveal how stunning they could be under all the dowdy self-doubt. But instead of going into all that, I simply said, "I just know all the tricks. What to wear, how to fix my hair, etc."

"That's the outside packaging. It's the inside you can't fake. That's where a woman is either beautiful or not." The vein that ran down his forehead pulsated as he took in a deep breath. I breathed in as well, shallow, trying to hide that it felt like it might be my last. We stood that way for a moment, my heart beating fast and the air dense and warm like another layer of clothing.

Then, with one hand, he moved the collar of my sweater an inch south, and with the other traced my collarbone using his index finger. "We don't see much of a woman's bones, even though we know they're there, supporting their amazing structure. Think of that—how perfectly the human body is designed—what a miracle it is. And the collarbone, how it protrudes just enough so it's this beautiful hint of what holds a woman together. So delicate, yet strong, like the women they support. Like the woman you are." He traced the left side collarbone, stopping for a brief second to rest his finger in the hollow of my neck before moving up to my ear, where my hoop earring dangled. "Your skin tells me you haven't spent much time in the sun." His voice, husky, was only a notch above a whisper.

"One of the benefits of working all the time, I guess." Had I said this out loud or only in my mind? I couldn't be sure. Either way, he didn't seem to notice.

He moved his hands to the sides of my face, stroking just below my mouth with his thumbs. "I've wanted to kiss this sassy mouth since the moment I saw you."

"Sassy?" I whispered.

"And strangely vulnerable all at once."

"I know you say this to all your women."

"You need to learn when to be quiet and let a man take the lead. You know, like a dance?"

"I don't dance for that very reason. I always try to lead."

"The key is surrendering."

"Surrendering? To a man? No."

He chuckled. "How about to the right man, and it doesn't have to be all the time—just in certain situations. It might yield good results."

"Are we still talking about dancing?" Given my breathless, wanton voice, I didn't even recognize myself. What was happening? Flirting with a man I'd met a few hours ago? A man who would soon be in my family? Again, that sliding feeling came, that feeling like I could not control anything. Chaos.

"If I don't kiss you, I may perish right here on the spot."

I laughed. "Perish?"

"Too dramatic?"

"A lit—." He stifled my answer with his mouth as his arms went around my waist. The kiss was delicate at first, with his lips parting mine. No tongue, just our lips fitting together. After a moment, he began to explore, ever so slightly with the tip of his tongue. My arms went around his neck, pressing my breasts against his chest. He let out a soft moan and his kiss turned hard. He pushed into my thighs with his own, our muscles tense. We kissed for what seemed like days, with the room receding to nothing until it was a space where only he and I existed, like two hothouse flowers in a glass container. I could not get enough of the taste of him, and he seemed to feel the same, for the second I thought we might stop to catch a breath, we picked up again.

Finally, breathless, hot, and damp, I said against his mouth. "What're we doing?"

He withdrew slightly, looking into my face, his cheeks flaming red. "That was the best kiss of my life, that's what we're doing."

Despite myself, I whispered, "Like magic."

"Magic. Exactly."

"You should go."

"Yes, I should go," he said.

"Before this goes any further."

"Yes, before this goes any further."

We kissed again at the counter, then again by the fire before he put his boots on, and again at the door as he slipped into his jacket and hat. Finally, breathless, I pushed him out into the frigid night, listening with my forehead pressed against the door as his boots crunched in the icy snow on the steps. The room went cold without him. I imagined that the warm air had followed him out the door, allowing an arctic wind to invade. Shivering, I went to the window and watched Ciaran's shape that seemed a shadow make its way over to the big house and did not turn away until the lights in the yard went dark. And in that inky night with a billion stars above, the time between us began to feel like a dream, like I'd somehow conjured him from the recesses of my heart as dark as the scene before me. Had I stumbled from a dream to this window that felt icy against my fingertips? I touched my lips. They felt bruised, almost bloody, but hungry still for more. More Ciaran. I closed my eyes for a moment, remembering the ways his hands had caressed my body, how he'd whispered, how clearly I'd felt his desire. It was real. Ciaran Lanigan had kissed me, and in those moments I'd changed. The porous nature of my skin had betrayed me, had allowed this man in and made me alive and confused and more frightened than I'd ever been. I stood for a long time at the window, wondering, fretting about the future and my newly softened heart—peering into the darkness as if answers might appear like matches struck at midnight on the darkest day of the year.

CHAPTER 14

THANKSGIVING MORNING I WOKE AROUND NINE to the sound of my cell phone ringing. It was Henry calling to see how I was faring. Listening to his tone of voice, I tried to figure out his mood, but it was the usual clipped accent with no inflections whatsoever. How had the date gone? I hoped he and Mrs. Pennington had kissed as passionately as Ciaran and I. Ciaran. I almost let out a groan at the mere thought of him.

"Did you hear what I said, Miss Heywood?"

"No, I'm sorry. What was that?"

"I said we need to understand the details for today. The agenda and all."

The agenda? Could Henry be more uptight? It was possible he needed to have sex even more than I. "Come at three. All of you."

He cleared his throat. "Mrs. Pennington as well?"

"Depends. How did last night go?"

"Fine." Aha! I detected a smile in his voice.

I decided not to torture him by teasing him. It was Thanksgiving after all. "Can you bring them all out? Moonstone, too?"

"Yes. About that." He paused. "She and Sam. Well, they seem to be...how shall I say it? Becoming close?"

"How close?"

"She seems to think she can hear his thoughts. The two of them have been huddled up together on the couch since early this morning. It's... I don't know how to describe it."

"Weird?"

"Right," said Henry.

"Moonstone's a weird one. No doubt. But she's harmless."

"I don't want to see him get hurt."

"What's this, Henry? You going soft on me?"

"Hardly. We'll see you at three."

"Splendid. Did I sound British just now?"

A sigh from the other end of the phone. "Not even slightly."

I called my sister next, confirming that the guests were arriving at three and asking when I should come to the big house to help her cook. She laughed at the suggestion. "No need to help in the kitchen. I have Rori."

"What? I can help," I said. "You know, stuff the turkey or whatever one does on this gluttonous holiday."

"You're going to stuff the turkey?"

"Uh. Sure. If you need me to." I shuddered, thinking of the inside of a turkey carcass. "Do you have any plastic gloves?"

She laughed. "Don't worry, the turkey's already in the oven. Rori and Lola are here helping me cook and Ciaran's bringing a few dishes. You and Clementine can set and decorate the table. How's that?"

"I'm as talented as an eight-year-old. Great."

"Well, you might consider taking instructions from her, actually."

I flushed, remembering the microwave incident from last night. "Any idea when Ciaran's coming over?" Was that a guilty squeak in my voice? If so, Blythe didn't seem to notice.

"Three or so. He just called and said he's elbow deep in sweet potatoes. He's making a soufflé."

A soufflé? That sounded serious.

We hung up and I got out of the warm bed, shivering from the chill of the room.

After dressing in yoga clothes, I went through my daily routine of poses in front of the fireplace, then showered, fixed my hair and face but dressed in the robe I found hanging in the bathrobe instead of clothes. I smiled, thinking of Henry and his request for the agenda. Lounging in front of the fireplace was my agenda for this morning, I thought, as I perused the novels in the bookcase before choosing a mystery set in Seattle. Perfect vacation book, I thought. I put the book on the coffee table and went in search of food.

Grapes, a boiled egg and a piece of toast made a fine breakfast as I sat on the couch eating and gazing out the window. The clouds had parted to let in a sliver of sunshine that made crystals sparkle on the blanket of snow. Tree limbs heavy with snow hung low like the curve of a white swan's neck. My thoughts went to Ciaran, unfortunately, wondering if he had thought of me at all this morning. After my meal, I wandered back to the kitchen, deciding a cup of coffee sounded like the perfect partner to a good book. I found a bag of coffee grounds in the freezer and located a small maker under the sink. I scooped a generous amount into the metal filter, liking my coffee strong, and had just hit the start button when a knock on the door startled me. Probably one of the little girls, I thought.

But when I opened the door, it was Ciaran. He held two oblong contraptions made of orange canvas encased by metal with a dangerous looking clamp in the middle that reminded me of an animal trap.

"What are those?" I asked, afraid to hear the answer. "Please tell me those don't go on a person's feet."

"They do, indeed. Snowshoes."

I looked down at his feet. He wore a pair of the contraptions and they were covered in snow. Behind him on the porch were two backpacks and two sets of poles. "Snowshoes? For me?" I asked.

"Yes. Your gateway to the great outdoors even during snowy season." He shook them above his head like they were trophies. "I've come to take you snowshoeing. No better way to see the property than walking."

Snowshoes? I knew nothing of these awkward looking things and had no intention whatsoever of walking in the snow or anywhere else with them attached to my feet. No, I would stay inside with my book rather than go out into the elements. Much safer on all counts.

"I kind of made plans to stay in and read this morning." I clutched the collar of the bathrobe, feeling quite naked and vulnerable underneath. "I'm not dressed, as you can see."

His eyes ventured lazily down the length of my body. I felt my nipples harden and moved my arm to cover them. "I can see that." He moved his gaze back to my face.

"I thought you were cooking?" I asked.

"I am. And I need your help." His eyes twinkled. "With the microwave."

"Very funny."

"Actually, I'm all finished. I woke early this morning. Restless. I can't imagine why." He raised an eyebrow before glancing behind me. "Is that fresh coffee I smell?"

"I suppose you want a cup?"

"Sounds delicious. Thank you for offering."

"Fine. Come in, but I'm not going snowshoeing." I stepped back and indicated that he should come inside, knowing I might never get rid of him and not even sure I really wanted to.

He unsnapped his feet from the snowshoes, stamped his boots against the floorboards of the porch and followed me inside. He set the snowshoes meant for me, and his bag, on the table and hung his jacket and cap on one of the hooks near the door. I hadn't noticed the hooks last night—apparently too distracted by the company, I thought, glancing at him. His hair stood up in all directions. I wanted to run my hands through every strand of it. Instead, I went to the refrigerator and pulled out the pint of half-and-half I'd spotted earlier and set it on the counter. "Cream?" I asked, turning back to look at him. Folding my arms over my chest as if that would protect me from my desires, I leaned against the counter, watching him. In two steps he reached me and picked up the ends of the robe's belt. "Are you wearing anything under this?" His voice was gruff but teasing.

"None of your business."

"So you aren't?"

"I might be," I said.

"I could have you undressed in under a second." He fingered the collar of my robe with one hand and traced my lips with the other. "I couldn't sleep a wink last night thinking about you."

"Really? I slept fine." A lie.

"I must not have done a good enough job getting you as worked up as I was then. Not even the cold ride to the house calmed me down." He untied the bathrobe's belt, inch by inch, all the while staring into my eyes. "But I happen to like a challenge."

I held my breath until he leaned in to kiss me, soft at first, pulling at my bottom lip with his, then harder. I gasped as his fingers found their way under the robe to the bare skin of my waist. "This isn't a good idea," I said against his mouth.

He stopped, leaning back an inch or so to peer into my face. "Why?"

"It's so complicated. Us. The family." I paused. "What I know of your reputation."

Cocking his head to the left, the sides of his mouth curved into an almost smile. "I'm supposed to teach you how to have fun. Wasn't that the agreement?"

I nodded in the affirmative, feeling vulnerable and fragile, like a woman perched on the side of the cliff so precariously that all it would take was a soft breeze to push me over. A memory of a drive to a swimming hole in my hometown of River Valley came to me. The best hole of all—Six Mile, the locals called it. A spot on the river over forty feet deep and a sandy beach with rocks to jump from. But to get to it you had to take a skinny road with bends and curves for miles up the side of a mountain. As you climbed, if you dared to look down— Blythe did but I couldn't—you could see the river, snaking through the canyon. One wrong turn and your car could tumble from the road and bounce against the side of the mountain until you landed in the river, nothing but a ball of metal with your crumpled body inside. Ciaran was like the bend in the road that tossed you over or maybe the car coming around the corner until it was too late and both cars were lost to the canyon below.

"Well, sex is fun," he said. "Especially with me."

"I am familiar with the concept."

"I'm sure you're more than just familiar."

"It's been a while, actually."

"That's just wrong."

"Wrong or just unlucky?" I touched the side of his face with my fingertips. He'd shaved since last night and his skin was smooth. I caught the scent of his lime shaving cream. A smudge of residual suds made a quarter-moon shape below one ear that he'd apparently missed when wiping his face. Did he wipe with a towel or run water over his face, I wondered? The thought of him in that intimate setting—a towel wrapped around his waist, shaving, made me shudder. It was either that or the way his hand was moving from my waist to my hip and then down to my backside as he pulled me closer.

"We could just agree to enjoy one another. No strings attached?" He leaned over and teased my earlobe with his tongue before moving his mouth down my neck. "It's not like you're moving here or anything. Just stay a couple of weeks. Let me show you a good time."

I turned my gaze to the ceiling, trying to reason through what he was saying, which was no small feat given how my body was reacting. I'd had arrangements like this in the past. Why was I hesitating now, with this particular man? I'd never been as attracted to someone as I was to Ciaran—there was no question of that. Was I was afraid the family would find out about us, or was it that I was afraid I might fall for him? Or, a combination of both? "Women like me shouldn't get involved with men like you." Unless they wanted to get hurt, I thought.

"Men like me?" He slid his other hand under the robe and found my breast. He cupped it gently and then moved his thumb against my nipple. I sucked in my breath and let out a whimper of pleasure. "What's wrong with a man like me?"

"You don't stick around for long."

His hands went still as he looked into my eyes. "But I'm sure fun when I'm here." He grinned for a second before turning sober. "I would never lie to you or mislead you. I am what I am. We're both adults with no one in our lives who would get hurt if we spent some time together."

I moved my arms to wrap around his neck. "What about our families?"

"No one has to know," he said. "It's not their business anyway."

"You make it so I can't think straight."

"Good. You think too much." He kissed me again, quickly this time, and released his hands from under my robe, tying the belt like I was a child about to go out to play. "But I'll let you run away if you want. Go get dressed. I promised you fun, and I shall deliver."

"Now?"

"Yes. I'm going to teach you how to snowshoe. You'll love it. Great exercise, which will hopefully help get my mind off taking you to bed."

"I have nothing to wear."

He pointed at the bag on the table. "Blythe sent over some of her snow gear for you to use."

"You told her you were coming here to ask me?"

"She suggested it. Said it would be fun for you to try something new."

"What if I fall? I'm not supposed to hit my head."

He grinned and tossed the bag to me. "You won't fall. Anyway, I'll be there to catch you.

"What about boots?" I asked, stalling for time.

"Damn. I forgot about boots."

"It's Thanksgiving. Nothing will be open." I paused. "Is there even a place to buy boots in Peregrine?"

He nodded but looked distracted, running his hands through his hair. "I guess we'll have to take the truck to my house."

Just then my cell phone rang. I left him and went into the bedroom. It was Blythe. "Hey. I forgot to send boots over with Ciaran. I have an extra pair—they've never been worn."

Darn. We had the same size feet. I was stuck now. I would have to go out into the elements and try to walk on snow with dangerous-looking contraptions stuck to my feet. Why couldn't Kevan have had a second home in Hawaii instead of godforsaken Idaho? I threw the phone on the bed, trying to think of an excuse, when I heard Ciaran say my name. He stood in the door frame of the bedroom, watching me.

"That was Blythe. She has boots for me."

His face lit up. "Excellent.

"Great. Cooking and snowshoeing. The fun never stops with you."

"Now don't spoil the mood by being snarky. You'll have fun, trust me." In what seemed like a second, he'd grabbed the bag of clothes from the table and emptied the contents on the bed: snow pants, sweater and ski jacket, along with a cute hat with a tassel. At least there was that. There were also a white cotton long-sleeved T-shirt and pants that reminded me of something an old man would wear to bed. I held up the pants. "What in the hell are these?"

"Long underwear. Nice and cozy for under your ski pants."

"It just gets worse and worse."

He ignored the last comment. "Once you're ready we can snowshoe over to my house and have a snack. Then, we can shower and be ready by three. Where we shower and with whom is optional."

"You're hopeless."

He raised an eyebrow. "Say the word and we can entertain ourselves inside."

I pointed toward the living room. "You may leave my bedroom now. And shut the door, please?"

He shook his head, as if saddened by a great loss. "I promise not to touch if you let me watch you get dressed."

"You're a complete perv."

He laughed. "Can't blame me for trying. Seriously, grab an extra pair of clothes to wear to dinner. You can dress at my house."

"I'll have to do my hair and makeup."

"That won't be a problem. I have mirrors."

"Please don't say hung on the ceiling."

Smirking, he raised an eyebrow. "That, my dear, is not my style."

"I don't have the type of clothes that pack well in a back pack."

"Fine. I'll take you back on the snow mobile in time for you to get ready for dinner. No more excuses. You can try to wear me down with your pessimistic attitude, but I promised you fun and I will not be deterred no matter what a pain in the ass you try to be."

"Fine."

"Fine." He left the room, closing the door behind him. Still, I felt self-conscious and took the clothes into the bathroom, dressing in the layer of soft cotton first. I had to admit it did feel lovely on my skin. When I had everything on but the ski jacket, I went out in my stocking feet to find the living room empty. Assuming he went to get the boots, I poured a cup of coffee and went to the window just in time to see him trudging back from the big house holding a large shoebox. Idaho boots. Hideous. Twenty-four hours in Idaho and already all sense of fashion had disappeared.

CHAPTER 15

AFTER I DONNED THE BOOTS AND THE SKI JACKET, Ciaran helped me clip my feet into the snowshoes and handed me a set of poles. He demonstrated how it was similar to walking on regular ground except that you must widen your stance an inch in either direction to make it easier on your hips. "Use the poles for balance and momentum but really it's not that different from hiking," he assured me.

He indicated that I should follow him. "Just try to mimic what I do."

I did as he asked, pleased to see that he hadn't lied. Snowshoeing was actually quite easy, although it was clearly a good cardio workout, as I was huffing and puffing in a matter of minutes. We kept on, passing by the big house, where my nieces stood in the front room watching from the window. When I waved with a pole, they clapped and jumped up and down like I was a star athlete in a parade. With one last wave of my pole, I continued watching Ciaran's backside, quite a nice view, in his black ski pants. We walked past the lake. The edges were frozen solid, but in the middle large pieces of ice floated in a haphazard pattern. We headed onto a flat section of property, blanketed in snow, Ciaran's tracks from earlier hinting to where we were headed. As far as I could see, the tracks continued across the meadow and into a gaggle of firs heavy with snow. The cloud cover had moved in again, and the gray sky possessed a stillness that comes before a snowfall. Close skies before a snowfall always made me feel lonesome, as if time had frozen and I was the only remaining person in the world. I was a yard or so behind Ciaran but kept pace, trying to match his gait but falling short by several inches so that our tracks became longer than if I'd been able to put my shoe in the exact same spot as his. He stopped, turning back to look at me as I approached. "You're doing well," he said. "I knew you'd be a natural. I'll slow up a bit so we can walk side by side?"

I nodded, catching my breath before making a comment about it being great exercise. He handed me a bottle of water and waited for me to take a sip before taking one of his own and sliding it into the mesh side pocket of his pack. We set out as promised, side by side. I didn't say much, concentrating on breathing, but the exercise seemed to energize him.

"Did Blythe tell you our mother didn't name us until we were two years old?"

I nodded yes. "She waited until she knew you, right? Tried to match your name to your personality?'

"That's right."

My sister and I had marveled over this strangeness, remarking that it was as eccentric as our mother, only in a different way. "Will you remind me what they all mean?" I asked.

He recited them, like a poem one learned as a child, so familiar that it simply rolled from the tongue with no effort at all. Kevan: gentle child, more comfortable with animals than humans. Ardan: high aspirations. Ciaran: little dark one. Teagan: beautiful. And the deceased brother, the second born, Finn: fair-headed, handsome, and wise.

"He was our mother's favorite, you know. Finn. Everyone's favorite. He was all those things, but also kind and generous. Only the good die young, you know." His gait slowed and his shoulders curved inward. Had his voice caught? I couldn't be certain. Our voices seemed to get lost in the expanse of the air, under this big sky with the close clouds.

"Did your mother name you all aptly? Are you all like your names?" I asked.

He shook his head with a grimace. "A little, I suppose. Kevan is more comfortable with animals than people. And Ardan has high aspirations, in that he's deeply spiritual and chose a life as a teacher despite the fact we're all rich enough that we don't have to work. But Teagan and me? Our names describe our appearances, not who we are. Little dark one? I used to be little, now I'm only dark. My mother couldn't predict that I'd be the tallest of the brothers. And Teagan—she is beautiful, but it's been more of a curse than a blessing. My father only wanted her to be a little doll that looked pretty, without any views or opinions of her own."

"What about you?" I asked. "Are you more than your looks?"

He cocked his head to the side and looked down for a second or two before looking over at me. "Does it answer your question that I desperately want you to think so?"

Before I could answer, he continued. "Maybe we're both trying to outrun our names, Bliss Heywood?"

I waved my pole at him. "Maybe so, Ciaran Lanigan."

We were about twenty or so feet across from what I assumed was a dormant meadow below the snow, when Ciaran stopped. Grateful, I halted as well, catching my breath, watching him. He knelt, dropping one pole to the snow and using the other to dip into the track in front of him, like he was measuring its depth. Standing, he left the pole upright like a flagpole with no flag and then tugged off one glove, scratching under his cap at the back of his head while looking toward the wooded area. "What the hell?" he murmured, just loud enough for me to hear. For a moment I thought he'd forgotten I was next to him.

"What's the matter?"

He looked up with a blank expression, before cocking his head to the side as his eyes flickered, like it was a surprise to see me there. "These tracks look wrong."

"Wrong?"

"Deeper than my tracks would be on my own and facing the wrong direction, like they were walking to my house not from it, as I did this morning. I think someone came through after me."

Although I was hot from the exertion, I felt a chill speed through me. It held the same dread as the still and close clouds above, waiting to spill snow. "Someone? Like who?"

"Kevan or Cole maybe. Don't know why they would be headed toward my place though. And Ardan's not here." Using his pole as a pointer, he gestured to the right. "His house is the other direction anyway, so it can't be that he decided to surprise us." He tugged at his cap, pulling it further down over his ears. "Never mind. I'm sure there's a good explanation. Come on now, we just have a quarter mile to go." He pointed with his pole again. "Do you see the bank of trees? My house is just behind." His voice sounded hollow and distracted.

I nodded and took a step closer, now close enough to see the pores in his skin. "Are you worried about something?"

"What? Of course not. Let's go. If we pause too long we'll get cold." He grinned but it seemed more like a Halloween mask with a false, stretched mouth and dead eyes than the usual way he smiled with his whole body. He seemed like a bad actor trying to portray a false confidence. Through the thick layers of his jacket, I suspected every muscle was tense, like an antelope sensing danger.

"Let's have a little water and then get going. The hot tub will be warm by now, and there's juice and scones in the fridge if you're hungry." He took off his backpack and rummaged inside before pulling out a water bottle. He took a swig and then handed it to me. "It's easy to get dehydrated doing this kind of exercise."

I did as he instructed without taking my eyes from his face. Something had spooked him, I was certain of it, but even with my limited knowledge of men, I knew when to let something go. After another sip of water for both of us, we headed toward the trees, falling into our previous rhythm. Fifteen minutes later, we arrived at Ciaran's house.

It looked like a ski lodge, all high, broad beams and stained-wood siding. The second-story patio wrapped around the entire front of the house. Exposed wooden beams and large windows, a roof covered in a layer of snow. I half expected Santa and his reindeer to appear at any moment.

We took our snowshoes off in the mudroom, which also housed several pairs of skis, a snowboard and golf clubs. As he locked the door behind us, I sat on a wooden bench, taking off my snowshoes. I slipped out of the boots and stored them near the door and hung my jacket but left my snow pants and sweater on, remembering how thin the long underwear ensemble was underneath. I shook my hair free of the cap, running both hands through it to loosen damp hair from my neck and scalp. Putting my hands to my cheeks, I felt the warmth there too. Vigorous exercise had made me feel quite alive, I thought. I couldn't remember feeling better, head injury be damned.

Snow melted from our boots and snowshoes, making clear puddles on the tiled floor. Ciaran wiped them with a towel and then hung his jacket next to mine. "You want some juice? You hungry? We wouldn't want your stomach growling like last night."

"Sure," I said, smirking, following him into the main part of the house. "I'm starving, actually."

"Snowshoeing will do that to you," he said. "You like peanut butter and jelly sandwiches?"

"That's my favorite."

"What kind of jelly?" he asked.

"Strawberry preserves, if you have it. That's what Blythe always made me when we were kids. She saved the strawberry preserves for me and ate just plain peanut butter on her sandwiches."

"Because she didn't like preserves?" he asked.

"No, we were poor and had limited jelly resources. She sacrificed it for me." My eyes stung, remembering.

He halted as we entered the front room, and took my hand. "You were lucky to have someone love you that much."

"She's the only one who ever has, but she did it so well it made up for the rest."

"Well, I happen to have an unopened jar of strawberry preserves in the fridge. It came in one of those gift baskets I get from my mother for my birthday. I'm more of a blackberry jam kind of guy."

"Good, more for me."

"Absolutely."

The entire main floor was an enormous great room with an exposed kitchen, separated by a counter. Large windows looked out to Blue Mountain from a sitting area, replete with a stone fireplace. High ceilings and rustic wood exposed beams. Rough, wide plank flooring. As I gazed around the room, Ciaran began to make our sandwiches in the kitchen while explaining that he'd asked the architect to design the main floor of the house for family gatherings and parties. "Everyone always congregates in the kitchen, so I decided to make everything one big room."

However, there was no furniture in the room. No couch. Nary a chair. Not a rug or a lamp. Just empty space. I raised my eyebrows and looked over to Ciaran. He was at the refrigerator, kneeling with his head inside like a teenaged boy looking for a snack. With his head still inside he called out, "Do you want milk with your sandwich, madam?"

"Of course." I walked the length of the room, stopping in front of the fireplace. A charred log lay in the grate, in the shape of an alligator's mouth. I glanced at the mantle. No photos on the mantle or art on the walls, either. "Why don't you have any furniture?"

He finished spreading peanut butter on two pieces of bread before answering. "Commitment issues. I can't decide what I want." Grinning, he held up a jar of strawberry preserves. "See here?"

"Of course. Commitment issues." Not that my condo and the ones of the past were much better than this. Although, I did have some furniture and photographs of my nieces, thanks to Blythe. At least something personal adorned my space.

"Right after I finished building this place, Finn died and my family blew up. The idea—the dream, I should say—of all us having homes on the old property and raising families together died with Finn. He was the glue that bound us together. Once he was gone, we all fell apart."

"I'm sorry."

"It doesn't bother me anymore. Don't worry about it."

So we were both liars about certain things. Not bothered? Hardly.

"Anyway," he continued, "I haven't been here enough to figure out what I want other than in the bedroom. I do have a *bed* and a couple pieces of furniture up there." He grinned that wolfish smile. "Emphasis on the word bed."

After rolling my eyes at him, I went to the window and looked out over the snowy landscape. The back of the house had a similar patio as the front, only this one had an outside kitchen and hot tub, steam hovering about like early morning fog on a lake. The water was hot, I thought, longingly. How good it would feel to submerge my already sore muscles into that warmth.

Ciaran joined me, handed over the sandwich and then gestured toward the outside kitchen. "Sadly, I haven't used my outside kitchen once. It's funny how things work out. I thought I'd be out there all summer, barbecuing with my brothers."

"Life's never as we imagine. It's best not to wish for things."

He studied me, locking my gaze to his for a moment before I looked away, pretending to examine my sandwich. "Are you really that jaded?"

"Not jaded. Realistic." I took a bite of the sandwich. It was perfect, with just the right amount of peanut butter relative to strawberry. We ate our sandwiches standing side by side at the window. His finished his in four bites, whereas I took seven. "I think everything tastes better in Idaho."

"I agree." He smiled, looking down at me like I was a morsel to devour as he brushed back my hair and kissed the side of my neck. I shivered.

"Cold?"

"Not cold, no," I whispered.

He kissed my mouth, exploring the soft flesh of my mouth with his tongue. My arms slid up and around his neck. He tasted like peanut butter and smelled of the same aftershave he'd worn last night, spicy and intoxicating. After a moment, we were breathless and so tightly pressed to one another I felt his excitement pushing against my leg. When he pushed me against the wall, the material of our pants slid against one another, making a noise like two plastic bags. "Did you say something about milk?" This was said against his mouth, the words garbled.

He pulled away, smiling. "You're awfully demanding." As he walked over to the kitchen, I turned to look back out the window. The sky continued to have that smoky, close feeling. However, I didn't feel my usual sense of loneliness. Just as I had that thought, I spotted the first flake. Large, fluffy, falling slowly until it reached the patio and disappeared into the already fallen snow. Ciaran handed me a glass of milk. I drank several sips. Milk tasted better here, too. The air became speckled with snowflakes before our eyes.

"Have you ever been in a hot tub while it's snowing?" he asked.

"I don't think so."

"You would remember."

I didn't answer. There was no way he was getting me into that hot tub. With him mostly naked, there would be no way to control what I wanted to do to him.

"It would definitely count for the fun list," he said.

"No swimsuit." I made a helpless gesture with my hands before heading for the kitchen, where I set my now empty milk glass in the sink. This time I was safe. He couldn't just pop over and get one of Blythe's like he had the boots.

He watched me as I crossed back to him. "I promise I'll behave," he said.

"Not likely."

The skin near his eyes crinkled as he smiled and kissed me, pushing me against the window. It was cold against my backside even through my layers of clothing. "You don't need a suit," he said. "No one can see us from here."

"You can see me."

"Yes, but I'm harmless." He made a sound at the back of his throat that was halfway between a growl and a moan, then kissed me again. "Just give into it," he whispered. "Let me take you upstairs."

"I've known you less than twenty-four hours."

"Yes, but we've spent many hours together within that period, so it almost counts as three dates."

"Three dates?"

"My previous companions tell me this is the requisite amount of time before testing to see if we're physically compatible."

"No offense, but your companions sound kind of easy."

Laughing, he twirled a bit of my hair around his fingers. "You talk a big game, but I know you're no innocent."

To distract him from this line of reasoning, I pointed outside to the hot tub. "Do you have a pair of boxers and a T-shirt I could borrow?"

"I go commando."

"What? All the time?"

He chuckled, rolling down the waistband of his snow pants to reveal the top of a blue set of boxers. "I'm just kidding." Taking my hand, he pulled me toward the stairs. "You'll be way sexier in them than I."

Not likely, I thought, stifling a shiver. Not likely.

We climbed the suspended spiral staircase to the second floor, talking as we made our way to the top. "These stairs make me think of *Vertigo*," I said.

"The movie?"

"Right. Classic Hitchcock." I said this with enthusiasm, feeling with some authority that it was one of the greatest movies of all time.

"I wouldn't know."

"What? Everyone's seen that movie."

"I don't watch scary movies," he said. His voice sounded odd, almost hollow. I glanced at him but his eyes were hooded and unreadable.

"I thought all boys liked scary movies."

"Not this one. Real life is scary enough."

"I didn't think you were afraid of anything," I said, thinking of his athletic pursuits.

"Well, that's where you're wrong."

Pausing for a moment at the ledge that overlooked the empty room below, he put his arm around me in a way that felt familiar, like we'd been a couple for a long time. "My mother's appalled by my lack of furniture."

"Ah, well, she doesn't have to visit then."

"That's the spirit." He grinned at me. "I like you, Bliss Heywood. You like me too, just a little, don't you? Come on. Just admit it."

"You're okay." I smiled at him, feeling my insides melt into warm chocolate.

"Well, *okay* will have to be good enough for now." He pecked my lips with his and then moved his arm from my shoulders and pointed down the hallway. "My bedroom's this way." Guest room across the hall, but there's no need to go in there. No furniture. My office is at the other end of the hall."

"Also empty?"

He shrugged, steering me toward his bedroom by putting his hands on my hips. "I have a desk in there, if you must know. But I rarely use the office. I'm more of the work-in-bed kind of person."

"Does everything out of your mouth have to be an innuendo?" I turned to look up at him.

He raised his eyebrows, laughing, and took my hand. "I'm wounded by your assumptions. Anyway, I actually meant it. I usually work on the bed with my laptop perched on my legs."

"I do that, too."

"Stop with the innuendos," he said. "Please."

"Shut up."

We were at this bedroom now. He let go of my hand and moved aside so I could enter before him. He hadn't lied. The room did have a king-sized sleigh bed covered by a heavy feather comforter without a duvet, a dresser and a couple of nightstands with lamps, all made of some rich wood, probably cherry. Bare white walls. Simple accordion shades hung over the windows instead of curtains. Precarious looking stacks of jeans, sweaters and T-shirts covered the dresser. Disheveled clothes spilled out of several open drawers, arms of sweaters seeming to reach out to the room as if they wanted out. A suitcase lay discarded near the window, with several books and what appeared to be toiletries in the side pockets. "Don't you unpack?"

He waved away my comment with an impish flutter of his hand. "You don't cook. I don't put things away." He walked over to the dresser and picked through several piles, coming up with a pair of red boxers and a blue T-shirt with "Sun Valley, Idaho" across the front. After tossing them to me, he lifted his sweater over his head. I caught a glimpse of his lean, muscular stomach before he pulled a white cotton, long-sleeved shirt down over the waist of his pants. His shirt was made in that tiny waffle texture material that I always found irresistible on a man. I swallowed and took a deep breath as Ciaran tossed his sweater into the middle of the muddle on the bureau, knocking a haphazard pile of various colored T-shirts on the floor.

To my dismay, his shirt clung to his torso in all the right places, revealing muscular shoulders and back. I wanted to press my face against the middle of his back where the shirt crinkled just above his tailbone. I should tell Henry about waffle material, I thought. Henry should wear one of the waffle shirts in front of Mrs. Pennington. I made a mental note to order him a couple and have them delivered to Moonstone's.

To distract my twitchy hands, I rubbed my thumb against the boxer shorts he'd thrown me. Soft, probably made of some expensive silk blend. What did these boxers look like on him? An image of my hands moving up his thighs to tug them off came to me in a sudden flash. Teasing him with my fingertips. Making him beg me to keep going.

"Hey, you still with us?" Ciaran held a pair of swim trunks in his hands, staring at me with obvious amusement.

I blinked and cleared my throat, as I flushed what I'm sure was a shade away from fuchsia. "Yeah. Where should I change?"

"Change here." He put up his hands in a defensive gesture. "Don't say it. I'm leaving. I'll change downstairs. Just come on down when you're ready."

I followed him to the bedroom door, closing it firmly behind him, and listened until I could no longer hear his footsteps. After peeling off my sweater and the undershirt, I stood for a moment in my bra. Should I take it off? If I did, it would be my own wet T-shirt contest for sure. If I kept it on, it wouldn't be very comfortable. Leave it off, I decided. I'd just slip into the hot tub quickly and stay submerged. Good plan. I unclasped my bra, bringing it to my nose to make sure I hadn't perspired to the point of stinking, but it smelled of my perfume and body lotion. Apparently, I hadn't sweated too profusely during my entanglement with the great outdoors.

Realizing I needed to use the toilet, I went into the bathroom, which was only slightly smaller than the size of my bedroom, with marble floor and granite tiles, high ceiling with a skylight. Large soaking tub set high with five rectangular windows that displayed the view of Blue Mountain. The room housed a shower with traditional twin showerheads on both sides, plus a large, round one in the middle with a dozen or so holes and six nozzles hung horizontally so that water came from every angle spraying all parts of a body like I'd seen at spas. Two could shower at once quite easily, I thought, with a shiver. A bench ran across the back, perfect for shaving legs, or other things, which I didn't allow myself to think about now.

The bathroom was clean, thankfully, but as untidy as the bedroom. A can of shaving cream without its cap in perfect unison with a tube of topless toothpaste on one side of the double sink, the other with a bottle of cologne on its side and an unplugged electric toothbrush. I held the shaving cream can to my nose; it smelled of Ciaran's face. Then I picked up the cologne and sniffed, closing my eyes to the intoxicating smell that was Ciaran's neck. Get a grip, I told myself, setting it aside, and looking around the rest of the bathroom. A towel lay crumpled like a toddler after a day at the zoo on the floor near the heating vent while the chrome hangers remained empty. Several *Sports Illustrated* magazines, opened to pages crinkled from water (did he read in the bathtub?) cascaded from the back of the toilet. The toilet seat was up; splashes of urine speckled the rim. Think about that, I told myself, when lustful thoughts come to you in the hot tub. He's messy. His toilet has pee spots. After putting the seat down and emptying my bladder, I tugged off my ski pants and used the last three sheets from the roll of toilet paper to wipe. After washing my hands, I plugged the toothbrush into an outlet between the two sinks, righted the cologne and put the caps on the toothpaste and shaving cream.

I looked at my bare torso in the mirror. My breasts were not bad for a woman of almost forty. Gravity and my lack of children had been kind to them. Blythe had told me hers were a mess after nursing two children. That said, although perky, mine were barely a B-cup, which for my tall and medium-boned frame appeared quite small. I had long, trim legs. I could be grateful for that, I supposed, as I pinched the skin at my waist. Not exactly a perfectly flat stomach like Ciaran's little actress in that tiny bikini. Damn those cookies at the office. I took off my pants and looked at myself from the back. My black thong underwear left little to the imagination, including a few dimples on my rather round butt cheeks that I'd rather not have. Why did I look so much better in clothes? Ciaran would surely be disappointed if he saw me naked.

I dismissed these thoughts. He was not going to see me naked. Absolutely not. I had to put all this kissing to a stop as well. We should be friends. We were practically siblings, for heaven's sake. I peered into the mirror, leaning over the sink for a closer look, and examined my skin. Hardly any sign of wrinkles. I could thank the fact that I barely came out of the office for that. I guess it hadn't all been in vain. My eyeliner had smudged. All that rigorous exercise wreaked havoc on a girl's makeup. Taking a tissue from the box on the floor next to the fallen towel, I swiped under each eye. What would I look like after sitting in the hot tub with snow falling into my face? "Never mind," I whispered out loud. "Just have fun."

I remembered the empty toilet paper holder then, and decided I better replenish it in case I needed it later. Without much hope of finding any, I opened the cupboard under the sink. To my surprise, a dozen rolls were stacked neatly on the far left-hand side. I leaned down to get one and what I saw made me gasp. Toward the back of the cupboard, behind the drainpipes, was a shotgun. At least I assumed it was a shotgun. It was long and black. An image of a panther came to mind. Why did Ciaran have a gun in the bathroom? Is this how they did things in Idaho? But why was it in the bathroom next to rolls of toilet paper?

I went back to the bedroom, leaving my clothes on the bed. For some reason I couldn't explain, I went to the right-side bedside table and opened the drawer, slowly in case it squeaked. I needn't have worried. It was one of those expensive sliders that felt like opening a silk handkerchief. The drawer was empty. Committed now to my treachery, I went to the other and opened it, this time with little regard for sound. A handgun, made of dull black metal with tiny ridges on the handle, rested on top of a book of Mary Oliver poems. The juxtaposition of these two things duly noted, I closed the drawer.

Slightly shaken by my discovery of two guns within ten feet of one another, I dressed in the boxers and T-shirt, having forgotten my worry over whether or not to wear a bra. Owning guns is not that odd, I assured myself, as I descended the spiral staircase. People in the country owned guns. There were bears and cougars and other dangerous creatures. But a handgun by your bed? It seemed out of character for playboy Ciaran. He certainly did not seem like the gun type. Not that there was a type, I supposed. People from all sectors of society owned guns for a variety of reasons. Gun for political reasons, for sport and hunting, and for safety. Which of these were the reasons Ciaran owned them? I thought of the tracks again. Ciaran had seemed distinctly unsettled, even afraid. Was there a reason for this? Was he afraid of something, or someone?

Ciaran was downstairs by the glass doors dressed in nothing but his swim trunks, holding a bottle of red wine in one hand and two plastic glasses in the other. Outside on the patio, he'd shoveled a path to the hot tub. I sighed, resigned that I was clearly out of my mind. Red wine and a hot tub with Ciaran? I was doomed.

CHAPTER 16

HE WAS RIGHT ABOUT ONE THING. Snowflakes falling while your body was submerged in hot, swirling water? Perfection. Ciaran and I sat across from one another, our glasses resting in cup holders built into the sides of the tub. Neither of us spoke for some time, seemingly in agreement that the setting required no conversation. Sinking down until my neck was covered by the water, I watched him, letting the flakes fall on my face. Ciaran sat with his shoulders above the water, occasionally sipping from his glass of wine. His eyes darted around the yard from time to time in a way that made me wonder if he was worried about an intruder, thinking of the footsteps we'd seen earlier.

"You ever get scared out here all by yourself?" I asked.

One shoulder came up and down in a shrug. "I have an alarm on the house."

"What about when you're out here?"

He picked up his glass, shaking his head. "I don't come out at night for the most part."

"Bears?"

"Sure." Flakes of snow settled on his thick, brown hair, then melted almost immediately from the steam, to be replaced immediately by more. Why did I have the feeling he was lying? It wasn't bears that had him frightened.

"Do you have guns?" I asked, keeping my voice light.

"Everyone has guns in Idaho."

"For the bears?" I asked. "And other critters?"

"Right."

I sighed with contentment, moving my hands under the water, feeling warm and relaxed, both from the tub and his answer. Of course that's why he had guns, I assured myself. Bears and other critters. Just to be safe. He wasn't in danger.

I looked up to see him staring at me. "Why did you ask that?"

"No reason," I said.

He set his glass into the cup holder, rising slightly from the tub, his skin pink from the hot water. Perching on the side with only his legs in the water, he slicked wet fingers through his hair. Creases I hadn't noticed before lined his forehead. He seemed to be considering whether he should say something or not.

"What is it?" A chill ran up my spine. I felt my skin turn to goose bumps in the hot water. "There's something you're not telling me. Those tracks in the snow made you nervous, didn't they?"

"It's probably nothing."

"Probably?"

"It makes no sense, but sometimes I just get these feelings—like darkness—like I won't be alive much longer."

Something clicked in my head just then. "Do you think it's because your brother Finn was murdered? Has it made you fearful the same thing could happen to you?"

"No, it's not that. I've felt like this since I graduated from college. I'm certain someone's trying to harm me."

"What do you mean by harm?"

"Serious harm. Like death."

"Like someone's trying to kill you?" I asked.

"I know it sounds crazy. But I've had several near-death experiences in the last year alone."

"Several?"

He spoke with reluctance, the way you do when you know if you say something out loud it will seem more real. When you keep it to yourself, you can remain in denial. "There was a fire in the cottage where I was staying in the south of France last spring. The entire place burned to the ground. The authorities thought it was intentionally set. I would have been killed if I hadn't been staying over at a friend's house that night." A friend? A woman, I had no doubt. I tried to ignore the pang of jealousy that shot through my middle as he continued. "In New York City last summer, after seeing a play, I stepped onto the crosswalk—it was a green light for pedestrians—and all of a sudden this car pulls out from in front of the theatre, headed straight for me. I froze in the middle of the street, watching like it was slow motion or something. If the person behind me hadn't grabbed the collar of my jacket and pulled me back, I would have been killed. There have been other incidents I can't explain, but they weren't as obvious as the ones I described. At least one a year."

"When did you say it started?"

"It started in my early twenties. I think."

"Is this why you're afraid to make commitments?" I thought of his empty house.

"Maybe."

"Why would you build the house, then? If you think you won't be here to enjoy it. Why not just stay at your brothers' homes?"

"Because it's ridiculous to live your life like you could die tomorrow."

"Who would want to kill you?" I thought immediately of jealous husbands and boyfriends of the women he bedded. "Who have you made angry enough to want you dead?"

He slipped into the water. The noise of the bubbles seemed louder, more pronounced, in his silence. "I do not sleep with other men's women, if that's what you're thinking."

How had he known that was what I was thinking? "I didn't say anything of the sort."

Smiling, he picked up his glass and took another sip. "You should not take up professional poker for a second career."

Ignoring him, I continued. "Most crimes are crimes of passion, you know."

He raised his eyebrows. "That right?"

"In novels, anyway." I paused, looking up at the sky. The flakes continued to fall. A few landed in my lashes. "Are there any women you've hurt, you know, who've fallen in love with you only to be dumped?"

"I don't dump women. They know when they get involved with me that I'm not the relationship kind. They know the score before we sleep together. They're women like you."

"Like me?"

"Yes." Using his fingers, as if counting off items for a grocery list, he rattled off four qualities. "Independent. Highly intelligent.

Don't need or want a man for anything other than a physical relationship. Purposely stay clear of romantic entanglements."

"Is that how you see me?"

"Am I incorrect?" His eyes glittered, watching me. There was a quality in his voice I hadn't heard before. What was it exactly? I had a sudden image of a day trip I'd done for an executive retreat. We'd all gone out on a fishing boat in the San Diego bay, and I'd watched as one of my team members pulled in a fish. Was he fishing for something? A confession of sorts? What did he want the answer to be?

"I suppose," I said.

"I understand the first three." Again he held up his fingers. "But the fourth perplexes me. Why do you stay away from romantic entanglements?"

I took a deep breath and let it out slowly, thinking. "It wasn't purposeful, exactly. I wanted a career. I didn't see how to have a relationship, a husband, and be as ambitious as I wanted to be. I've lived in almost a dozen places since I left business school and spent a lot of time on the road. No offense to your gender, but most men couldn't deal with that. Plus, Blythe and her first marriage certainly confirmed that women have to give up half of who they are in order to accommodate a man. She practically disappeared when she was married to him."

"Do you think that's every marriage? That someone loses themselves to accommodate the stronger personality?"

I shrugged. "No. I think your brother and my sister are a good match. Evenly matched."

"Do you think you'll feel differently about marriage now? For yourself? In this new chapter?"

"You mean since I got canned, knocked myself senseless, and decided to come to Idaho?"

He laughed. "Precisely."

I looked up the sky, never tiring of watching the flakes fall, the way they seemed to come down in straight lines until they were right above you. "I like to make my own decisions. I'm not sure I could ever adjust to being someone's wife. I can't imagine spending my life with just one person, having to compromise to make it work, not being able to do what I want, when want."

"We've already established you don't have fun. What do you do?"

"Binge-watch Netflix shows, eat salted-caramel ice cream, read, do yoga, spend whatever I want at Nordstrom. Work. I like my independence. Anyway, it's too late for me now."

"Why?"

"I'm forty next month. Everyone knows women over forty are more likely to get hit by lightning than get married."

"That can't possibly be true. Look at Blythe and Kevan."

"Blythe's special."

"I can't argue with that," he said.

I turned my gaze to him. He held his wine glass just above the water, his gaze down, as if studying the bottom of the pool. "What about you? What's your real reason for avoiding romantic entanglements?"

"I'm unable to commit to anything long-term. But I'm careful not to break anyone's heart. I did it once. I'll never do it again."

"When?"

"College. Willa Fletcher." A look of pain crossed his face.

Suddenly overheated, I rose from the water to sit on the ledge, steam rising from my body, the T-shirt clinging to me. "What happened?"

He splashed water on his cheeks, like a little boy washing his face. "I dated her my junior year of college. Pretty shortly into the relationship, I realized she was unbalanced to the point of being obsessive."

"Obsessive?"

"About me, to be precise. We were in college. I wasn't mature enough to want something serious. Two months in, she started hinting about getting married. I liked her, but I knew I didn't want to marry her. So I ended things, thinking it would be for the best. But she started following me around campus, waiting for me after classes. One night I came home from a party and she was in my bed at the frat house. Naked."

Of course he was in a fraternity. Came home from a party and not the library. "What did you do?"

"I insisted she get dressed, telling her in no uncertain terms that if she didn't leave me alone I would report her to the campus authorities. The minute I said it, I realized I had made things worse.

She started crying, asking if it was because she was fat." He made a face like he was perplexed. "I don't know why women who are not even close to fat think they are. Let me tell you a secret. Men are not nearly as critical of your appearance as you are about yourselves."

I nodded, thinking of myself in the bathroom just minutes ago.

He continued. "I felt terrible that I'd hurt her, but it had nothing to do with how she looked." He hesitated, looking toward the woods. When he spoke, his voice cracked. "She left, and later that night slit her wrists."

"Oh my God. Did she succeed?" I stopped, hoping it might not be true.

"No, her roommate, Patricia, found her in time. Willa left school afterwards and I never heard from her again. Patricia told me her parents had sent her to a place to get better. She never came back to school. I don't know what happened to her. I kept in touch with Patricia for a year or so afterwards. I felt responsible and wanted to make sure Willa was okay. But I lost track of Patricia when I moved to Europe after college. Recently she sent me a friend request on Facebook—lives in Los Angeles—but we haven't exchanged messages or anything. I just see occasional pictures of her kids—you know how it is on Facebook. I'm friends with people I don't have close friendships with, like the women who are part of my charity work or acquaintances from college like Patricia."

"I'm sorry, Ciaran." No wonder he was afraid of commitment.

He took a sip of his wine. "I've never looked to see if Willa is on her friend list. It makes me feel guilty every time I think about her."

"It wasn't your fault. People break up every day and don't try to commit suicide over it."

"Yes, but certain women are vulnerable. When I thought about things afterwards, and trust me, I went over and over it in my mind, there were indications about her fragility that I ignored. I was too young and immature to understand that a woman's heart must be treated carefully. I don't want to ever hurt anyone like that again, so I make sure to choose wisely and that they understand the situation before we get involved." He paused, taking another sip of wine. "So, to answer your question, there are no psycho women out there mad enough to want me dead."

I swallowed, hoping to get rid of the lump in my throat. Poor Willa. I'd known several girls like her when I lived in the dorms as an undergraduate. Vulnerable. Unbalanced. Craving a man's attention. College-aged women are still young, even though one doesn't think so at the time. Everything seems important, heavily weighted, like your life depends on one thing or the other happening. Romantic loves seem larger than they really are. I knew all this from Blythe, of course, not having loved anyone in college. I was much too busy studying to be distracted by boys.

I looked over at Ciaran. He had his neck resting on the cushion that covered the ledge of the tub. His eyes were closed. The snow fell steadily, landing on his face and hair and quickly melting.

"What about business associates? Or people you've worked with in your philanthropic roles. Have you made anyone angry?"

He opened his eyes, turning his head to look at me. "Not that I know of. For the most part I play very well with others."

"Have you told anyone about this?"

"About my suspicions?"

"Right. Like the authorities?" I asked.

"You're the first person I've told."

"Why me?"

The bubbles from the tub suddenly stopped. Snow fell in silence. In the distance, the howl of either a dog or a wolf penetrated the quiet.

"You have a quality that makes me confess things. Must be the boss-lady quality thing you have going." He splashed water toward me.

I rolled my eyes and made an exaggerated sigh. "I'm certainly not the boss of you and never want to be."

"I'd love you to boss me around."

"Seriously, maybe you should tell the police what you just told me." Shivering, I slid back into the water and scanned the yard. Nothing but white on white except for the green of the fir trees.

"I have nothing to tell them. No proof of anything other than anecdotal evidence. I'll sound paranoid. Fearful thoughts of the idle rich. They'll assume drugs or mental illness." He paused, his expression somber. "Let's face it, the whole thing makes me sound pretty insane." His tone lightened. He poked my foot with his. "The fact that you're taking me seriously proves how unbalanced you are, because half the time I don't even think it's real myself."

I had to admit he was most likely right about the authorities taking him seriously. Regardless, that didn't change the fact that his instincts told him someone meant him harm. Another howl from the woods interrupted the silence. "Please tell me that's a dog." I gestured toward the woods.

"A wolf. But don't worry, they're too scared of us to come close to the house."

"What if I am insane?" He emphasized the word 'am' while peering into his drink. "It has occurred to me."

My heart thudded. Like last night, I felt like the pores of my skin become wider, letting feelings inside that I didn't want. A softening. I was softening. "You're not insane. That's me. Remember? Ever since I fell, I've been doing things I would never have thought I would do. Might I remind you of Sam and Sweetheart?" Without intending it to be so, my voice had quieted, as if someone might hear me in the hushed wood just a few feet away from us.

He laughed. "Right. But are insane people able to recognize one another?"

"We can spot one another in an instant."

"Wait, I'm lost. So does that mean we are insane or not insane?" he asked, reaching for his drink.

"It means we can decide between the two of us."

"Then I vote for insanity. Cheers." He toasted me with his drink and took a sip, then set it back in the holder. "For years now I've been expecting to die on any given day. I'm surprised I'm still here, actually. Every day is a gift when you think of it that way."

"Is that why you've had so many adventures? Trying to fit them all in?"

He took a long time to answer. When he spoke, his voice was husky. "Try to imagine what it feels like to think every day could be the last one." He took another sip of his wine, looking at me over the rim of the glass. "It makes you live in a different way. I don't ever think 'I can do that tomorrow,' so I do it today. It keeps me guarded, knowing that anyone who loves me is sure to lose me sooner rather than later, and it also makes me paranoid, so I'm in this middle ground between fear, gratitude, and this reckless approach to seizing each day."

"Ciaran, that's not so different from everyone else. We all know that we'll die one day and leave behind people who love us."

"No one thinks it could be tomorrow, though, really. We go into relationships imagining growing old together on the front porch. When unexpected things happen and someone dies young, we do not think it's the natural order of things. Mostly we're in denial that tragedy awaits around every corner. I'm not, therefore I live my life louder than most."

I thought about this. Everything was starting to make sense now, all the pieces of the puzzle taking their places. Ciaran lived like a man who was dying. His bucket list, his lack of commitments. His paranoia and darkness, loving life but thinking it could end at any moment.

To my surprise and utter alarm, I felt tears threatening. "Ciaran, this is no way to live. You need to get help." My voice cracked. Something raw was swirling around my gut, a mix of desire and vulnerability and intimacy. Whether he believed it to be true or not, he'd opened up to me in a way that belied his words that he only involved himself in casual affairs. The same could be said for me, of course. My outer persona was the independent, self-actualized woman that he felt sure he could not hurt, but inside I was a mushy mess of desire and stirred emotion. If I let him take me to bed, how would I be able to walk away? Could I go back to my regular life without him? Had I opened a space within me that would now be empty when he was done with me?

He moved across to where I sat, kneeling on the floor of the tub and pulling my legs around his waist. "That's why you should let me take you upstairs."

He was right, of course. Here were two consenting adults who had this unusual chemistry. We should seize the opportunity for pleasure. To deny it would be like slapping fate in the face. Was I just telling myself this, or was there some validity to the argument? Between Ciaran being almost naked and the warmth of the hot tub, I felt confused. He pointed at my wine. "You're not drinking. How can I expect to get you into bed if you won't let me get you liquored up?"

Laughing, I reached for the glass and took a small sip. It tasted of blackberries and tobacco. I took another before setting it back in its cup holder. "So good."

"See, no harm in a little wine." Leaning close, he whispered in my ear. "Let me take you upstairs. I promise you won't regret it."

"Ciaran." His name came out as a moan as I wrapped my arms around his neck and pressed against him, unable to stop my physical response to him. "This isn't a good idea."

He moved his hands to the uppermost spot on my thighs, wrapping his fingers around them so his thumbs were just above my pubic bone. Kissing his way up my neck until he reached my ear, he then flicked his tongue against my earlobe. "But you want me."

My breath caught as he pushed me against the wall of the tub. "A little."

"You lie. You don't do anything little." He kissed my mouth, pulling on my lip and exploring with his tongue, as he wrapped my legs tighter around him. "How can you expect me to keep my hands off you when you look like this? Feel like this. Your legs." He groaned softly. "They're like weapons against rational thought."

I pressed my breasts into his chest. My thighs tightened. I whispered his name again as I kissed him back without any thought to technique, having lost all control, like my careful switch had been suddenly shut off and it was my body wanting, needing, demanding. It was primal, all instinct. His mouth tasted of wine. I tugged at locks of his thick hair as I bit at his lips, and sucked his lower lip into my mouth. Tongues teased and fought. Everything ceased to exist but him. No water. No snow. No lonely wolf's howl. Just this moment. And Ciaran.

He pulled away slightly, looking into my eyes. "Should I stop?" His voice was more urgent now, his kisses hard, our breathing heavy. "If we go much further, I don't know if I can."

"No, don't stop," I whispered.

"Tell me you want me." With his fingers, he reached under my wet T-shirt and moved his hands up my torso until he found my breasts and stroked my nipples with his thumbs. My eyes closed as I let out a soft moan and pressed harder against him, feeling the evidence of his desire pushing against his swim trunks. His lips were once again on my neck. I arched toward his touch, wanting more, but he moved his hands from my breasts to pull the T-shirt over my head, tossing it over the side of the tub. He wrapped his fingers around my upper arms, not tight enough so that it hurt but enough so that I felt captive, unable to move except for the pounding of my heart and the flutters in my stomach. "Tell me. I need to hear you say it."

"I do. So badly." I swallowed and fixed my gaze on his neck, trying to catch my breath.

"Bliss, look at me." He continued to hold my arms captive.

I did as he asked, as if I were in a trance, raising my gaze to his eyes. The color of strong tea, I thought. "It's been a long time since someone touched me, and it's making me confused."

"Confused?"

"This is not the sort of thing I do." My voice wavered.

He cocked his head to the side, the lines on his forehead creased. "But maybe it's time you did."

"I don't like messiness. This is messy. Our families. Lives we'll go back to."

"Sometimes a mess is just what you need." He let go of my arms and placed his hands on my face, stroking his thumbs under my eyes as if tears had fallen. "Speaking of beautiful, the way you look right now—I've never seen anyone as exquisite. If this moment lasted forever, it would not be long enough."

Tears came to my eyes then. I was helpless to stop them. "It won't. Last, that is," I whispered. Tender, I thought, as I stared into his eyes. This is a tender man. Despite all his bravado to the contrary, he was not just a party. He was a man with a past, with a conscience. And, I liked him. Truly liked him, which, as we all know, is different than lust or even love. He'd moved me. Made my pores open, and seeped inside.

"I know it won't. But can't it be enough that I want it to?" He brushed the tears that had mingled with snow and steam from my face.

"I want it, too."

"Come upstairs."

"Yes," I said. Just that one short word. Yes. And a world opened.

CHAPTER 17

I CLIMBED OUT OF THE TUB and padded carefully across the patio, the freshly fallen snow already an inch thick on the path Ciaran had shoveled. It was cold on my bare feet, and I started to shiver.

He came up behind me, wrapping a large towel around my shoulders. "Come inside." His voice sounded hoarse, like he'd screamed for hours at a sports match. I couldn't look at him. Wanting him. I stepped inside. Water dripped from our shorts onto the hardwood floors.

"You sure about this?" he asked.

"I'm sure." He held out his hand and we walked to the stairs and began to climb up the suspended staircase shaped like the curl of a woman's hair. My mind was blank now. I cared only that we get to the bedroom as quickly as we could. And then we were there in his disheveled bedroom, the unmade bed tousled like one might expect after lovemaking, not before. Behind me, I heard cloth sliding against wet skin. Taking off his shorts, I thought, my heart pounding harder than I'd ever felt it before. Then, his footsteps and what was probably the sound of the top of a laundry bin opening and shutting. I stood near the bed facing away from the bathroom, still in my wet shorts with the towel wrapped around my shoulders.

"Let me take this. It's making you colder." He was behind me, separating the towel from my shoulders as if it were a silk pashmina, then moved my hair to one side and kissed my neck, then my shoulder, before moving away to toss the towel on the chair in the corner. He missed, and it fell to the floor next to a crumpled sweater, but he did not kneel to fetch it. I watched him move—muscular but lean, tan except for his pale backside. By the window, he pulled down a shade and then another, and the light dimmed. He turned, moving back to me. I kept my gaze above his waist, not knowing what to do when confronted with a naked man in the middle of the day in Peregrine, Idaho. I braced myself, imagining he might tease me when he sensed my unease, but there was none of that. He picked up a dry towel from the end of the bed. His eyes glittered as they roamed down the length of my body. I began to shake, whether from the chill or desire, I could not say.

"Take off your wet shorts." He stood at the corner of the bed, several feet from me.

I peeled them from my damp skin, letting the shorts fall to the floor before I stepped out of them, not wanting to bend over in front of him. Why hadn't I stayed away from those enchiladas last night? I felt his gaze on my body but I could not look up. I watched his feet step nearer and nearer until they stopped in front of me. He lifted my chin until my eyes found his. "You're nothing if not contradictions," he said.

"What?"

"You're shy. I didn't expect that."

The sound of the heater coming on penetrated the silence. Water dribbled from the ends of my hair. "I'm not shy," I said, finally.

"Again with the lies." He smiled and began to dry the wet ends of my hair with the towel. "Don't worry, I'll be careful with you."

"You don't have to be too careful." A fallen eyelash rested on his cheekbone. I brushed it away, letting my finger linger, surprised by the heat of his skin. His chest expanded with a breath, in and out. A tremor in his voice contradicted the confidence in his gaze. He dropped the towel to the floor. I traced my finger over his jawline and up his chin until I reached his bottom lip. Capturing my hand with his, he brought my palm to his mouth, and kissed it. With his other arm, he nudged me to the bed. I fell backward onto the bed. He paused, his eyes roaming the length of my body. "Gorgeous," he whispered.

I still could not look below his waist, but when he covered his body with mine I felt how much he wanted me. He kissed me, pulling my hips up slightly with his hands. He teased my nipples into hard nubs with his thumbs before drawing each one into his mouth, flicking his tongue over them while his hand moved to the spot between my legs. I moaned, and arched against his hand.

"You're so wet." His voice was gruff, animal like.

My legs spread and reached around his torso, but he put his hands on them so that I couldn't move, and nibbled the insides of my thighs. His grip grew tighter. His mouth hovered over me, then just a flick of his tongue, and then another. I writhed under him.

He moved, covering me with his body once again. My legs wrapped around him. He pushed my hands over my head, and kissed me. "I want to make you wait, but I can't stop myself." He entered me, slowly, moving his hands to my legs. He lifted my right leg higher, moving it so that it rested against his chest. He thrust into me deeply, and then again. A rhythm of slow, slow, fast, rubbing in all the right places. I closed my eyes, my breath fast, a soft moan escaping with each fast thrust. Knowing how close I was to climax and not wanting it to end, I tried to calm down. Perhaps he felt my resistance, because he whispered, "Just let go. Let go and trust me."

"I do. I do."

"You're driving me crazy. You know that?"

His words did nothing but take my excitement higher. "I..." But I couldn't finish because the shuddering had begun. My head drove into the pillow as the orgasm came in like three shock waves, one after the other. I cried out at the last, only vaguely aware of how he'd made one final push and groaned as he spilled inside me.

CHAPTER 18

IT WAS NEARLY TWO by the time Ciaran dropped me off at the door to the guesthouse, both of us giggling like naughty children. Once inside, I showered and did my hair and makeup, and put on a violet-hued sweater dress that clung nicely to my curves. Outside, snow continued to fall. I was just zipping up my high-heeled boots (I'd wear them, damn the pain, just to catch Ciaran's eye) when my cell phone rang. It was Blythe, saying Kevan was going into town to fetch my friends in his four-wheel drive. The roads would be slick, and he didn't think it was safe for Henry to drive the town car out to the house.

"How was snowshoeing?" she asked before we hung up.

"Fine."

"Isn't Ciaran a kick to hang out with?"

"Yeah. A total kick." I swallowed, guilt rising up from my stomach into my throat.

"Did something happen between you?" A note of concern had crept into her voice.

"Of course not."

"Okay, well, come on over whenever you're ready. Clemmie's dying to see you."

After promising to come right over, I headed outside, pulling on my hat to protect my hair. I was only several feet away from the guesthouse and had slipped twice when I spotted Ciaran headed my way. Great. A lecture about my boots was sure to ensue.

When he reached me, I opened my mouth to defend my boot choice, but before the words could come out of my mouth, he leaned down and scooped me into his arms. "If you insist on wearing these boots in the snow, I'm going to insist you wear them later with nothing else."

I laughed, speaking softly into his ear. "Nothing else?"

"Yeah, just the 'throw me on the bed' boots and nothing else."

"You've named my boots?"

"I have a less polite name, but I'll refrain."

"So restrained of you."

"The boots plus your legs—the combo makes it impossible to get through dinner without wanting to forego the stuffing and jump you. And, that's saying a lot, because I love stuffing."

A feeling of unease traveled up my spine. "We have to be careful. Act like friends. Promise me? I don't want Blythe to figure this out."

"I can't promise." He grinned, his breathing heavy as we trudged across the snow. "Unless you promise to meet me in the bathroom between turkey and pumpkin pie."

"That's not going to happen."

"You'll like what I do to you in there," he said.

I shivered with desire, and changed the subject. "I'm too tall for you to carry. And heavy."

"You're right on both counts. Good thing I work out."

"That's very nice." I lowered my eyes to stare at his mouth, remembering all too the well the taste of him.

"I'm just teasing you."

Despite the chill, I was hot under my coat. At the house, he kicked open the door with his foot (it had been left open a crack) and deposited me onto the bench in the mudroom. I unbuttoned my coat, skin damp under my clothes, unable take my eyes off him as he shrugged off his outer layers.

I hung my coat, and then knelt to brush the melted snow from my boots. When I stood, I found Ciaran staring at me with an impassive expression. "What?" I asked.

"That dress. It clings to all the right spots." His eyes skirted up and down my body. My nipples, betraying me once again, hardened under my bra. He moved close, pinning me with his thighs against the wall, and speaking softly into my ear. "I won't be able to keep my eyes off you."

"You have to."

"I'll be covert." He grinned, tracing my bottom lip with his finger, before leaning down to kiss me.

The sound of footsteps on the hardwoods made us jump apart. Tiny feet, obviously running, could only mean Clementine. Ciaran turned his back to me, fussing with something in the pocket of his jacket that hung on one of the hooks. Clementine bounded into the mudroom, wearing a shiny pink dress with a wide layer of tulle around the skirt. She began chattering away like a bird on a spring morning, about the dinner, setting the table, how pretty my dress was, how she'd watched Ciaran carrying me from the window. "You looked like Cinderella and her prince." She looked from Ciaran to me with shining eyes.

"There's no such thing as Cinderella," I said. "What did I say about this?"

"Cinderella is a fairytale brought back to life for the purposes of selling unrealistic dreams to hopeless young women." She spoke the sentence by rote, like an amateur actress saying a line she'd memorized for a play, but with no sense of the meaning behind the words. Clementine, obviously, didn't agree with my assessment of Cinderella, although she had the sentence mostly right.

"I don't think I used the word hopeless," I said.

Her eyes looked to the left, thinking. "What word was it then?"

"Desperate," I said.

She didn't comment on my word choice, instead turned to leave, motioning for me to follow, her black patent leather flats squeaking on the tile floor. "I think Mom's calling me. She needs my help. She told me she can't do it without me." Stopping in the doorway, she did a ballerina-type twirl. "Do you like my outfit?"

"It's very fancy," I said.

"Yours too, Aunt Bliss. And guess what?"

"I couldn't possibly guess."

"Mom brought all kinds of Thanksgiving decorations." Jumping up and down, she clapped her hands. "I'm so excited, but she says we have to wait a little longer to decorate the table because she can't remember where she put the candles she bought. Aunt Bliss, you can't believe how many things she doesn't remember." With that, she was off, running down the hallway, her shoes making a tapping noise on the hardwood floor.

Ciaran, at my side, spoke quietly as we walked down the hallway. "Do you think she saw us kissing?"

"No way. She would've made a comment. She thinks kissing is gross." I giggled.

"What's so funny?"

"Sneaking around like a couple of teenagers."

"It's so hot," he said, giving me a wicked smile. "Why can't you let her have Cinderella?"

"I don't want her to expect, or want, a man to rescue her. She needs to make her own life."

He chuckled. "She's eight. I think she can have Cinderella and Barbie for a while longer."

"That's exactly what's wrong with our culture. Men, and I do mean men, selling dreams of unrealistic waist sizes and giant boobs and the idea that the only way to have a good life is to have a prince race down a staircase with a glass slipper made from magic for your tiny foot."

"No wonder you don't have a boyfriend."

"Very funny, Mister 'I don't want to get married.'" I made quotes in the air.

We stopped just outside the doorway to the main room. "I never said that."

"You most certainly did."

"I said I don't get involved with women who want to get married."

"That's the same thing."

"Not exactly." He smacked me on the backside. "Don't be so quarrelsome or I'll have to punish you."

I rolled my eyes. "Should I start calling you Mr. Grey?"

"Did I mention my secret room?"

We were laughing as we stepped into the front room. Except for Lola curled up reading a book by the fire, Shakespeare at her feet, the room was empty. I heard Clemmie's voice from the kitchen calling out to her mother. "Aunt Bliss is here, Mom."

Lola looked up from her reading only long enough to flutter her fingers in an absentminded greeting. It gave me a start to see her there, as if I had taken a time machine back to myself at eleven. I watched her for a moment, as I breathed in the scent of the wood-burning fireplace, then perched on the arm of the chair nearest the hearth.

Ciaran moved the grate to the side and added another log from the iron basket to the modest flames. After setting the grate back in place, he knelt on his haunches, his face toward the fire. He warmed his hands, holding them in front of him, the muscles of his thighs bulging against the fabric of his jeans. The new log caught fire, making rather fierce crackling noises. Several fiery splinters of wood plopped against the grate and turned to charred remnants on the floor.

I excused myself to go say hello to Blythe. She was in the kitchen, wearing an apron and looking at a cookbook. Clementine was at the stove, standing on a footstool and stirring something in a saucepan. Rori sat at the counter, snapping beans.

"You needn't worry, ladies. I'm here to help save this dinner," I said, teasing.

"Oh, I think I have plenty of help." Blythe laughed before looking over at Rori. "Bliss isn't really the cooking type." She walked to the refrigerator and pulled out the vegetable crisper.

Rori smiled at me. What a lovely young woman she was, I thought. "I'm not really a cook either, but Blythe's teaching me things."

"And me too, Aunt Bliss. I bet Mom could even teach you to cook," said Clementine

"Let's not get crazy." I kissed the top of Clemmie's head as I peered into the pan. Crimson cranberries with shavings of orange peel bubbled. "Did you make this all by yourself?"

"Well, Mom helped a little. But I poured the sugar in. That's the most important part. Right, Rori?"

"That's right," she answered.

"Clemmie, you can turn the cranberries off. They've cooked long enough," said Blythe, her head still in the refrigerator.

Clementine did as asked. The bubbling ceased. I caught a zesty whiff of the orange peel.

"Where's Cole?" I asked.

"He's visiting his mother," said Rori.

"She's not feeling well," said Clementine.

Blythe and Rori exchanged looks as she shut the refrigerator. Cole's mother had drug problems, I remembered from previous conversations. What a way for Cole to spend Thanksgiving, I thought, thinking of my own mother.

Blythe had several ingredients for a salad in her hands: lettuce, carrots, and baby tomatoes. She set them next to Rori, telling her they were already washed.

"Seriously, do you need help with anything?" I asked, feeling slightly guilty. "Everything smells so good in here." The aroma from the baking turkey made my stomach growl.

"We've got it under control," said Blythe. "Go enjoy yourself. Relax." She asked me to send Lola to the kitchen. "She wants to me to teach her how to make a pie."

"How sweet," I said, hoping she would not ask me to join them for the lesson. Making a piecrust sounded like the ultimate lesson in futility. The closest I would ever come to making a pie was ordering it from a bakery, and I was just fine with that. I slipped back to the living room before Blythe got any big ideas

"Your mom says it's pie-making time," I said to Lola.

"Awesome. She's been promising me this forever." She grinned, set aside her book and waltzed into the kitchen with Shakespeare following her.

Ciaran stood from where he had knelt by the fire, brushing his hands on his jeans. "I'm going to grab some more wood before it gets dark." Leaning over, he tucked my hair behind my ear, and kissed the side of my face. "You do look a bit like Cinderella, you know. Just as beautiful."

"With the heart of the evil stepmother." I dropped my gaze, wanting to hide how much his compliment pleased me.

"No one believes that, you know." He knelt on the floor, cupping my face in his hands. "Especially me."

I opened my mouth to utter another sarcastic quip, but he placed his index finger against my lips. "No, whatever you're going to say, don't. I know better. You have the heart of the fairy godmother, Bliss Heywood. Bringing Sam and Sweetheart here? That's a special kind of magic that required no wand, just your good heart." Rising to his feet, he crossed the room, disappearing into the hallway.

I turned my gaze to the fire, thinking about Cinderella and the happy curve her life had taken with a couple of swipes from a magic wand. Ciaran was correct, it was the fairy godmother I resembled at this time in life. Of course it was. Not Cinderella with her tiny feet and her beautiful gown and the prince that twirled her across the floor in perfect rhythm. Pushing forty, with the magic that money brings, but no discernible life of my own. No man to twirl me across a ballroom floor or even the kitchen. What would it feel like to have a man love you enough to search a kingdom for you? Would it change me if a man wanted to protect me, keep me from harm, to call me his own? I would likely never know, what with the way I'd chosen ambition over love. Now I was a fairy godmother, able to make magic for others with the contents of my bank account, for which I was grateful. And yet, in the light of the fire that crackled before me, I understood something I had not previously known. I was lonely. Not just for friends, but for a man to love—for a man who loved me. I'd covered loneliness with the pace of my life, and for years and years it had been enough. But now, in the silence of the falling snow, I'd become still. And in my stillness, in the quiet, the truth had been given a space in which to enter. I'd never known what it was like to have a man love me, and I wanted to.

I thought of my father. He should have loved me, but didn't. During his lifetime he lived like a ghost, lurking in the shadowy corners where cowards and deserters gather. According to my mother, he was unwilling to embrace my mother's descent into the counterculture, uncomfortable with drug use and her desire for an open relationship. I was a baby when they divorced, and he moved thirty miles up the Oregon highway to a town just like the one we lived in, Dairy Queen and all. He continued his pencil-pusher career, one of those premature balding men with a comb-over, pocket protector, and plaid pants sitting behind a gray, metal desk at some county job no one ever heard of but paid for with their tax dollars. He married again, the only thing he ever did that was different from the moment before. Our stepmother was completely opposite from our mother in every way, except one. Despite my mother being a stoned hippie dressed in a gypsy skirt and Nannette a repressed Baptist dressed in a polyester pantsuit, they had only one similarity. Neither of them had any interest in my sister or me.

Every other Sunday afternoon, Nannette declared shortly after their wedding, between the hours of two and four were visiting times for her new husband's offspring. I have no memory of this, being only two at the time, but Blythe says he picked us up in his yellow Ford pickup that smelled of rubber and gasoline (her memory not mine) every other Sunday for several months. Throughout theses visits we sat side by side on a couch encased in a plastic cover, as was all the furniture. I vaguely recall the feel of cold, sticky couch cover on the backs of my bare legs and how my feet didn't reach the floor. Blythe recalls that the room was small and smelled of potpourri, and decorated with modest furniture that Nannette managed to make look fussy with an abundance of knickknacks, mostly in the form of three-inch ceramic dolls and a collection of antique teapots and cups that were displayed on shelves and end tables. Not a book in sight. If someone's character can be explained by the books on their shelves, surely no books means no soul.

All went as dictated by Nannette until one Sunday I spilled apple juice on a rose-embroidered throw pillow. As it inevitably and inexplicably does when you're a child, the glass simply slipped out of my hand without warning or explanation. Blythe jumped up and then wiped at it, nearly hysterical, with the sleeve of her sweater, but it was no use. The yellow juice had seeped in, making a stain the shape of Texas across the embroidery. Apparently, there were no plastic covers for throw pillows.

Nannette called me a "careless heathen" as she snatched the pillow from Blythe's hand while simultaneously ordering our father into the kitchen with a mere penetrating glint of her scary, green, cat eyes (Blythe's description) in his direction. My sister heard her shrill voice coming from the kitchen while the two of us sat hip to hip on the couch, now decorated with one less ugly pillow. "They're not to come into the house. Not ever again. You take them out somewhere." She continued on, cabinet doors slamming.

Blythe told me this story during one of our late-night phone calls after Michael left her. That's the way it is with grief. It opens you up, makes all this truth come out instead of the usual mundane discussions of the weather or what we'd had for dinner or even our accomplishments. After her divorce, raw and painful feelings that had been supposedly been grieved over and tidily put away, spilled out of her. Stories surfaced I'd never heard. This was one of them.

"The remarkable thing is, I cried but you didn't," she said. "I'm seven and you're two—so tiny and sweet with these big, intelligent eyes that took everything in, and yet the whole time she's screeching at him, it's me sobbing, thinking we might not ever see him again."

"What did I do?" I asked her.

"For a bit you were perfectly still next to me. But as the tirade continued, you patted my leg three times like an adult might do to a child. "No cry. No cry, Bythe.' You couldn't say your 'l' sound. Then, you turned toward the kitchen and gave them the finger." Blythe started laughing, deep in her chest with that shaky laugh after you've been crying that sounds like courage would if it were a sound. "It stopped me crying, I can tell you that."

"At two? How did I know what that meant?"

"Sally's friends weren't exactly discreet around us." I heard her shifting the phone from one ear to the other and the creak of bedsprings, probably adjusting her legs to sit cross-legged on the bed with a pillow on her lap, as was her habit. "I thought of it just yesterday. How you gave them the finger and I cried. The memory just surfaced. I don't know why."

Of course it had. Damn Michael. "I'm sorry," I said.

"For what?"

"That you cared."

"Don't be sorry. I had you. That was all that really mattered, in the end."

"I'm sorry about Michael, too."

"Don't be. I got the girls out of it. They're all that really matters in the end." The bitterness in her voice made my stomach ache.

Blythe continued the story, and as much as I didn't want to hear it, I knew the telling of it gave my sister something intangible that she needed.

We continued to see him during the Sunday window. Not every scheduled Sunday, mind you, because often he had to meet an obligation at the command of his wife. But sometimes, he would pick up us and take us all to the Swap Meet, where we perused old things that smelled of mildew and dust.

As Blythe talked, fuzzy memories came to me, ones long forgotten. I remembered the two of us traipsing behind him as I held Blythe's hand. I felt afraid. The noises of the crowds, shouts and murmurs, voices and more voices. So many people. Bumping into us. An elbow to my head. A knock of my shoulder. We were trapped in a sea of pants, coats, and boots. Smells overwhelmed me: cooking grease, wood smoke, boot polish, stale cigarettes, spilled beer. Old ladies stopped to fuss over us, and when they knelt to get a better look at my freckles, I spotted whiskers angrily poking out of their chins and thought of witches in the fairy tales Blythe read me.

Hot months brought hot, bare legs, sticky next to my face, smelling of unwashed skin, baby oil, patchouli, and other scents I could not name. Rays of summer sun sizzled the tender, exposed area of my scalp where my hair had been parted precisely by Blythe and made into pigtails. Later I would have a stinging sunburn there, then flakes that Blythe would brush out at night with a comb. Other times it was cold and I had to bury my hands in my jacket pockets instead of holding onto Blythe, so I made sure to match her steps, my feet only inches from hers at all times because I knew the crowd could swallow me and take me away from my sister. My sister was home. I did not want to lose my home.

I was five, Blythe went on, when one winter Sunday I refused to go with them. Blythe tried to convince me to come by saying there might be ice cream today if we were good. When that didn't work, she used guilt as a tactic. "Dad will be so disappointed if he doesn't get to see you," she whispered, so our mother wouldn't hear.

Nothing could penetrate my resolve. "He doesn't care, you know, if we stay or go." I folded my hands over my chest. "I'll stay and read the books you got me from the library. This Sunday. And next. All the Sundays. I'll never go to that place that smells like old lady's sweaters ever again."

"Honestly, Bliss, where do you get these things?" Blythe stood looking at me, pulling on her ponytail, trying to figure out what to do with me, the expression on her face somewhere between amusement and irritation. But she knew me better than anyone. And she knew when to give up. "Fine, but don't forget to eat a little something. You know how cranky you get if you don't have a snack in the mid-afternoon."

Blythe continued to see our father every other Sunday, but I refused. Now, sitting in Kevan's peaceful home with the glow of the fireplace warming my hands and face, I thought about this bold declaration I'd made as a five-year-old. It was, quite simply, me. I refuse to do things I don't want to do; whether out of conviction, stubbornness, strength, or weakness, I could not say. No one has ever been able to dissuade me from my own ideas, my own ways, not even my sweet and sensitive sister whom I love more than anyone in the world. While she cries, I give them the finger. While she complies, I rebel. Which one is better in the long run, again, I couldn't say. But I know this: Blythe has a home with people who love her. I do not.

My sister's muffled voice and Clemmie's laughter from the kitchen, then the sound of a car coming up the driveway, pulled me from my musings. I went to the window. It was Kevan's Range Rover, coming up driveway with Henry, Moonstone, Mrs. Pennington, and Sam. Sweetheart's head was near the window, looking out like a tourist on a bus. That dog was enough to break my heart.

CHAPTER 19

MOMENTS LATER, MY FRIENDS HEADED toward the house. Henry had his hand resting on Mrs. Pennington's back, as if protecting her from the snow. Sam, behind them, his eyes darting about, seemed to be taking in the scenery and the house. Sweetheart was close by his side with her nose in the air, sniffing. Moonstone was chattering away to Kevan, who nodded his head every so often, obviously listening carefully.

Ciaran came into the room with his arms loaded with firewood. After plopping it into the basket by the fire, he came to stand beside me at the window. He stroked my wrist with one of his fingers, once, then twice. "What had you so deep in thought?"

I wouldn't tell him of my further thoughts on Cinderella or my father. Too revealing. Instead I chose a safer subject, one that would not reveal so much of the inner workings of my heart. "Yesterday, driving out here, I had the sensation we were all characters in *The Wizard of Oz*," I said. "All of us in search for some character attribute we think will elude us."

"What quality are you looking for?" he asked.

"Not me. The others."

"Ah. Right. Of course."

Without saying anything further to Ciaran, I walked down to the mudroom to greet my friends. I did not need to look back to know that he did not follow me. The attraction between us was like an invisible electric current. I knew when he was near.

Amidst much chatter and taking off of outer layers, Mrs. Pennington gave me a warm hug. She smelled of an exotic perfume, more spicy than sweet, and wore a light blue sweater made of expensive cashmere that draped just so over black silk pants. Her makeup was understated but perfect, with a pink lipstick that complimented the flush in her cheeks. A flush that was not there yesterday, I thought. I inspected Henry with a careful dart of my eyes. He seemed about twenty years younger than the last time I'd see him. Had their dinner last night turned into something more?

Mrs. Pennington squeezed my hand as we walked toward the front room. "Your meddling has caused me to have a terrible hangover."

I looked at her, surprised. "My meddling?"

"Henry and I closed the bar down last night. I can't remember how many glasses of wine I had, which is not typical for me, I can assure you. I'm completely mortified." She laughed and squeezed my hand harder, giving me the distinct feeling that she felt the absolute opposite of mortification.

"My sister met Kevan at that same bar. It must be something about the place mixed with this high altitude that turns proper ladies scandalous." I couldn't imagine Mrs. Pennington stumbling anywhere, but perhaps the wine and the altitude had made her daring and wild?

She leaned closer, whispering in my ear. "You can't imagine what I've done."

"Do tell," I said. We entered the front room. No Ciaran. Where had he gone? I glanced back into the hallway. Sam, Henry and Moonstone had stopped to examine a painting with Kevan as their tour guide. Sweetheart was at my heels, wagging her tail, but stopped when she saw Shakespeare, back at his perch by the fire. Shakespeare rose to his feet as Sweetheart approached him tentatively, tail wagging. Then, as if they'd already worked it out between them, both lay down by the fire, side by side.

"Let's just say I didn't wake in my own room this morning."

I coughed. "Oh. Well."

She smiled and pushed back a lock of hair from where it had fallen just over her eyes. "And we skipped breakfast."

It was my turn to blush. My matchmaking scheme had worked. I knew it. I was right about the two of them.

"In my experience, it's the quiet ones who are the best in bed," whispered Mrs. Pennington.

I blushed further. "Really?"

"Oh, yes. I believe it's because they spend so much more time observing than talking. They know how to make a woman respond. But goodness, I have a headache. Moonstone suggested a little hair of the dog, but I have no idea what she meant. Is it some kind of hippie herb?"

I laughed. "No. She just means have another drink as a cure for your headache."

As if on cue, Ciaran entered, carrying a bottle of champagne and a bottle of white wine. I made introductions quickly, avoiding Mrs. Pennington's gaze for fear she'd see the attraction between us. Two could play at the matchmaking game. The others had come in by then, as had Blythe and the girls. Introductions were made and gratitude expressed to our host and hostess for the invitation. While all this was going on, Ciaran moved to the bar, setting the bottles on the counter. He smiled at my new friend, then took her hand and brought it to his mouth like a man from another century. "You're positively stunning, Mrs. Pennington."

Mrs. Pennington curtsied. "Oh, please, call me Lauren." Mrs. Pennington, reduced to a shy schoolgirl in less than thirty seconds, I thought. No wonder I was unable to resist him. He was like one of those super-human strains of bacteria in a science fiction novel that took out an entire continent. Or, like the norovirus on a cruise ship. There was nowhere to hide.

"Lauren, has anyone ever told you that you look like Grace Kelly?" Ciaran let go of her hand but remained close, seeming to take in her every detail.

"Well, I can't lie. I have heard it once or twice."

I sighed. I had my analogies wrong. Ciaran wasn't like a strain of bacteria but more like the love potion in *Midsummer's Nights Dream*.

"Did I hear something about a hangover?" he asked her.

Once again, she giggled. I looked at him, amazed. How had he heard us? We'd spoken quietly, so much so we'd had to lean into one another. "I'm afraid so," said Mrs. Pennington.

"I have just the cure," he said. "But you have to trust me, because the ingredients are a little strange."

"Well, I suppose I could take a chance on your suggestion. As long as it doesn't make me feel worse."

His face lit up as he offered her his arm. "Follow me. I have to search for some of the ingredients in the kitchen, and I think there's a blender in there, too."

"Something blended?" said Mrs. Pennington as they walked toward the kitchen. "My favorite."

Blythe approached me then, quietly asking me to stay and entertain our guests. "I have last-minute things to do for the dinner," she said. "It's best not to have anyone underfoot."

"Are you sure you don't need me?" I asked.

"No, you're more use to me in here. Try and keep Kevan and Ciaran civil."

After I promised to do my best, Blythe left for the kitchen. My nieces, apparently uninterested in the adults, scooted off to watch a movie in the television room while they waited for dinner. I took a good look at Sam. He looked well rested and was dressed in a pair of the slacks and one of the new sweaters I'd gotten him. No one would have believed that three days ago he was living on the streets. I turned to examine Henry once again. He had clearly gotten some action the night before. I think I would have known even if Mrs. Pennington hadn't already spilled the news. His face seemed relaxed, and his stiff British posture less ramrod straight. There was just a slight curve on either side of his mouth, like a permanent half smile.

I sidled right over to him, taking his arm and guiding him over to the bar. "Henry."

"Miss Heywood." He nodded with a slight tilt of his head.

"How was your night?" I asked with the most innocent voice I could conjure.

"You can't possibly believe I'll give you the satisfaction of the details, do you?"

"Oh, come on, Henry. You're no fun at all." I sat on one of the bar stools and motioned for him to do the same.

Kevan was behind the bar now. "What can I get everyone to drink?"

Moonstone asked for a glass of wine and informed us that Sam wanted a root beer. "Sweetheart isn't thirsty," she added. Sweetheart had already found a spot near the fire, looking at us all with her chin perched on her paws. At the sound of her name, she wagged her tail.

"A little hair of the dog for you?" I whispered in Henry's ear. "You've given poor Mrs. Pennington a hangover."

He gave me a look meant to wither the hardiest of hothouse lilies, before resting his forehead in his hands. "Women can never keep a secret."

"Is it a secret?" I asked, enjoying torturing him more than I should.

"No, no, of course not." He stuttered and flushed. "Just, please, don't make a big fuss about it. I don't want her to feel embarrassed."

I felt bad for teasing him, and relented, although Mrs. Pennington seemed anything but embarrassed. "I'll behave. I promise."

He let out a thankful sigh, as he took a bottle of beer from Kevan. After Kevan had walked away with the other drinks, Henry leaned closer to me, whispering. "You really do need a young man."

"Why's that?" I whispered back.

"It's amazing what it does for one's attitude."

"You mean sex?" We continued to whisper.

"Miss Heywood, vulgarity in a woman is not attractive. But yes, that, amongst other reasons. Some love in your life might help with your bossy disposition."

"Oh, Henry, you say the sweetest things."

He sobered, glancing sideways at me before continuing to speak in the same hushed voice. "Speaking of young men. The brother. He's looking at you like he wants to eat you for Thanksgiving dinner. I don't like it." Henry took a long swig from his beer.

"Is it that obvious?"

"Be careful, Miss Heywood. Not to sound like a sad country song, but he's a heartache waiting to happen."

"You don't have to tell me, Henry."

"No?" He cocked his head, examining my face. "Oh for pity's sake, you slept with him already, didn't you."

I remained silent, tracing the paisley pattern on the cocktail napkin with my fingers.

"This is not what I meant by finding a young man," he said.

"I can handle it, Henry. It's just right for me. I'm having fun. No strings attached."

"Miss Heywood, it continues to surprise me how little self-awareness you possess."

"Self-awareness?"

"A woman who rescues a homeless guy and his dog is not someone capable of having a casual affair with a playboy."

"How do you know he's a playboy?"

"I follow the news, Miss Heywood." He took another sip of his beer, and then wiped the bottle clean of condensation with the cloth cocktail napkin. "Not to mention that it's obvious from the moment I spotted him. Men like that are never satisfied with one woman. They live for the chase."

"Well, it doesn't matter because I have no expectations. I don't even believe in all that love nonsense. Not for myself anyway." I smiled at him, desperate to change the subject. "I believe in it for others, though, like you and Mrs. Pennington. And Blythe and Kevan."

"Do you think it's possible to fall in love overnight?" he asked.

"Henry! Are you in love?"

"I'm not a one-night-stand type of fellow, Miss Heywood."

"I know you're not." I patted him on the shoulder, speaking without a hint of teasing in my voice. I could tell he was serious and that it pained him to speak openly to me about his feelings. The poor fellow was eager to talk, I thought, if he was confessing to me. "Blythe says she fell in love with Kevan after only three days. So, yeah, I guess it's possible. Plus, I'm a little in love with Mrs. Pennington as well. When you guys get married, will you adopt me?"

He chuckled. "Oh, Miss Heywood, you don't need anyone to adopt you. We'd just get in your way. You're what my mother would have called a force to be reckoned with."

"Is that a good thing?"

He smiled and patted my hand. "Most of the time."

CHAPTER 20

LATER, AFTER STUFFING OURSELVES the same way Blythe had so expertly stuffed the turkey, Ciaran insisted that he would do the cleaning. Henry, not to be outdone by chivalrous behavior, chimed in with his pledge of support. Sam was up first and began collecting plates, but Kevan stopped him, asking if he would come in the other room, as there was something he wanted to discuss with him. Earlier we'd agreed that Kevan would offer him the caretaker position after dinner. Rori and Cole excused themselves and headed back to Cole's mother's house—he'd arrived back at the house just before dinner— to deliver a package of food Blythe had put together.

"Please be careful on the roads, Cole," said my sister.

He promised her he would, reminding her gently that he'd lived here all his life, before the young couple left the dining room hand in hand.

"Mrs. Pennington?" Clementine asked in a small, shy voice, very unlike her usual spirited tone. "It's stopped snowing now. Would you like to help us build a snowman?"

Mrs. Pennington set her napkin on her empty plate. "Miss Clementine, I would love nothing more."

Clementine beamed at her as Lola chimed in that she would like to help as well, and the three of them scampered off. At the doorway, Clementine slipped her hand into Mrs. Pennington's. The look the older woman gave to the child brought tears to my eyes, remembering how she'd wanted a child but hadn't been able to have one. *Family finds us.* This phrase came to me, like it was on a banner over Clementine's and Mrs. Pennington's heads.

Blythe, Moonstone, and I retired to the front room where we proceeded to chat about this and that—a movie we all wanted to see, how Moonstone's inn was faring, when and where Blythe and Kevan would get married. As evening turned the picture windows to black, Blythe told Moonstone of Kevan's plan to offer Sam a job.

"So he's staying? Here, in Peregrine?" asked Moonstone.

"If he wants to, of course," said Blythe.

"He'll want to," I said.

They went on to discuss the little cottage where he would live, what the duties were like. Moonstone offered to help if they needed to communicate with him. "I can be your conduit when you're not here," she said to Blythe.

I only half-listened to their conversation, feeling distracted by Moonstone's hair and makeup, both of which made my hands itch with a desire to make her over. It would take some doing, but I could strip down all the bright colors to find her natural beauty. The orange hair dyed a shiny auburn and cut to her shoulders with some curls that reminded me of waves in a bay that were such the style now. Nails cut and polished with a French manicure. Purple eye shadow and dark pencil exchanged for soft charcoals to bring out the green in her eyes. When Moonstone excused herself to use the bathroom, I turned to Blythe, ready to pitch my ideas. But she put her hands up before I could start speaking.

"Don't even think about it. She likes herself the way she is," said Blythe.

"How is that possible?"

"Don't be mean."

"I'm not. I just see potential under that horrific makeup and hair." I shuddered, thinking of the split ends I'd spotted during dinner. "It's my duty as a woman of taste to help her."

"Never mind that." Blythe leaned closer, peering into my eyes. "What's going on with you and Ciaran?"

I made my eyes wide like I was surprised by the question. "Nothing other than he's taken it upon himself to show me how to have fun."

She hadn't taken her eyes off me. How could I escape? The longer I sat here, the more likely she was to figure out my true feelings.

"I saw how he looked at you at dinner. He barely took his eyes off you. And, he was unusually quiet. What have you done to him?"

"What've I done to him? It's the other way around."

"Oh, God." She continued to stare at me with those laser eyes. "Please tell me you haven't already slept with him. Was it the hot tub?" She banged her head three times against the hard back of the couch. "It was the damn hot tub. What was I thinking, encouraging you to spend time with him?"

"Nothing happened. As a matter of fact, half the time I want to punch him." Never in my life had I lied to my sister, although the punching part was true.

I jumped when Moonstone spoke, right behind us. "There's a reason the two of you have crossed paths. You and Ciaran, that is." She'd reapplied her lipstick. Same purple as her nails, glistening like tinsel on a 1970's Christmas tree. God help me.

We both turned to look at her as she came around the couch and took the chair by the fire.

"What does that mean?" I asked.

She fluffed her hair with those pointy nails, as her eyes closed. "I'm not entirely certain, but there's a gray haze over him. Something sinister threatens him. You're to assist in some way. I can see this when you stand next to him. The haze disappears, which indicates you're to save him somehow. I can't make it all out just yet, but you're important to one another in the ways that matter most. Clear light indicates true love."

I exploded in a burst of rueful laughter, mostly to hide the anxiety Moonstone's words had given me. "I can barely stand him. He's everything I hate about men."

"You're a cosmic challenge to one another," said Moonstone.

"But he's Kevan's brother," said Blythe. "Isn't there some rule against siblings dating siblings' siblings?"

"Blythe, we're not romantically involved. Stop worrying." Well, it wasn't romance, but attraction. There was a big difference in the two. I shook my head as if this whole conversation was tiresome, when inside I wanted to scream out, *tell me more.*

"More details will come to me. Probably in dreams if I meditate on the two of you before sleeping," said Moonstone.

I looked over at Blythe, fully expecting her to roll her eyes and laugh at such nonsense. But this new Blythe, this Idaho-influenced

Blythe, seemed to believe in such things. She looked concerned, not skeptical. Had Moonstone truly heard my thoughts? I needed to be more careful. I flushed, thinking of my Moonstone mental makeover that had so distracted me from the conversation just minutes before.

"Promise me you won't get involved with him," said Blythe. "Nothing good can come from it."

"Don't worry. Ciaran Lanigan is the last thing I need," I said.

My sister looked somewhat relieved. Moonstone, however, just looked down at her hands with an eerie half smile on her face. "The universe has spoken. I'm afraid it's not up to you." Then, she looked up at me. "Now about this makeover—when can we start?"

I flinched, like someone had cracked a whip over my head. Crap. The woman really could read minds.

Pretending that it was not out of the ordinary whatsoever for this woman to have been inside my head, I leaned toward her. "Does anyone do hair in this town?"

"Yes. You met her yesterday when you first arrived. Do you remember? Ida Smart. Moved here last year—lives with her brother out on Maple Loop. She doesn't have a salon, but she does do house calls. I could call her tomorrow." Moonstone smiled at me with a hopeful glint in her eyes, suddenly looking like a little girl.

"I thought she was a masseuse," I said.

"Oh, that too," said Moonstone. "She prefers to call it 'body work'."

Body work? That sounded like something our hippie mother would say.

"But Moonstone, I thought you were happy with your appearance," said Blythe. "Why do you want to change it?"

"Bliss is right. Once I saw myself through her eyes, I realized that I might be in need of a few changes." She scooted forward on her chair and lowered her voice. "And Sam. Well, you know."

Blythe cocked her head, wrinkling her brows. "I do not know."

I stared at her. "You like him—I mean, *like* him like him. Is that it?"

"Exactly." Moonstone sat back and crossed her legs. "And he likes me, but not that way."

"How do you know?" asked Blythe.

"It doesn't take a psychic to know when you're in the friend zone," said Moonstone.

"But Moonstone, he's homeless," said Blythe in a tone of voice that implied we had lost our minds.

"Our possessions do not define us," said Moonstone.

"But we don't know enough about him. He might be dangerous," said Blythe.

"He's not," she said. "I know." She looked back at me. "I need a complete overhaul." She swept her hands down the entirety of her torso. "Operation 'get out of the friend zone'."

"Game on," I said.

"Game on." Moonstone pointed at her mouth. "Can I keep the tinsel lipstick, though? Glitter makes me deliriously happy."

I shook my head. "God, no. Absolutely no glitter. If this is going to work, you have to trust me. Can you do that?"

She sighed. "No glitter. Ten-four."

CHAPTER 21

KEVAN TOOK OUR NEW FRIENDS back to the inn around nine. The little girls and Blythe had said good night, leaving Ciaran and me in the mudroom, preparing to venture out into the cold. Ciaran had run over earlier to fetch my Idaho boots, so I carried my others with the soft leather of the upper boots draped over my forearm like dishtowels.

"I'll walk you back to the guesthouse before I head out on the snowmobile," he had said in front of the others. We both knew he wasn't going anywhere the moment we shut the door behind us.

Tying the boots, I thought about Moonstone's words earlier. What was she seeing about Ciaran that none of the rest of us could? I squinted, looking just above his head, hoping to see some hint of what she saw. But nothing. Just regular light over his ridiculously handsome face.

"You all right?" he asked.

"Fine. Yeah."

I held onto his arm as we headed toward my temporary home. The path he'd shoveled for us was icy, and I was happy to have the practical boots. When we reached my place, he opened the door for me. There was something somber about him; he'd been this way after he'd come in from outside when everyone was gathered around having another drink and playing various games. He hadn't participated, instead, sitting in the chair nearest the fire, seemingly lost in thought. I'd seen my sister watching him several times with a worried look on her face.

"Do you think it's safe to come in?" I asked him. "Is anyone watching?"

He glanced at the other house. "All the lights are out."

"What about Kevan when he gets home? Won't he see your snowmobile?"

"I parked it around back." He grinned and raised an eyebrow. "Thinking ahead."

"Ah, smart man."

He followed me inside, closing the door behind him. I took off my boots and headed toward the fireplace, turning it on with a flip of the switch. He remained at the doorway, still in his jacket and hat, watching me.

"You were quiet after dinner. Is everything all right?"

He shook his head, shrugging his left shoulder and took off his hat, tossing it on the table. "That dark feeling came over me while I was shoveling snow. It's like smoke hovers around me. Hard to explain."

A chill ran up and down my body. Hadn't Moonstone described it as a gray cloud, like smoke? What did she see? What did he feel? Was it possible that it was something supernatural that haunted him? But that couldn't be. There was no such thing as ghosts or demons. It had to be something of this world that threatened him. Someone. Was there something in his past, someone who felt wronged and wished him harm? It was either that, or there were mental issues here that he should deal with.

He sank onto the couch, running both hands through his hair so that it stood up like a little boy's in the morning. It made him appear vulnerable, like I imagined he'd been as a child growing up the youngest of four tough boys, having to harden everything on the exterior so nothing could penetrate, nothing could hurt. I sat on the couch next to him and put my hand on his knee. "Do you ever feel safe?"

"Yes." Leaning closer, he cupped my chin in his hand. "I feel safe right now." He lowered his eyes my mouth; his lashes fanned out against his cheekbones.

"I'm glad."

He kissed me with a tenderness we hadn't shared earlier, his hands on either side of my face. "Can I stay with you tonight?"

"I would like that very much," I said.

He took my hand, leading me toward the bedroom, stopping only long enough to turn off the fireplace, grinning at me as he did so. "I'm a good boy scout. Never leave a fire burning."

In the bedroom, we stopped at the side of the bed. He lifted my sweater dress over my head and snapped the clasp at the back of my bra, freeing my breasts from the soft lace. The next second he pushed me onto the bed, his hands clumsy now as he tried to pull off my panties while kissing my neck.

"I'll do it," I said. My voice didn't even sound like me, coming out hoarse like I'd just run a marathon.

"Yeah, good." He stood and slipped out of his sweater, tossing it onto a chair.

I felt suddenly self-conscious, even though the room was dark except for the light coming in through the open door from the other room. I tossed the extra pillows onto the floor before pulling down the quilt and blankets to slide between the sheets. He did not take his eyes off me as he took off his own jeans and socks. I wanted him to stay standing so that I might take him in, but he joined me on the bed, moving the sheet off my body. "I want to see you," he whispered, before he kissed me. "There's nothing but beauty here."

* * *

Afterward, Ciaran held me against him, spoon to spoon, with his right arm under my neck. I expected to feel stiff in his arms, unused to having a man in my bed, but I relaxed into the strength and warmth of his body. This is what it feels like to be held by Ciaran Lanigan, I thought. Lovely. Warm. Languorous. As if no other woman had ever been held as gently. As if he had never held another. This was the magic, I realized. It wasn't Ciaran's beauty that attracted women. Instead it was the ways in which he made them feel beautiful, cherished, seen. I took in a deep breath, my legs shaky from how tightly I'd wrapped myself around him, and shivered. "Are you cold? Should I get another blanket?" he asked, his voice sounding low and sleepy in my ear.

"No, I'm fine." But I was not, really. The space he left would be more noticeable now that I knew what it felt like to be possessed by him in moments of passion and then held by him. "It feels good to be held."

"You should be."

"Held?"

"Yes. A woman should always be held during the night."

"Keeps the demons away, I suppose?" Trying to sound light, but I heard the loneliness in my voice. The light of day would come and this man would be gone. Henry was right; he was the leaving kind, the type of man who was the subject of too many country songs.

"I used to have a teddy bear." His face was in my hair. "I couldn't sleep without him. Used to hold him like this until I fell asleep. He was shorter than you, though. And furrier. Not nearly as sexy. I called him Toddy. My brothers teased me unmercifully."

"What happened to Toddy?"

"I outgrew him I suppose. Don't really remember when I stopped sleeping with him. Just one day he wasn't part of my night any longer."

"Replaced with women?"

He chuckled, and squeezed me tighter. "No, that wasn't for years after I abandoned Toddy. Now go to sleep. I'll tell you all my secrets in the morning."

The snow had started up again. I saw it falling gently outside the window, illuminated by the porch light. "It's so pretty," I said.

"Yes, you are."

I fell asleep listening to his soft breathing that broke the silence of this winter's night. My last thought before I drifted into nothingness: snow falls without sound.

I awakened near five a.m. needing to use the bathroom. The dresser and bookshelf appeared as black shapes in the dark room. From behind the window shade, a bit of light from the outside lamps fell in a rectangle across the top end of the bed so I could see Ciaran's face. He slept on his back with his head angled toward my side of the bed and his arms tucked under the covers. His breath came in long, even gusts of air, in and out of his nose with just a slight high-pitched noise at the end of each pattern. In sleep he appeared boyish and innocent; I suddenly had an image of him as a child with his teddy bear in his arms. I reached out to touch his face—my hand seeming to have its own mind—but pulled back just in time. I didn't want to risk waking him and have him leave before it turned light, the way men do. The few times I'd slept with men I hadn't known long, they always slipped out before light, as if they might turn back into a rat with the light of day.

I crept from the bed, careful to lift the covers only enough to slide silently to the floor. Cold seeped in, I knew, when blankets were disturbed. I tiptoed through the cold to the bathroom, wincing when a floorboard creaked. Glancing back to the bed, I felt relief to see Ciaran's long body splayed out as I'd left him. Outside it was still dark. The snow had ceased and the cloud cover had moved away. No moon this early, I guessed, as I could see only scattered stars sparkled in the dark November dawn through the glass windows. Before I sat on the toilet, I flicked on the overhead fan, self-conscious of the sound of urine hitting water. Decidedly unsexy. I rubbed my eyes. My hands carried the scent of Ciaran and sex. How long had it been, I wondered, since a man had touched me? At least a year. Sometime after my short-lived involvement with "Man-Bun Yoga Teacher." Some trip for work, I'd met a man in the bar of the hotel. Where had I been that trip? I couldn't remember if it was Chicago or Boston. Regardless, I'd met a man in the bar while eating a late dinner. We'd chatted about business for an hour or so. He had no ring on his left hand, so I'd let him buy me a second drink, which went to my head enough that when he offered to walk me to my room, I accepted, knowing full well what would happen when we got there. It had been what anyone might expect when you have sex with a stranger, more like a sporting match than making love. But today and tonight with Ciaran had felt different, even though we'd only just met. Why was that? Was it because I knew I would see him again, that he would be in my life from now on? Or, was it just that I felt a connection to him, despite my intentions to the contrary?

I tiptoed back to bed, slipping under the covers, then turned to face the wall. Not daring to hope for further sleep, I closed my eyes anyway, listening to the sounds of the Peregrine dawn. So this is the country, I thought. Quiet. Nary a sound, except the soft breathing of Ciaran. After a few minutes, I rolled onto my back, disturbing the covers so that a draft of cold air slivered in and gave me goose bumps. As I'd feared, it woke my slumbering partner. He stirred next to me and wakened as I shifted to look at him, his eyes glittering in the shaft of light coming through the space between the shade and the window. "Bliss?" He said it as if surprised to see me, rolling onto his side and resting his hand on my hip.

"Sorry I woke you."

"I didn't know where I was for a moment. Too many mornings of waking in a strange place." His voice was thick with sleep.

I moved to my side, touching his face with my fingertips. Pure instinct, I thought, to touch him in this familiar way, as if we were longtime lovers. "Go back to sleep. It's early."

"It's cold. Stay close." He scooted down a few inches and buried his face in my neck. "You smell like home."

"Like home?"

"Like something familiar. Someone familiar." He pulled me under him, peering at me with his thick hair brushing my forehead.

I didn't answer with words as I ran my hands down the muscles of his back, thinking only that I must memorize the feel of him for the cold day that would come.

Thus, on my second morning in Idaho I didn't witness the dark dawn slip away, pushed aside by morning light. It was only Blue Mountain's son and the silent sound of falling snow.

CHAPTER 22

THE LONG WEEKEND EVAPORATED and suddenly it was Sunday. Sam had agreed to take the job, after some encouragement from me, and for the remainder of the long weekend Kevan and Ciaran helped him get settled into his new cottage. They spent time showing him the extent of his duties, with Ciaran agreeing to answer any questions that came along in the weeks that were to come. Henry had agreed that we should stay at least another week, so we could make sure Sam was settled comfortably, but I suspected it had more to do with Mrs. Pennington than worry over Sam. Henry and I both felt Sam was in good hands with Ciaran remaining in Peregrine until the end of the calendar year. The rest of my Thanksgiving weekend days were filled with snowball fights, hot cocoa, competitive Scrabble games, reading on the couch, and Blythe's delicious meals. At night Ciaran snuck into the guesthouse.

On Sunday morning, Ciaran took Blythe, Kevan and all the kids, including Cole and Rori, to the airport in Hailey. Kevan encouraged me to stay in the big house and to drive his Range Rover if I needed, but I decided to stay in my small, temporary house instead. Already it had started to feel like home to me, and I didn't want to amble about the big house all by myself anyway.

When Ciaran left for the airport, he promised to be back in an hour or two so that he could take me to Moonstone's to begin our makeover, knowing I wasn't able to drive yet, per the doctor's instructions.

As promised, he arrived by mid-morning and drove me into town, although he declined to come inside the inn, saying he wanted to get a workout in and asking that I call him when I was finished. After lingering over a kiss, I jumped from his truck and headed inside to the lobby. Moonstone was sitting at her desk talking on the phone. The voices of Henry and Mrs. Pennington carried in from the parlor, and when I peeped in to say hello, they were sitting next to one another with a newspaper spread out over the coffee table, with several half-eaten scones on a plate. As I neared, I saw they were working on a crossword puzzle. They looked up as I approached.

"We hear there's a makeover today." Mrs. Pennington smiled, holding a pen like a baton between two fingers. "Perhaps I should be next."

At the same time, Henry and I said, "You don't need one."

She smiled. "Well, how nice of you to say."

Henry gestured toward the upstairs as I perched on the side of the coffee table. "Ida came by with her tools but remembered at the last second she'd forgotten something."

"I'll do Moonstone's makeup first. I hope this Ida knows what she's doing. Forgetting something isn't a great sign," I said. All Moonstone needed was a bad color and cut on top of what she already had going on top of her crazy, lovable head.

"Not that I would know one way or the other." Henry lowered his voice. "But since you mentioned it, she is a bit on the jittery side. I noticed it the first time we met her, but today she seems even more so."

"Jittery?" I made a face. "That doesn't sound good." Was this just Henry being grumpy as usual? "Like shaky hands?"

"No, he means more mentally jittery," said Mrs. Pennington. "Fragile might be the better word."

"Miss Heywood." Henry set aside the paper. "On another matter."

"Yes, Henry?"

"When would you like to return home?" he asked.

I hesitated. Mrs. Pennington put down her pen and picked up a fork, spearing the corner of a scone.

"I'm not sure. I don't feel like I want to leave here anytime soon." I went on to tell them that I'd seen Sam that morning helping Ciaran stack firewood. "He seems fine, and Ciaran's here to look after him so he doesn't really need us to stay longer than a week, I suppose."

Henry patted my hand. "You've done a good thing, Miss Heywood. I'm proud of you."

"Henry. A compliment?" I asked. I kept my voice light but a lump had formed in my throat. Was I this desperate for a father figure's approval? Pathetic.

Mrs. Pennington, without meeting my eyes, pulled the fork from the speared scone and brought it to her mouth, as if to take a bite. Did she realize there was nothing on it?

"What is it," I asked. "Is there something you want to ask me?"

"The thing is, Miss Heywood, is that I'm thinking of staying longer than a week." Henry's eyes darted to Mrs. Pennington. "We've taken a fancy to the place and would like to stay through the winter."

"We?" I asked, teasing

"Well, yes, we." Mrs. Pennington's cheeks were flushed as she looked over at me. "I'd already thought I might stay awhile, and now that I've met Henry, I have even more motivation to do so. Moonstone gave me a wonderful rate if we commit to staying until March."

"But, I'm worried, Miss Heywood, about sending you home alone. I feel responsible for you, it seems."

"There are flights out of Hailey, Henry," I said. "It's no problem."

"That's not what I mean, Miss Heywood."

"What he means, Bliss, is that he's worried about sending you back to Portland without a job or friends. We both feel strongly that it would be good for you to consider also staying the winter."

I stared at them, suddenly feeling eight years old in front of my parents. It felt good. "I could use a rest, I suppose."

"A rest? This doesn't sound like you, Miss Heywood," said Henry.

"But maybe it should." I turned to Mrs. Pennington. "How can I expect to make changes in my life if I just go back to the same life?" *Nothing different than the day before.* Was that the phrase Blythe had used to describe our father once? It was time to do something different than the day before. I wasn't certain what, only that I must in order to survive. "I can think here. It's so quiet. Maybe I can figure out what I want if I stay a couple of months."

"I couldn't agree more," said Mrs. Pennington, patting my hand. "Good girl."

"And Henry's right. I don't have anything to go home to." But there was the problem of Ciaran. The longer I stayed, the less likely it was to feel like a fling and more like a relationship.

"But what about the young man?" asked Henry.

I smiled. "We're just having fun. I doubt he'll stay after the first of the year. Maybe I'll be ready to go then, too. Don't worry, I have it all under control."

Mrs. Pennington squeezed my hand. "Just be careful, dear. Our heads have a disturbing way of not listening to our hearts."

"And Ciaran Lanigan is bad news," said Henry. "I don't want you to get hurt. You've been through enough."

"Henry, you're getting soft on me." I gave them both a kiss on the cheek. "Does this mean you're officially adopting me?"

Mrs. Pennington laughed. "I'll have my attorney send the papers right away."

From in the lobby, I heard Moonstone hang up the phone. "Have to run. Makeover time starts now," I said.

"Good luck, dear," said Mrs. Pennington.

I waved my fingers in the air. "Not to worry, this is what I'm born to do."

I found Moonstone standing at her desk, staring straight ahead. Should I interrupt her? Was she having a vision? Her eyes fluttered, then she went perfectly still for a second before shaking her head like she'd suddenly remembered something. She looked over at me, blankly at first, until her expression rearranged into one of recognition. She held out her arms. "Bliss, I'm like a kid at Christmas." Coming out from behind her desk, she pulled me into her ample chest and squeezed me. As instructed, she'd scrubbed her face clean of makeup.

"Game on?" I held out my bag with my makeup kit.

"Game on."

I had her sit behind her desk and asked if she had brought her own makeup, which she had. My plan was to use as many of her own products as I could, so she wouldn't have to purchase more and could duplicate what I'd done when she tried on her own. Using her foundation and a clean sponge, I put enough on for coverage, which wasn't much as she had surprisingly beautiful and unflawed skin for a woman in her late forties. Maybe psychics didn't go outside much, either? Giving instruction as I went, I added blush and a set of light brown and taupe eye shadows, complimented with brown eyeliner. After I added mascara, I handed her a mirror.

"What do you think?"

"I look amazing," she said.

"You really do." The soft makeup brought out her eyes, and the way I'd evenly spread out the foundation gave her a dewy appearance.

Just then, Ida came into the lobby, carrying a small bag. "Sorry to keep you waiting," said Ida.

Moonstone introduced us, reminding Ida that we'd met before, although there was no recognition in her eyes. To my surprise, Ida had a warm and soothing voice, in complete contrast to her appearance. "Your makeup looks very nice," said Ida.

"Thank you. I can't wait to have you fix my hair." Coming out from behind the desk, Moonstone smiled and clasped her hands over her ample chest. "Oh, Bliss, just one thing. While Ida's working on my hair, would you mind hanging out near the lobby? I have an unexpected guest arriving in an hour or so." She pointed at the desk. "I left her keys. Just show her to her room. I took care of everything else."

I agreed, happy to help in the cause of Operation Moonstone Makeover. We went up the stairs, past the antiques displayed in crowded clusters on the shelves: an old phone, a typewriter, glassware from the '30s, a child's wooden rocking horse, various books with tattered covers. She pointed down the hallway. "Ida, I thought we could use the room Blythe stayed in when she first came here. Good karma in there. But my new guest's room is Room C. The guest's assistant made the reservation and asked for the biggest room I had. I hope she won't be disappointed."

"Is it someone just passing through, or are they visiting family here?" I couldn't imagine staying here unless either one of those things were true.

"She didn't say. All I know is she asked for an unlimited stay. No checkout date, which is thrilling because I could use the money. The reservation is M. Madison."

All thoughts of this new guest left my mind when we walked into the room set aside for the cut and color. I knew immediately Mrs. Pennington was right about Ida's fragility. It wasn't merely that her unusually thin frame made her appear physically fragile; there was a skittish quality to her eyes, like a cornered animal unsure whether you were friend or foe, but ready to run either way.

Regardless, her hands appeared steady, if not her mind, and that's what mattered now. On the writing desk by the window, scissors, a comb, several round brushes, some product, and a hair dryer waited for their usefulness. A plastic robe, like those found at most salons, hung over the back of the chair.

The room itself had the feeling of another era. A patchwork quilt with geometric shapes in several shades of pink covered the bed, in unity with an antique, brass bedframe. Delicate lamps with roses embroidered on their shades donned bedside tables on either side. Outside, Blue Mountain loomed in the distance. From wherever I was in Peregrine, the mountain was a reassuring presence.

I explained to Ida my vision of changing Moonstone's hair color to a rich auburn and cutting off six inches, so that it would fall at the tip of her shoulders. "She can wear it with curls or not," I suggested. "Don't you think, Ida?"

She nodded, motioning for Moonstone to sit. After Ida had secured the wrap around Moonstone's shoulders, she put her hands in that mass of thick, orange hair, holding several tufts out from her head like one of Medusa's snakes. "Dye first. Cut second." Moonstone, with an excited shine in her eyes, smiled at me as she followed Ida into the bathroom.

I excused myself and went downstairs, remembering that I was to wait for the new guest's arrival. The lobby and sitting room were empty but smelled of fresh coffee and baking cookies. Looking around, it occurred to me that at one time it must have been the formal dining room, as I could see the kitchen just through the next door. An older woman was bent over an oven, taking out a pan of cookies. Moonstone had mentioned a woman who not only cleaned rooms but baked the cookies and scones as well. This must be her.

I wandered to the window. I wasn't sure if this was the case with all Victorian dining rooms, but this one had a window seat built into the curve of a picture window, which looked out onto the small grocery store. It reminded me of the stores you see near recreational spots that sell ice and beer that always smelled of old wood and popsicles the minute you entered.

I plopped onto the couch, wishing I could take my boots off, and close my eyes. The discarded newspaper was folded neatly on the coffee table, Mrs. Pennington's abandoned pen next to it. Where had they gone, I wondered? Probably upstairs together, which led to a visual image of Ciaran tossing me onto the bed last night. Stay focused, I thought, feeling that familiar twinge between my legs at the mere thought of how he'd hovered over me, his voice thick with desire. *You're beautiful.*

I got up and ambled over to an antique bureau where Moonstone had left a self-service breakfast. Only several dry-looking scones on a plate remained, other than pots labeled coffee, hot water, and decaf. A basket held assorted teas. I thumbed through them, picking an apple-cinnamon packet, and wandered to the window. The street, clear of snow, was wet, and occasionally vehicles, mostly trucks, passed by with a dirty spray of water onto the white snow. Snowdrifts, presumably made by the plow earlier, were at least four feet high on either side of the road. I held the tea packet to my nose but could smell nothing through its thick packaging. I went to the bookshelf and ran my fingers along the paperbacks. Vacation-type reading material for the most part: mysteries, romances, thrillers. I imagined their owners over the years, reading them under the patchwork quilts late into the night, only to leave them here after they'd gone back to their real lives.

I grabbed a romance from the shelf. Yesterday a mystery, today a romance—I chose not to examine that choice too closely as I made a cup of tea and settled onto the couch to read. I was five pages into the book—the heroine had just crashed her car and was wandering up to a poorly lit mansion to ask for help—no doubt her soon-to-be-lover, a troubled millionaire, awaited behind the heavy oak door—when I heard the ping of the bell that indicated someone had just come into the inn. Remembering my promise to Moonstone, I reluctantly got up and walked into the lobby.

A slight woman, dressed in a black ski jacket, leggings and Idaho boots with flair (faux fur at the top) held a small suitcase in a gloved hand. Her head was covered entirely in a ski cap, black to match the rest of her outfit, and she wore sunglasses, without any indication of taking them off even though she'd just come into a dimly lit room.

"Is Moonstone here?" the woman asked. Her voice sounded so familiar. Where had I heard it before?

"Moonstone's busy, but I have your key. Everything's ready for you."

"Great." She took off her glasses first, then her hat. Long, blonde hair fell about her shoulders. No makeup, except for a little mascara and lip gloss. Flawless skin. White teeth. A symmetrical face with small features, except for her eyes—round and blue, framed by dark lashes. She set her suitcase on the floor.

It took me a split second to realize who she was: Hope Manning. Hope Manning, right in front of me. My mind tumbled to the next thought. Had she come to see Ciaran? My gut twisted with jealousy. Had she come to spend the week with him? Was there something between them? Had he lied to me? Did he know she was coming?

CHAPTER 23

HOPE MANNING GESTURED TOWARD THE DESK, with a weary look that told me she knew I had quickly figured out who she was. "Let's get to it then, shall we? I believe the reservation is under M. Madison."

Scurrying behind the desk, I found the keys that Moonstone had left and handed them to her, telling her that I would take her up and show her the room.

As I came around the desk, Hope started for the stairs, leaving her bag behind. Apparently I was to take it up with me in my temporary role as innkeeper! Just then, the front doorbell chimed and opened. A cold draft swept into the room. We both turned to look. Ciaran, dressed in jeans and a striped blue and white sweater, with hair wet from the shower. I caught a whiff of his cologne as he closed the door behind him.

Hope let out a yelp and ran toward him, throwing her arms around him. "Surprise!"

His arms went around her waist, as he caught my eye. I looked away, my stomach turning sour. So this is what jealousy felt like, I thought. "What're you doing here?" he asked.

"I came to see you. Get away from the paparazzi."

"You know they'll find you here, right? They always do. And it'll fuel all the rumors." He sounded irritated. I glanced at him. His expression matched his voice.

"Not this time. I managed to get here without anyone finding out. They think I'm in France with you. We let out a false rumor that we were staying at the Four Seasons in Paris. The idiots are all camped outside the gates, driving the real guests insane, I'm sure. It's been all over the rags. Have you not been keeping up?"

He glanced over at me with a slight smile. "I've been busy."

She stepped away from him, turning to look at me as if seeing me for the first time, then turned back to him. "Busy?"

He crossed the room to stand next to me, putting his arm around my shoulders. "This is Bliss." He'd emphasized my name in a way that left no doubt in anyone's mind that we were sleeping together. The writhing jealousy swirling around my gut subsided, replaced by warmth that ran the length of my legs.

"I see." A pink flush in the shape of an inkblot appeared on the left side of Hope's neck. The vein that ran down her forehead swelled and became visible under her white skin, like she'd just done vigorous exercise. I'd seen it happen in certain highly emotional scenes I'd watched in her films.

I knew it then. Hope Manning was in love with Ciaran. She might not know it herself, and he most certainly did not, but it was plain as the bulging vein on her forehead. The question was, what happened when they both figured it out? Hope did not seem like a woman who would let anything keep her from what she wanted.

With these thoughts running through my mind, I approached her and held out my hand. "It's wonderful to meet you. I'm a huge fan of your work."

She smiled and shook my hand. Her skin felt cold and dry, like rice paper. An image came to mind of my neighbor's prissy white cat with one of those squished faces. Precisely, the moment right before Candy lunged at my hand with her sharp teeth, drawing blood and leaving a permanent scar just above pinky knuckle. "Ciaran's girls always are," she said.

I stifled a gasp, as I withdrew my hand. Ciaran's girls? How many had she met? Girl? I was certainly not a girl.

Speaking to Ciaran, as if I wasn't there, she said, "Although she's against type, Ciaran. That's new."

What did that mean?

She turned back to me, as if I'd asked the question out loud. "Usually he likes petite little nubile things that could blow away in the slightest of winds." Her eyes swept my body, lingering for a moment at my waist. "You're sturdy enough to conquer a hurricane." She said this all with a smile on her face, as if she were complimenting me.

Taking in a breath, I backed away. Ciaran took my hand and gave it a squeeze. Perhaps this is why the press hated her and she had the reputation of being difficult on set. She was a mean girl. *Bring it,* I thought. Two can play mean girl just fine. Remembering the room key, I held it out to Ciaran. "She's in room B. I mean C." Had I just stuttered?

Hope turned her beautiful blue eyes back to Ciaran. "Anyway, regarding the paparazzi, no one will ever think I'd stay here." Fluttering her hand around the room, she gave him a knowing look. "Reminds me of my grandmother's old place. Doesn't it?" I knew what that was. The whole "talk about old times routine," so as to exclude me from the picture. As if to say, *See, you do not matter. We have a past. We go way back. You're new. And temporary.*

Ciaran didn't comment, but reached down for her bag. "Come on, I'll take you up."

She sighed and headed toward the stairs, without another glance in my direction. "Good. I need a nap before you make me dinner tonight. Do you have a dining room table yet?" She knew he had no table?

"I have plans with Bliss tonight." He twisted his head to wink at me and mouthed the word, "fun."

Setting one foot on the bottom step and grasping the rail with one hand, she stopped and looked over at him. "You've got be kidding me with this." Then, she let out a long sigh and walked up the stairs. She had the straightest back I'd ever seen and held her head like a queen. When we were kids, Blythe and I used to practice walking around with a book on our heads to instill good posture. This girl could walk with a stack of five books and not have one shift.

I rubbed the scar on my hand and shivered.

*   *   *

While I waited for Ciaran to come down, I paced the floor in the sitting room, stopping every minute or so to sit on the couch and read, but my attempts at distraction only lasted a second or so. Fidgety and agitated, I couldn't focus on the words, let alone the story. After ten minutes, I decided to go upstairs and see how our makeover was going. When I got to the second floor, I heard voices behind the door of room C. I couldn't make out words, but I had the distinct impression that Ciaran and Hope were having a hushed argument. About what, I wondered? Me? Or something else?

I walked by the room on tiptoe, not wanting them to know I was there. At room B, I walked in without knocking. Moonstone was in the chair, having her long, now auburn, hair combed out. "Bliss, what do you think?"

"The color looks fantastic," I answered.

"She's going to cut it now," said Moonstone. "This is the scary part."

Ida, scissors in hand, smiled like she was interacting with an indulged toddler. "It won't hurt, I promise."

As Ida began to snip, long strands of hair fell to the floor, reminding me of the tails on those play coon hats the boys used to wear in elementary school. Fortunately, Ida had put newspapers all around the chair to catch the clippings. While she cut, I filled Moonstone in on the arrival of the latest guest. Both Ida's and Moonstone's eyes went wide when I told them the true identity of M. Madison.

Apparently Moonstone hadn't predicted this turn of events. "What's she doing in our little town?" she asked, meeting my eyes in the mirror. Ida hands moved fast, the scissors snipping like the beaks of a hungry baby bird. Already I could see the shape of the cut forming.

"She's here to see Ciaran," I said.

The scissors went still. Ida's gaze remained fixed on Moonstone, as if thinking about what to do next. Tiny slivers of hair floated in the beam of sunlight that had appeared through the window. Then, just as suddenly as she'd stopped, Ida began to cut again.

"So it's true? What they say in the magazines?" asked Moonstone.

"No. According to Ciaran, they're just friends. They went to high school together," I said. But even as I said it, I felt uncertainty and jealousy swirling around my gut.

"You have no reason to doubt him," said Moonstone. "I know this for certain. "

I sat on the edge of the bed. "So how does it work? How come you know some things but not others?"

"The universe decides. It's not up to me. My job is to remain open so the waves can come inside."

"Well, can you tell the universe that about now it would be really helpful if I knew if they were involved or not?"

"You've fallen for him," said Moonstone.

"No, it's not like that. We're just having fun, enjoying one another. That's all it is. I'll probably go home next week." I looked at her, pausing. Why did I sound like I was trying to convince myself?

"Men always want fun," said Ida, surprising me by speaking. She held her scissors at her side, and opened and closed them three times. Alligator jaws, I thought. She continued, still holding the scissors at her side. "Women are not capable of staying casual after having sex."

"No, that's not true," I said. "I'm not interested in serious, either, but I don't want to be lied to. If he has a thing with her, and she's here, then that isn't my definition of fun."

Ida shrugged and went back to cutting Moonstone's hair. "Men are liars. Some worse than others."

"The problem is, with matters of the heart, or desires of the flesh, we have to decide one way or the other, do we trust this person?" said Moonstone, sounding like a self-help advisor on *Oprah*, airy voice and all. "He told you they're not involved, so you have to decide if you believe him or not. But don't stay in the middle place between doubt and belief. Choose one way or the other."

I had to admit that Moonstone's advice was good. And my instincts told me that despite his phobia of commitment, Ciaran was not a liar. He'd been upfront from the beginning, as had I. The problem was that, to Ida's point, I wasn't sure I could maintain my end of the agreement. Feelings for him had crept in, despite my best efforts. I'd believed at the moment of decision that I could truly treat this as a casual, fun, and satisfying fling. But at the first appearance of Hope Manning, jealousy had appeared with a swift force. My reaction, this swirling in my gut, was not in conjunction with someone satisfied with a casual affair.

"You're afraid to get hurt." Moonstone stated this as fact, like she'd commented on my taste in chocolate.

"I'm impossible to hurt," I said.

"Didn't think you had it in you, did you?" asked Moonstone.

"As I said, I don't. Her arrival was surprising, that's all."

During the last part of this interchange, Ida's hands had not stopped moving with that assured and practiced way great hair stylists possess. It had always amazed me how sure they were, how they did not hesitate to cut with what seemed like wild abandon and yet at the end every strand fell in exactly the right place. Moonstone's haircut was complete. Ida set down her scissors, crossed her skinny arms over her concave stomach and looked at her work for a moment before picking up a can of mousse. "Straight or wavy?" she asked Moonstone.

"Straight?" Moonstone looked over at me. "Bliss?"

I remained perched on the side of the bed. "Straight sounds great." Putting aside my thoughts of Ciaran and Hope Manning in a room alone, I focused on my makeover project. "Watch how she does it so you can duplicate it," I said.

Moonstone nodded consent. As Ida turned on the dryer I waved good-bye, saying I would wait downstairs. I walked slowly past Hope's room; there were no voices. Had Ciaran come downstairs to wait for me? Or was he in there, making silent love to her? The thought made me feel as if I might retch. I sped up my gait as I went downstairs, almost slipping on the sleek wood, but reached for the rail just in time.

To my relief, I found Ciaran in the sitting room, stretched out on the couch, with his eyes closed. Was he asleep? Approaching with silent steps, I sat on the coffee table, resisting the desire to put my trembling fingers in his hair. His breathing was even and his upper lip made a little fluttering noise with each outward breath. Watching him sleep felt intimate, I thought, as his hand twitched where it rested on his stomach. Dreaming, I supposed. Of what?

I shifted slightly and accidently knocked one of the forks left from Henry and Mrs. Pennington to the floor. He opened his eyes at the sound of the metal clanging against the hardwood floor. "Hey, Bliss." Smiling, he put a hand on my knee. "For some reason, I can't imagine why, I'm tired today. It's like someone kept me up half the night."

I smiled back at him, running my fingers through the soft hair on his forearm. "We could go home and nap, if you wanted."

Shifting into a seated position, he swung his feet to the floor, and then pulled me onto his lap. "I can think of nothing better." He nibbled on my neck. "But let's eat first. I'm starved."

"What about Hope?" There it was, that high-pitched tone at the end of the sentence, betraying my feelings.

"She'll probably sleep the rest of the day. Jet lag and too much wine on the plane." He tucked hair behind my right ear. "Is something bothering you?"

I didn't say anything, focusing my gaze on his neck, swallowing the lump in my throat.

"You're not jealous, are you?"

"Of course not. I just don't want you to sacrifice spending time with her to take me out or whatever. I know you guys go way back."

His mouth puckered in apparent amusement. "Her being here has no influence on our plans." A flash of annoyance crossed his face. He lowered his voice. "Between you and me, one of the reasons I came to Idaho for the holidays was to get away from her." He took in a large breath, his chest expanding. "Yes, we're good friends, but she drives me crazy—like a spoiled sister might. I don't know if you've noticed, but she's a bitch. Not to mention a surly drunk."

I let that information sink in, trying to detect if it was false or not. "Why do you spend so much time with her, then?" I had to ask it. I had to see what he would say.

He cocked his head to the side. "It's complicated."

"Complicated?" Again, my stomach clenched with jealousy. Complicated implied involvement, perhaps of the sexual nature. "I know we're just having *fun*." I made quotes in the air around the word fun, appalled at how jealous I sounded. Damn, I could not get it together. "But I don't want to share you with another woman while we're here. That's where I draw the line."

"Duly noted," he said, no louder than a mumble. "I'm hungry for lunch. Let's eat at the grill."

"Are you changing the subject?"

His arms tightened around my hips. "Bliss, I'll tell you everything. Just not here. Over lunch." It was the first time he'd ever spoken to me with impatience. It sent a shooting pain through my chest.

"Fine."

His grip relaxed. He touched the side of my face with his fingertips. "You're kind of cute when you're jealous."

"I am not jealous." I dipped my face into the side of his neck.

"You don't need to be. Not of her or anyone. Come on, you need a good meal and so do I."

CHAPTER 24

WALKING INTO THE PEREGRINE BAR AND GRILL was like entering a shabby version of a western film set. The bar itself was made of light oak with matching backless stools. Walls covered with tattered and fading burgundy wallpaper and shelves filled with liquor in no apparent order, an old-fashioned popcorn machine, a cash register with manual keys and an actual money drawer. The wide plank floors scattered with peanut shells, dingy. On the restaurant side of the building the walls were brick. Five booths on the far wall with rubber seats split in places, foam poking out, as if waiting for the right moment to escape, were in juxtaposition to the tables and chairs made of the same faded oak as the bar, like a late 1960s set decoration had been accidently placed in the wrong movie scene. Everything needed a good scrubbing if the splatters of ketchup and mustard on the legs of the chairs were any indication. I shuddered to think how many pieces of gum were stuck under the tabletops. Empty of patrons, it smelled of dust, and coffee too long on the burner, with undertones of stale beer.

A waitress, middle-aged, with a worn-out slump to her shoulders, wearing loose, high-waisted jeans that did nothing for her skinny frame and a Peregrine Bar and Grill T-shirt, greeted us. She snatched a pencil she had placed in the middle of a mousy brown-and-gray bun, and gestured around the room with it. "Sit anywhere you like." During the day, the bar was closed, she informed us, but the restaurant served breakfast or lunch before shutting down at two p.m. and re-opening for dinner at five. "Don't get much business this time of year." She sounded apologetic, as if it were her fault that tourists hadn't flocked to this town the size of a large city block.

Then, she grabbed plastic menus from the cashier's desk and handed them both to Ciaran. "We don't have the Salisbury steak today. I suppose you'll want waters?" This was said as if we were from an exotic land where waters were audaciously served to everyone.

Ciaran smiled, thanked her, and led me to a booth at the back of the restaurant set with silverware the texture of a tin can wrapped in thin paper napkins, salt and pepper shakers with a film that I knew would make them sticky to the touch. Mustard and ketchup in plastic bottles propped up a drink menu between them. The plastic covers of the benches felt cold under my leggings as I slid into one side of the booth and Ciaran the other. I shivered and pulled my jacket tighter around my middle.

"I don't think they heat this place during the slow months." He glanced toward the kitchen where our waitress had disappeared behind a swinging door. "Can you see my breath?"

I chuckled. "It's not that cold."

"Well, I'm ordering the soup." He took off his gloves, setting them next to him, and rubbed his hands together.

I glanced at the menu. Split pea soup was the soup of the day. With a shudder, remembering school lunches and peas the color of army greens, I dismissed the idea.

After deciding that the turkey sandwich with wheat bread was the safest bet, I glanced over at Ciaran, to find him watching me, looking amused. "What?" I asked.

"You're such a snob."

"I am not."

"When was the last time you ate in a place like this?"

I shook my head, unable to remember. "I grew up in a town just like this one, you know. I'm quite familiar with this type of establishment. Anyway, I'm not a snob. I simply choose carefully."

Laughing, he poked my foot with his. "So, it's the boy named Sue phenomenon again."

I made an exaggerated sigh, and pulled my foot away from his. "What does that mean?"

"Just that you stay as far away as possible from anything resembling your childhood, including dive bars, which can be fun, you know. If you're in the right company, that is."

"Meaning you?"

"Precisely."

"Kevan and Blythe fell in love at the bar, you know." I pointed over to the bar area, hoping to change the subject.

The waitress came before he could respond, bringing the scandalous waters in bumpy plastic cups the color of weak apple cider. We ordered and she left.

Ciaran rubbed his eyes and sighed. "So, you want to know about Hope."

I shrugged like it didn't matter. "I guess."

He raised one eyebrow like he always did right before he teased me. But instead, his expression sobered. Picking up his set of utensils, he unwrapped them from the napkin. "This is a long story. Hope and me, that is."

I gestured around the room. "We've got nothing but time."

"I don't talk about this with anyone." He picked up his fork, pushing it against the pads of his fingertips, the tongs making dents in his flesh. "At least not lately."

I couldn't think what to say and held my breath, waiting for what was to come next. A muted sound came from the kitchen—the crash of broken glass and our waitress cursing, then a lower voice answering. I took a sip of water. It tasted of minerals.

"When we were kids, Hope's father was an equipment supplier for my father's trucking company. Metal items and such. I won't bore you with the details but basically they made parts that we put into our trucks. Their quality was important to the safety of our rigs, and it was a relationship my father took very seriously. He was intensely loyal and also felt strongly that whenever possible, he wanted to partner with vendors local to Idaho.

"My dad insisted that all of us get a job once we turned fifteen. I went to work for Hope's dad in the warehouse, doing various tasks, but I was clever with numbers and spreadsheets and that sort of thing, so I quickly moved into more of a desk job, essentially the assistant to one of the buyers—the guy responsible for procuring a lot of our materials. Again, without boring you with the details, I noticed a discrepancy in the paperwork and figured out that the metal they claimed to use for all of the parts they made for us was really a cheap version of it, one that, as it turns out, was not safe. I snuck into the office in the middle of the night and went through every piece of paper in the files and figured out that it had been going on for three years. Almost exactly the time that Hope's family had moved to our neighborhood in Boise and started attending the same private school as me and my brothers."

I stared at him as this story unfolded. He paused, taking a deep sip of water. "Anyway, I told my father what I'd figured out, and once he confirmed it for himself, he cut ties with Hope's father, recalled three years' worth of trucks and sued for damages. He won.

"It bankrupted them. Hope's mother left her father for one of the attorneys that defended them in court and took Hope with her—she was their only child. Her father, by the time we graduated high school, managed to kill himself in a drunk driving accident."

"That's awful," I said.

"Yeah, so through it all Hope and I remained friends. She sided with her mother, of course, who hadn't known any of what was going on, and basically just divorced herself from his life, acting like she'd never had a father, which was odd because growing up she had always been a daddy's girl and the type to fight with her mother. I have no idea how she feels now about the whole thing because she never talks about it. She rarely speaks to her mother, which is the only indication that it all still bothers her. I'm the only one she stayed in contact with from the old days. So, there you have it. I feel responsible for her, to her, all of it."

"But you did nothing wrong. As a matter of fact, you probably saved countless lives."

"While I know that's true, I also know that my actions destroyed a family. Hope has never been the same since then. Believe it or not, she used to be kind of a sweetheart. Now we only see that side of her when she's playing a part." He took another large drink from his water. "Anyway, we're not lovers. Never have been. Honestly, I wish she'd meet a decent guy and get married, but she chooses idiots every time. Ironically, all of them are liars, like her dad."

The waitress brought our food. Ciaran asked for a beer. I took off my coat and bit into my sandwich, without much enthusiasm. My stomach was in knots, waiting for the rest of his story. He ate several spoonfuls of his soup, both of us quiet.

"Why do you want her to get married?" I asked.

He sighed. "Because it would let me off the hook as her 'go-to' guy. I'm the person who always picks her up after her mistakes. It's exhausting."

I had a sudden thought. "Maybe this is why you haven't wanted a real girlfriend? Have you thought of that?" It was out of my mouth before I knew it.

"That has nothing to do with it." The waitress returned with his beer. He thanked her and set down his spoon. After taking a sip of his beer, he wrapped both hands around the pint glass.

"Have you ever thought that she's sabotaging you with all her drama? Keeping you from having a girlfriend because she's in love with you?"

"No. Absolutely not. There's nothing between us."

"Maybe from your end, but I saw the way she looked at me when you introduced us." I paused. "She acted like a crazy ex-girlfriend."

"No, that's just the way she is. Bitchy. Maybe it's true she wouldn't be thrilled if I had someone in my life, but she knows my stance on marriage, so there's no threat to her. I can be the best friend she calls at two a.m., and no one will care either way."

I thought about that for a moment. Did Hope know why he didn't want to marry? Had he shared with her his fears? "Does she know why?"

"No. No one but you." His face went dark. "Okay, that's about all I can stand on this subject."

I let it go. Pushing him was not a good way to get more information. As we ate our lunch, mostly in silence, I thought through what he'd shared with me. As much as I worried Ciaran was mentally disturbed, I did not believe he was a liar. If he said he wasn't sleeping with her, I believed him. The real problem was that she knew I was sleeping with him. Women like Hope Manning made trouble. Mean girls are mean girls forever. And now I was sleeping with the man she loved. Whether she realized her feelings for Ciaran or not, I knew enough to know she would try and sabotage us if she could.

Ciaran's beer was almost empty, along with his bowl of soup and the chunk of bread that had come with it. Despite my lackluster interest in the food, I'd eaten most of my sandwich, when he reached across the table for my hand. "I have an idea."

"What's that?" I asked.

"There are two full moons this month."

"Blue moon. I love that," I said.

"Full moons are special, right? And if there are two this month, that means something."

"I'm not following," I said.

"I think we should stay through New Year's. Just the two of us out at my house. No one has to know if you went back to Portland or not. We can just have a month of fun with no obligations to anyone."

"One month?"

"Right. Why not enjoy each other's company and check out for awhile? Enjoy the full moons."

A whole month with this man and no work? Nothing had ever sounded better in my entire life. "What about Hope?" I asked.

"She'll be gone in a day or two. It's way too boring here for her. Plus, she'll start jonesing for the press. She'll do something to make sure they know where she is."

"But why would she miss them? They hound her."

"She likes it. Feeds her ego to think everyone's interested in her every move."

"Actresses." I rolled my eyes.

"Don't I know it?"

"Don't remind me how well you know it," I said.

He laughed. "I told you not to believe everything you read in the papers."

"You're not worried I'm going to get attached to you if we're together a whole month?" I asked, teasing.

He shook his head, smiling. "You're not capable of getting attached to me or anyone. That's why you're perfect for me."

"And Sam?"

"He'll be the only one who'll know we're staying here together, but if you ask him to keep it quiet, I'm positive he will."

That was true, except that Moonstone seemed to be able to read his thoughts. But she wouldn't say anything if I asked her to keep our secret. But still, it was such a big lie to tell Blythe. "You know, it isn't like we're never going to see one another after the month ends. There are endless family holidays in the next forty years."

"Doubtful I'll be at any of them."

I wasn't sure what he meant. Did he mean because of the riff between the brothers or because he wouldn't live long enough to have to worry about it? For the hundredth time I wondered if his suspicions were true or imagined. Regardless, to spend time with him was something I wanted, I realized, as I sat across the table. Something I wanted that would lead nowhere, would open no path, but was simply pleasurable for pleasure's sake. I thought then, how would you live if the future was not guaranteed? Would we live more as we pleased? Would we seek pleasure over esteem or ambition? For the first time in my adult life, I felt as if the future was not clear. I did not know what I wanted to do next, no plan, no ambition. And I felt free, light. Was this what it felt like to be happy in the moment? Nothing to prove. Nowhere to go. No obligations fueling my energy.

Squeezing his hand, I nodded, yes. "Through New Year's."

"Through New Year's." Then he stood, and came around the table to give me his hand. "Let's go look at Moonstone's new hair."

CHAPTER 25

MOONSTONE WAS IN THE LOBBY when we arrived back at the inn, standing in front of the mirror near the door, smiling at her reflection. Turning to us, she twirled around to let us look, with the same shy but hopeful look Clementine has when she shows me one of her new tutus. "What do you think?"

I walked in a circle around her, amazed at the transformation. Never underestimate a good makeover, I thought. It was cut and styled exactly as we'd discussed, with long layers that fell to her shoulders except for side bangs that apparently they'd decided on after I left. I had to admit they were a great addition, taking ten years off her appearance. Bangs, the free facelift, I thought. The rich auburn color was striking and shiny.

Ciaran took her hands. "You look beautiful. He'll be in love with you in no time."

"Do you really think so?" Moonstone looked up at him with such hope in her eyes that I had a sudden image of Blythe when we were kids and our father would pick her up for their Sunday visit.

"Where's Ida?" I asked. "I want to thank her."

"She's upstairs packing up her things. She'll be right down," said Moonstone, back to looking at herself.

I remembered her nails then. "Did you make an appointment with your nail lady?" I asked.

"Yes. This afternoon. She was surprised to hear I wanted my acrylics taken off—I've had them since the 90s."

"Moonstone, you have no idea how much that scares me," I said, laughing.

"Will you go with me, Bliss? There are several shops in Hailey. You could help me pick out some clothes. Get your nails done."

I looked over at Ciaran. "I could be back before we go out tonight."

"You girls go. Have fun. I'm going home to take a nap." He winked at me. "I need a lot of energy for later."

I flushed several shades of red, I'm sure, as he kissed me on the cheek and headed out the door.

A second later, Ida came down, carrying a bag, presumably packed with all her supplies. We stood, chatting for a moment in the lobby, admiring Moonstone's hair. I wanted to pay for everything but wasn't sure how to bring it up, but lost my train of thought when Hope came down the stairs. She'd changed into leggings and a T-shirt, and unfortunately she looked beautiful in them, right down to her perfect, tiny feet.

We all stopped talking to look at her. She was like that—you couldn't stop looking at her. She halted at the bottom of the stairs. Moonstone introduced herself and asked if there was anything she could get her.

"I need a wine opener," said Hope. "I brought several bottles of white, knowing it would be hard to find anything decent other than in Ciaran's cellar." She winked at me, as if I was an old friend in on an inside joke. "But I can't locate my wine opener."

"Oh, yes, of course. Do you want ice as well?" asked Moonstone.

"Super. Yes," said Hope, continuing to look at me.

I realized Ida was standing next to me, probably hoping for an introduction. "This is Ida. Ida, Hope Manning."

Ida's thin face had flushed, her gaze on her hands. "Nice to meet you. My brother loves your movies."

Hope flashed her movie star smile. "Just your brother? Not you?"

"Me too. Of course. Everyone does."

Hope cocked her head to the side, observing Ida. "You look so familiar to me. Did you grow up in Boise?"

"No, Minnesota." As soon as Ida had said it, she closed her mouth, almost as if she were sorry to have admitted to her place of birth.

"Ah, yeah, I guess I hear a hint of an accent," said Hope, still looking at Ida like she was trying to figure out how she knew her. "Have you lived in Idaho long?"

"On and off." Ida continued to stare at the floor. Shy, I thought. Very sweet. If only she would eat a sandwich. It hurt to look at her, she was so thin. Maybe she was sick? As I counted out cash to pay Ida, I made a mental note to ask Moonstone.

Right on cue, Moonstone came back with the wine opener and a bucket of ice.

"Well, I'm off then," said Hope. "Jet lag's killing me, so I'm going to drink a glass of wine and take a sleeping pill." Once more, to Ida. "I usually never forget a face, part of the trade, but I must be mistaken. Maybe you just look like someone else I know." She took the ice and opener from Moonstone, then wriggled her fingers in a wave good-bye.

Ida, as if suddenly snapped out of her trance, took the money from my outstretched hand and tossed the handle of her bag over her shoulder, leaving without another word.

"What a strange little bird that one is," I said to Moonstone.

Moonstone whispered with a covert movement of her eyes to indicate upstairs. "Both of them."

"Is Ida sick? She's so thin."

"The poor lambie. Eating disorder. I think it has something to do with a man in her past, but I can't get a clear read on it." She pointed upstairs. "Now, that one. There's some evil lurking there."

CHAPTER 26

THE WEEKS PASSED IN A BLUR. Ciaran Lanigan was a party. I was the library. I did not think these two locations ever intertwined, but they had, and the result was thrilling. Ciaran, like the second full moon in a month, had appeared to sway the tide of the sea and the heart of a woman dedicated to accomplishment rather than love. I was having fun. More fun than I thought possible. We walked in snowshoes every day. I taught Ciaran yoga poses. We made meals together. He cooked and I was his faithful assistant. I had never been as happy or felt as alive. It was easy to deceive Blythe and Kevan, since I always called from my cell phone. As Ciaran predicted, Hope left Idaho after several days, much to my relief. Moonstone and Sam continued to spend time together, with Sweetheart by their side, although still in the friend zone, despite her makeover. Sam caught on quickly to the simple duties of caretaker and was a natural with horses.

One night I dreamt that Ciaran was birthed from Blue Mountain herself, like she'd opened up and allowed this beautiful creature out into the world, yet never fully let him go, ensuring that he always found his way back to the place that made him.

Five days before Christmas, on the floor of the front room of his house, we were wrapped in a blanket that smelled of sex and wood smoke. We'd made a bed of sorts by piling blankets and pillows near the fireplace. We had just devoured a loaf of French bread, a block of Oregon white cheddar, and the Walla Walla Syrah that Ciaran brought up from his cellar, sitting cross-legged on the pile of blankets, both of us suddenly ravenous after weeks of exercise and lovemaking. I was certain the food tasted better than anything I'd ever eaten, and he agreed. Nary a scrap of food remained on the bistro-style white plates. Our wine glasses were empty.

"We need another bottle, but I'm too lazy to get up." He was on his side, resting his face in his hand, his arm bent into a triangle, while I lay next to him, my head on a pillow.

I smiled and touched his cheekbone with the knuckle of my index finger. "Later. Don't leave me yet." I felt young basking in the glow of that fire and Ciaran's doting gaze, with the sound of crackling wood as it splintered in the flames. The years that had made me hard seemed to have disappeared, leaving someone soft and vulnerable. Night had come while we'd made love, warm despite the chill of the room because of our flesh on flesh and the fire, and now a half- moon hovered in the black sky.

"How about I teach you to ski?" he said.

"Ski? Sure. Looks fun." This was a lie. Nothing about skiing appealed to me. It seemed cold and treacherous. No, speed was not for me. I didn't even care for driving a car, let alone hurtling down a mountain with nothing but a couple of slick pieces of wood attached to my feet.

Not only had this man rendered me a giggling schoolgirl, I was now a liar.

*   *   *

Regardless, two days later, I was on a chairlift over Bald Mountain in Sun Valley, Idaho, dressed in a new and, I must admit, stylish purple ski jacket, pants, and boots, along with these magic socks that supposedly kept your feet warm despite the fact that I was soon to be headed down a mountain in blinding snow. In addition, I had this adorable purple and gold striped angora wool hat, a gift from Ciaran, which made my amber eyes pop. Just last night he'd whispered something about my beautiful eyes as he hovered above me in bed. This thought, not the cold, caused me to shiver with desire. Regardless of the possibility of death, I looked good. This was a small comfort. At least if this was the last thing I did in a life I'd spent mostly working, I would look good.

We continued to climb. The chairlift in front of us held three children wearing matching blue hats with green tassels. Seahawk fans, I presumed. They were everywhere, including the man next to me, outrageous in their zealous support of a football team. What were the children doing? Rocking their chair back and forth with purposeful intent? I closed my eyes for a moment, suddenly nauseous. Nothing but sex could have gotten me into this mess, I thought, stifling a small groan.

The chair moved in the wind like a Ferris wheel basket on an evening at the state fair. The nauseous feeling continued. Don't look down, I told myself again and again. I reached for Ciaran. He took my hand and placed it in his lap, giving it a little squeeze. You wouldn't think with these thick gloves I could still feel his touch, but it was the same spark as always, despite the layers. I breathed in and out, lecturing myself silently. *Don't look down. Don't start to hyperventilate. That would be exceedingly unsexy.*

I glanced at Ciaran. He gazed out over the mountain, looking ridiculously handsome in a black ski outfit and blue cap that complimented his olive skin and brown eyes. He'd shown me how to place my ski goggles onto my forehead, fixed in place over my cap, so that I could pull it down over my face when I was ready. Despite this, he wore his pair backward, so the strap was in the front, making it appear as if he had a face on both the front and back of his head.

For the hundredth time in the last month, the sight of him gave me pause. What was I doing here? Ciaran was a player. I knew this. At the end, when he'd grown bored, I'd be discarded for the next, and left to tears and ice cream. Don't sleep with players. Every woman knows this rule passed down through the ages. But I had. It was too late. Despite my pedigree—smart, successful, fully independent, slightly snarky, a product of the work of Gloria Steinem and scholarships for poor girls and breaking the glass ceiling—I had succumbed at the first erotic touch of Ciaran Lanigan's hand.

All these facts aside, the dizziness of lust made it so I didn't care. Not one iota, even knowing the ice cream and tears that were sure to come. I told myself to enjoy it without expectations of the future. It wasn't as if I loved him. This was an affair, a lark, a vacation, if you will, in a life thus far focused almost entirely on work. A man like Ciaran comes along only once in a blue moon, I told myself. And what a blue moon he was.

Regardless, the pages of the calendar kept turning, until soon it would be the day we said good-bye. It was for the best, I told myself. I had a life to go back to, a career to pursue. I was not a woman who wanted to marry or have children or any of the other impediments to a life of ambition and achievement. This time with Ciaran was a gift, nothing more, nothing less.

He turned toward me. "Don't worry. You got this." His dark eyes held my gaze. Those eyes—the hue of which was elusive—had the ability to hold me transfixed for hours at a time. I'd contemplated the exact shade for more moments than I cared to admit and had decided they were the color of strong tea—not quite as dark as coffee, with flecks of gold like wayward tea leaves.

"How did I let you talk me into this?" I asked.

"Wasn't it something about starting to have fun?"

"I wish I'd never told you that."

"You need a bucket list, sweetheart. And if you had one, "learn to ski" should be on it."

"Why?" Ciaran and his bucket list.

"Because it's exhilarating. Nothing better than speeding down the slopes. You'll see."

"I can assure you skiing is not better than multiple orgasms." I had no idea that multiple orgasms actually existed until twenty-five days ago. Until Ciaran.

I have a theory that almost every stupid choice made by a woman is because they were somehow influenced by sex. As women, we're led to believe men are more deeply influenced by their carnal desires, but I'm doubtful of this divide between the genders. How many times have we heard the quote about how men think of sex every seven seconds as opposed to our more respectable number of once a day? Is it really only once a day? I'm not certain if that's the true statistic, but let's stick with it for argument's sake, because I don't care what measuring tool one uses, it's impossible to quantify that in any accurate way.

Irrespective of statistics, the man sitting next to me had rendered me utterly useless. I thought of nothing but him, of his hands on my skin, of the way he threw his head back when he laughed. His smile with his straight, white teeth lit up a room, and he made me feel small and girlish even though I'm tall and muscular. And the way he made me laugh—that more than anything. I hadn't laughed much in my life, and it seemed I was making up for lost time every moment I spent with him.

Stop thinking about all that, I thought, looking down at the snowy slope below us. *You must focus on staying alive during this perilous feat you're about to undertake.* I calmed myself with the thought that surely beginners do not die on the slopes. It's always the skilled skiers on the black runs you hear about. Actually, I wasn't even sure that was true, because kids raised in poor households, like me, do not learn to ski. It's the same with golf. I've wished many times I could get through a golf game without extreme embarrassment, as many business deals are made on the green between men in their undying, unspoken boys' clubs. But poor kids don't learn the pastimes of the rich. We learn to scramble and scratch, making our own games on the streets or, in my case, the woods of southern Oregon. We learn of the world between the pages of books, our imaginations widening without benefit of physical experience.

No matter, I assured myself. Get through the morning, and afterward, Ciaran would take me back to his place to soak in the hot tub on his deck, snow falling softly while we sipped red wine.

As if he read my thoughts, he grinned in that wolfish way that made all my limbs go numb. "Glad to oblige on both items, Miss Heywood." Pausing to pull the tassel on top of my hat, he ran a gloved finger over my mouth. "You know what this means, though?"

"What's that?" It was ridiculous how I could just stare into those eyes all day long and not tire of it.

"You'll have to help fill one of mine."

I smirked. "You don't have anything left on your list."

"You don't know that."

"You've been all over the world. You know three languages. You've started a charity feeding hungry children in South America." I could go on, including, how many women he'd seduced, but I kept that to myself.

"It's true. Adventure wise, I've done everything I've wanted."

"What's left then?" I experienced a pang in my chest, knowing that whatever awaited him would be without me. I felt the cold suddenly, and shuddered.

"I have one or two items left." His lips twitched into a smile that didn't reach his eyes. I'd grown accustomed to these bouts of sadness, had accepted that this otherwise clever and charming man was more complex than I could ever have imagined on the occasion of our first meeting. Without predictability, darkness came with a sudden force like a summer storm. This period of gloom never lasted long, usually only a minute or so, but made me feel fearful and unsure.

"There are several things I want. I'm just not sure I can have them, or that I deserve them. Or, that there will be time."

"Ciaran, please don't say that." I was unable to think what to say next. He'd only spoken of it once, this feeling that came over him, claiming he'd never told anyone but me the cause of his dark bouts. As difficult as it was to fathom, Ciaran was certain someone was trying to kill him. He was equally certain they would succeed sooner than later. I dismissed his fears as paranoia, convincing myself that an otherwise well-balanced individual had this one small but troublesome quirk, one that influenced his every decision.

"Someday I'll tell you," he said.

"Fine." I pretended to pout. I had turned into a woman who pretends to pout, which did nothing but make him laugh, and just like that the darkness lifted.

We were almost to the top of the mountain. The people two chairs ahead of us departed, sliding effortlessly onto the packed snow, all the while talking to one another. I surely would not be able to speak, this I knew for certain, and was just hoping not to fall and get pulled under by the chair and subsequently crushed by the people behind me. Ciaran instructed me to slide forward on the seat and take hold of both my ski poles in preparation for departure. The chair advanced, up and up, until we were there, the snow just under us. He lifted the safety bar. It was time. My heart beat like the wings of a hummingbird. "I can't do it," I whispered.

"You're fine, just put your skis forward, stand up and lean forward. The snow and your skis will do the rest." Just then my skis touched the ground and seemed to take over as if an invisible rope pulled me from the chair. Before I could quantify what had happened, I was gliding down the small slope toward a flat section, with Ciaran beside me. But wait, I didn't know how to stop. How would I stop? Why hadn't I thought to ask him this? I called out to him but he didn't seem to hear me as he pushed into the snow with his poles and darted ahead. When he was several feet ahead of me, he made an abrupt turn with his skis, the snow splaying in the air like we were in a James Bond movie. Facing me, he held out his arms. "Just come to me, Bliss. I'll catch you."

As if I could stop, I thought, falling into him, my legs parting like blades of a scissor, in a half-split that I was positive damaged an internal organ. This was truly an awful sport. Ciaran tossed his poles onto the snow and put his hands under my arms, lifting me upright. My scissor blade legs were side by side once more. He grinned. "See, you did great. The chair wasn't so hard, right?"

"I think I hate you," I mumbled.

He laughed. "Well, at least you're not indifferent to me. That's the opposite of love, you know."

Ignoring him, I looked around. The top of the mountain was encased in fog so that I could barely make out a lodge-type building on our left and signs indicating various runs all around us. Falling snow caught in my lashes. I should have purchased waterproof mascara, I thought. I would be a mess in no time, if I weren't already.

After he instructed me to put on my goggles, he put his on and then picked up his poles. Using one as a pointer, he indicated the various ski runs, all marked with names and colors. "The runs are color-coded for difficulty. Green, blue and black."

Skiers, all looking fit and athletic, glided by us. How long until it felt as effortless as they made it appear?

"We're doing a green run, right?" I asked.

His eyes sparkled at me as he grinned. "Of course. Here's what we'll do. I'll ski ahead of you about ten feet and then stop and wait. You'll ski right into my arms. Like you just did."

"Is there any kissing involved during skiing?" I asked, stalling for time.

"Lots and lots of kissing." With that, he leaned down and put his mouth on mine and kissed me soft and slow. Why couldn't the kissing portion of this sport be the main event?

After the kiss ended, I gestured with my pole toward the bottom of the hill from whence we'd come. "I think I should've started with the bunny slope." From what I had discerned while watching the little children with their skis angled like a piece of pizza, I was certain it was the place for me.

"Come on now, you're not the type of woman who's scared of anything."

"The boardroom is different than an icy mountain with these things attached to my feet."

"You'll conquer this mountain in one day." He took off his right glove and unzipped my ski jacket, then pulled me close, inching his fingers under the elastic band of my pants, and spoke softly into my ear. "How about a kiss every time you reach me? And afterwards we'll go back to my house and I'll ravage you in front of the fireplace."

"I'm liking this sport more every minute." Only Ciaran could say the word ravage without making it sound ridiculous. With a promise like that, I'd hurtle down a black run with no questions asked. This man played to win.

As if he read my mind, he laughed as he zipped up my jacket. "You're a good sport, Bliss Heywood, not to mention beautiful, intelligent, and sweet under that feisty attitude, which just makes you almost unbearably hot." His voice softened. "I can't remember having more fun with anyone. Ever."

"Oh, I know that's a terrible lie," I said, smiling up at him, but flushing with pleasure. Could I dare hope he might have feelings for me other than lust? "I bet you say that to all your unsuspecting conquests."

"Not lately." Chuckling, he kissed me again before plunging his wicked, talented hand back into his glove. "I'll see you in ten feet." He waved with his pole as he started toward one of the green runs. I imitated what he did, moving my skis like skates, assisted by the poles, which wasn't as hard as I thought it might be. It was the downhill part that had me worried.

At the entrance to the run, we stopped, moving to the side so other skiers could go ahead. "Just do what I do, Bliss." With his poles, he pushed off, heading in a straight line down the side of the run for ten or so feet and then stopped with that same delicious spray of snow as he turned toward me with his arms outstretched, the poles like skinny extensions.

The falling snow blinded me no matter how I adjusted my ski goggles. My feet ached inside the rented boots. Sweat trickled down my back from the extreme effort it took to stay upright despite the chill of Bald Mountain. I yearned for the lodge and a hot toddy and my bare feet in Ciaran's lap. Maybe he'd rub my feet and ankles and then move his fingers up my legs until he ran out of leg. I shuddered, thinking of his hands on my skin, and the way his face twisted with pleasure the night before as my hair fell into his face. Sex. This was exactly how I'd gotten myself into this mess.

Yes, steamy, senseless sex all night will cause a brain to malfunction. For example, agreeing to ski when one does not know how to ski, I thought. But there was the fireplace waiting later and his muscular body and all the pleasures I could ask for. I pushed off.

I met the flakes of snow as I headed faster and faster toward Ciaran. What had he said about stopping? Make my skis like a piece of pizza as the kids were doing. How did one do that? It was too late to figure it out because I was upon him, fast and without any control. His arms were outstretched, his mouth turned up in a smile. And then I was there, barreling into him. Surely I would knock him over. But no. He caught me, as promised, wobbling only a moment before setting me straight. "Well done."

I had done it. I'd skied. Only ten feet, but still, it was something. Jubilant, I squealed, and tossed my poles down before throwing my arms around his neck. "It was scary."

"It'll get easier, I promise." He leaned over to kiss me but our goggles knocked together. "Hang on, let me get these out of the way." He put them on backwards as he'd done before. "That's better." Turning his head to the side to avoid my goggles, he kissed me.

We carried on like that for a while longer, other skiers passing by us with a few good-natured shouts of "get a room" or "go for it, dude." I didn't care. I was happy just then. Happier than I think I'd ever been in my life.

Finally, he started out again, without turning his goggles around. How could he see? Ten feet down, he stopped as before and held out his arms. He was as near to the side of the run as possible, I noticed, probably not wanting to disturb other skiers as we had my little lesson. Next to him there was a considerable drop. I really did not want to ski right off the side of the mountain. It was possible I could take us both down. Turn my skis inward to slow down, like a piece of pizza, I thought, for the second time. I could do that. No problem. If I could support my body weight on my arms in a yoga pose, surely I could this. I adjusted my goggles and took a deep breath. I turned to look at where I'd just come from, comparing steepness and stalling for time. Just then, a man, dressed in all black, and skiing without poles, shot out from the top of the run. In seconds he whisked by me, so fast and close I felt wind from his movement. I hesitated. I would let him get past Ciaran before I started out again. During that thought, the man curved slightly and pointed his skis right at Ciaran. Then, he was upon Ciaran. He reached out his arms and pushed on Ciaran's chest with both hands. With great force, I thought later, given how steady he'd been when I ran into him. Ciaran's skis slipped out from under him and he lifted in the air for a moment before disappearing over the side of the cliff. Before I knew what had happened, the man turned and sped down the mountain.

Screaming Ciaran's name, I forgot my fear and skied toward the spot where he had been pushed. I fell on purpose at the spot where he had waited for me and unhooked my skis from my boots. On hands and knees, sinking into the soft snow banks at the side of the run, I crawled toward the edge of the cliff. My heart pumped between my ears; a metallic taste filled my mouth. What would I find below? Please, be there, I prayed silently. As I reached the drop, I slid onto my belly and hung my head over the side. He was there, in a ravine about twenty feet below, his body crumpled into a semicircle, with skis splayed in opposite directions, one leg bent back unnaturally into the shape of a V. His arms covered his face, as if trying to protect himself. No visible movement. I could not discern if he was breathing or not. I sat up and started screaming, waving my arms. A skier stopped, pulling off his goggles and face mask. "What's wrong?" he asked.

"My friend's hurt," I screamed. "He's down below." I pointed toward Ciaran.

"Oh, crap. Okay."

"He was pushed off the side. He's not moving." Had I seen what I thought? Had the man pushed him? As it is when you see something shocking, I began to question what I'd actually seen. Had my eyes deceived me? My vision blurred from tears, I closed my eyes, seeing once again the man zooming down the mountain. He'd not only run into him but had pushed into Ciaran's chest with his hands. No doubt. It was a deliberate push.

I've always thought I'd die young, he said to me, just weeks before. Someone's trying to kill me.

"I'll ski down as fast as I can and get help," the other skier said to me.

"I'll stay right here," I said, more to myself than him, as he was already speeding down the hill.

I went back to my belly position, calling Ciaran's name over and over, hoping my voice might rouse him. But he was still and crumpled. I started to cry, the fear for his fate as cold and hollow as the ravine below. "Please, don't leave me, Ciaran," I whispered.

It was then I knew. I loved this man. My efforts of resistance and denial were fruitless against the truth. I had fallen in love with Ciaran Lanigan.

CHAPTER 27

THE DETAILS OF THE EVENTS that followed Ciaran's fall are blurry. I know I remained at the side of the mountain watching Ciaran's still body, but I have no recollection of how long—perhaps fifteen minutes, perhaps longer. But eventually the ski patrol came, along with the stranger who had gone for them. I was nearly incoherent, crying uncontrollably and shaking so that my legs felt they might not hold me upright, not to mention the cumbersome ski boots, all of which reduced me to a helpless state.

The ski patrol were paramedics on skis. Several of them came immediately to my side, asking if I was hurt. "No, but I can't ski down, I don't think."

I heard one of them call out to another. "Jesus. Dude, we need him airlifted out of there."

"We're going to get you down the mountain, don't worry." Two of the strong men lifted me and placed me on a toboggan, which was basically a stretcher with a curved bottom like a sled. Before I could comprehend what was happening, they had strapped me down. I started screaming that I needed to stay, to be there when they pulled Ciaran from the ravine. They exchanged knowing looks between them, which infuriated me further. "What is it? Tell me." I shouted through tears and grasped at one of their arms. "Please tell what's happening."

"It's going to fine. But he'll have to be rescued by helicopter. There's no way we can get to him."

"I want to wait," I said. "I'll wait for the helicopter to come."

The larger of the two nodded sympathetically, tucking a blanket around me, and explained in a soothing voice that it might take some time and that I would be in the way. "You'll get too cold. And it could take awhile."

"He was pushed. Someone pushed him. I need to talk to the police."

"We've already called the police. They'll want to talk to you when we get off the mountain. While everything's fresh in your mind. So we need to go now, okay?"

Right, of course. The police. They must know every detail. I relented. And then we were on our way, speeding down the mountain.

Once we arrived at the lodge, not far from where we'd rented my ski equipment, a young woman dressed in fitted black ski pants and a sweater greeted me, introducing herself as Susie. Dirty blonde ponytail, no makeup, freckles scattered across her nose and cheeks, no older than twenty-five with the compact, muscular physique of an athlete. Susie escorted me into a small office, where she helped me take off my boots, goggles, and gloves, then put a mug of hot tea in my hands. Still shaking, I couldn't bring the drink to my mouth and instead, just stared at it helplessly, unsure what to do.

"They're airlifting him to Seattle. Harborview Hospital," said Susie. "They just radioed me to let you know."

"Airlifted? What does that mean?"

"I'm not sure, Ms. Heywood, other than I suspect he needs surgical attention that the small hospital here can't provide, so they're flying him to Seattle as quickly as they can."

Harborview. Specializing in spine and head injuries. Why did I think that? Had I heard it someplace or was I mistaken? Was it my imagination or did I hear a helicopter overhead?

"But he was breathing?" I asked, my own breathing in question as I waited for the answer.

"Yes, Miss Heywood, but unconscious. We have no idea of knowing what internal or head injuries he's sustained." Susie sat next to me and took my hand. "Is there someone you want to call?"

I nodded. Blythe. I needed to tell Blythe and Kevan. My thoughts lurched ahead on high speed. They could meet him at the hospital. I would fly out as soon as I could. Henry would take me to the airport if I could get a flight out. I reached for my cell phone, tucked into the inner pocket of my ski jacket.

Susie left me alone to call Blythe. The minute she answered the phone I started blubbering incoherently. Somehow she was able to decipher where I was and what had happened. "What were you doing skiing with Ciaran? Have you been spending time with him?"

"I'll explain everything when I get there," I said.

"Please tell me you're not involved," she said.

"Blythe, please, just go. I can't get there for hours and I don't want him to be alone."

"Oh, Bliss, what're you doing?" She paused. Even over the phone I felt the internal conflict she was experiencing—wanting to know more but understanding that it wasn't the time to ask. "We'll head to Harborview now."

I called Henry next. He promised to come get me and offered to look into flights. "Just stay put. We'll be right there."

A police officer came into the office next and asked me questions. I tried as best I could to answer everything and tell him in detail what I remembered, knowing that I was the only witness to what had happened. He asked me a series of questions about whether Ciaran had enemies and all of the things one expects if there is suspicion of foul play. I told him everything I knew, including that Ciaran suspected someone had been trying to harm him for years but that he had nothing but anecdotal evidence and no clue who would want to hurt him, having no known enemies. It struck me that the cop didn't dismiss the notion, and that he seemed to believe there was validity to my story, including my assertion that Ciaran had been pushed.

"Is it hopeless?" I asked at the end. "With no leads, will you ever be able to solve this?"

"I won't lie. We don't have much to go on. But I will say this, Ms. Heywood. In cases like this, it's almost always someone the victim knows, someone in their inner circle. If that's the case, we have a much greater hope of solving this."

*   *   *

I arranged to take the next flight out of Hailey for Seattle. Henry and Mrs. Pennington picked me up in the town car, and we went back to Ciaran's so I could pick up clothes and toiletries before going to the airport. I had calmed enough by then that I was able to tell them what had happened as we sat in the small Hailey airport waiting for my flight.

As I told them everything, Mrs. Pennington held my hand, like Blythe used to when I was a child. I leaned my head on her shoulder. "I love him. I was pretending to myself that it was just a fling, but when I saw him there, hurt and helpless, I knew." I started to cry again, and she gathered me into her arms.

"I know you do, dear girl."

"I've never felt so scared in my life," I said.

"He's young and strong," said Henry. "He'll fight like hell."

"Especially knowing you're waiting for him," said Mrs. Pennington.

"That's just the thing," I said, crying harder. "That won't matter to him one bit."

Henry smiled at me, kindly. "I'm not quite sure you're correct, Miss Heywood."

"Just go to him," said Mrs. Pennington. "Being there will help him, I'm certain of it."

CHAPTER 28

BLYTHE AND KEVAN WERE WAITING FOR ME at the hospital, both pale and visibly shaken. They'd arrived just a few minutes after Ciaran was brought in and had been waiting in the lobby of the surgical ward during the three or so hours it had taken for me to arrive.

Ciaran was in surgery, they told me. Internal bleeding that needed to be located and repaired. His legs were broken in multiple places, as were several ribs. His right arm was shattered and would need intensive surgical repair.

"What about his head?" I asked.

"Trauma there," said Kevan, his voice cracking. "They don't know the extent of it yet. They don't know if he's going to live."

"No. No. He has to," I whispered.

"Bliss, tell us what happened today. Every detail," said Blythe.

We sat, and I went through it as carefully as I could, including his suspicions over the years that someone had been attempting to harm him.

"What're you talking about?" asked Kevan. "He thought someone was trying to kill him?"

I nodded. "I don't know if this is my place to tell you, but it's been going on for years. It's shaped all his decisions."

"What do you mean?" asked Blythe.

"For one, his lack of commitment to anything but his charity causes. And ticking things off his adventure list. He's felt certain that he'll die young." I started crying, but continued. "He's alternated between questioning his sanity—wondering if he was simply certifiably paranoid—or if it was true, that the incidents over the years indicated there was someone trying to kill him. Either way, it's kept him from close relationships. Romantic ones, in particular."

"Why would he keep this a secret from us? Why did he tell you and not me, or Ardan?" asked Kevan.

I reached into my jacket and pulled out a crumpled tissue to blow my nose. Behind us, we heard someone asking the front desk nurses questions about their loved ones. "I'm the only one he's ever told."

Next to me, Blythe took in a deep breath. "Because you two are in a relationship. You're sleeping together." My sister's eyes were red. Obviously, she'd been crying.

I went hot, knowing I had to confess. "Yes. It just happened. We didn't mean for things to go that way, but, well, they just did." Even as it was out of my mouth, I realized how trite it sounded.

"But why didn't you tell me?" asked Blythe.

"Because it isn't going to go anywhere, and we didn't want everyone to be awkward."

"For heaven's sake, Bliss, you're sleeping with my future husband's brother. It's not like you won't see one another again. Did you think through the consequences of this?" Blythe's voice was loud and an octave higher than her usual soft way of speaking. She peered at me with a horrified expression as her fingers clutched and unclutched the collar of her blouse.

"I did. I tried to resist him, but it was impossible." Angry, hot tears fell down my cheeks. I swiped at them with my hand. "You have no right to judge me."

"Blythe, she's right. Of all people, we know it's impossible to choose who we love," said Kevan. "I mean, look at us. It wasn't exactly without complications."

"It isn't the same thing at all," said Blythe, waving her hands in the air like she was swatting away a nasty fly. I'd never seen her as angry. "So, what, this was just a fling? Some fun?"

"It was supposed to be. But the plan went off the rails a bit," I said.

"You're in love with him," said Blythe. A statement of fact, as only a sister could level.

"Yes," I whispered. "I don't want to be, but I am."

Blythe sighed. "Oh Bliss."

"We agreed to just spend the holidays together. Enjoy some time off. I wasn't supposed to fall in love with him. Anyway, he's incapable of loving me back. Knowing someone was trying to harm him made him crazy, always looking over his shoulder, assuming he could die at any time. And now, I'm worried that whomever was trying to kill him might have succeeded."

I looked up at Kevan. Tears brimmed in his eyes. He reached for my hand. "Bliss, you have to remember, Ciaran's a fighter. You don't grow up the youngest of four rough boys and not be a little tougher than the rest. And if he knows what's good for him, he'll fight to get back to you, regardless of this ridiculous notion he has about being incapable of love." He stood. "I have to call Ardan and Teagan. Neither one of them will be able to make it here quickly. Ardan's overseas, and Teagan's, well, God knows where. We never know. But they should be on alert, in case..." He trailed off and then hurried toward the doors.

"You've never lied to me before," said Blythe. Her voice was no louder than a whisper now; the anger seemed to have subsided as quickly as it had flared. She sat looking at me, her face slack like a popped balloon.

"I didn't think you'd understand, and apparently I was right," I said.

"What I don't understand is that you lied to me. The other thing, well, Kevan's right. You don't choose who you love. It just happens."

"I'm sorry I lied," I said. "The whole thing has turned my world upside down. I love him so much it hurts." I started to cry.

"Well, I understand that," she said. For the first time, I noticed that we were sitting on a couch. Like when we were children, Blythe took my hand, and we sat like that for several minutes. Only today, I cried hot tears that seemed impossible to curb, as if the grief from forty years had welled up behind my eyes and was now unleashed.

My father came into my mind with a suddenness that surprised me. I was nine years old that day he became a real ghost, dying quietly and without fuss in a car accident, a shadowy lurker both in life and death. Blythe was fourteen that year. What did she remember of it? Had they taken him to the hospital when he died? Was he killed instantly, or was he in surgery as Ciaran was now? How was it I did not know these facts?

"Blythe," I said now. "The car accident—our dad—did he die right away?"

She flinched. I'd startled her. "Yes. It was instant, according to Nannette, anyway."

"Why didn't I go to his funeral?"

"There wasn't one. Nannette cremated him, and that was that."

"How old was he when he died?"

"Thirty-six," she said.

"I have almost no memory of him. It's like looking into the fog, knowing there's a figure there but not being able to see it. I regret it, you know. Not spending time with him. I feel like I squandered the chance to love him."

"Well, he was a hard person to know. I'm not sure I knew him much better, even though we spent a lot of Sundays together. Anyway, Dad was the one who should have insisted he see you. He was the grown-up. You were a little girl who should not have been allowed to dictate the relationship. It wasn't your fault." She squeezed my hand tighter. "And if Sally were any kind of mother, she would've known that a relationship with your father, regardless of your feelings toward him, is important to a little girl. His absence influenced who you became. They squandered love, not you. They taught you how to deny love, to seek everything but love. You should have been cherished. I wasn't enough." Blythe was crying now, too, and stroking my hair.

She was right about Sally. Our mother spent the better part of her life pleasing herself while hiding behind her flimsy principles, principles born of an era where free love, self-expression, and mind-expansion were sought after and valued more than what she would describe as the mundane ventures of commerce, hard work, and family.

Blythe was right about me, too. I was a survivor, meeting my parents' squandering of love with equal scarcity. I learned to keep love hidden, to squelch it and waste it, choosing business over relationships, career over love. I put everything I had into our American version of success. And damn, I was good at it. For years and years, I was good at it.

The problem with squandered love, I thought now, crying in the arms of my sister, is that it has a way of capturing you eventually. When you're a child, even a young adult, the power of your moral convictions, your indignant assurance that you're righteous and wronged is enough to fuel a life. But after a time it occurs to you that your choices have rendered you a ghost. All the ways you've rejected love out of fear are a boiling pot of regret, for at the end, when we have nothing but our memories, we know then that all we wanted was to love and be loved. It is all that matters, all we're left with at the end.

Perhaps that was it, I thought. When a life, like a sweet perfume, was boiled down and distilled into the essence of what mattered, its fragrance was the thing of importance, the sweetness that remained, not the process itself. What would we think of at the end of our lives? What memories would emerge? I suspected it was the smallest of moments. The sound of the screen door slamming, letting you know that someone you loved had arrived home. The scent of lilacs along a country road on the drive to school. Dancing in the kitchen with your sister. A beloved niece twirling in her tutu. The way he reached for the radio dial to turn up a song he liked. His arms reaching for you during the dark night when the demons wanted to snatch you. *I got you.*

"You want to know what I remember?" I asked, swiping at the tears that fell down my cheeks.

"What's that?" She spoke softly, resting her head against my shoulder.

"I remember how you made my sandwiches every day with just the right amount of peanut butter spread evenly across the bread, and how you saved the strawberry preserves for me, even though you loved it."

Blythe kept her head on my shoulder. "I had to hide the preserves from Sally in an old coffee can in our room. One jar lasted a month if I saved it only for you. I worried all the time if you had enough to eat. When you got home from school you always had these dark circles under your eyes, and you were so skinny. I learned to cook to try and fatten you up."

"After you left home, you can't imagine how I mourned those sandwiches."

"We'll have them again. Ciaran will get better and we'll have them together. All of us."

"He loves peanut butter as much as I do."

"Are you sure he doesn't love you?" asked Blythe.

"I can't let myself hope that he does."

She turned on the couch to face me, taking my other hand so that she held them both. "Bliss, I'm not always right about everything, especially as it relates to men. Need I remind you of my former husband? But sometimes you just have to go with your instincts, no matter what your head or your cautious older sister tells you."

"I just want him to live, even if I can't have him."

"That, Bliss, is love."

We went back to sitting side by side, Blythe still holding onto one of my hands.

"Who would do this to him?" she asked me, after a few minutes passed. "Who did this to him?"

Just then, Hope Manning walked through the emergency room doors.

CHAPTER 29

SHE WAS ALONE, dressed in dark glasses and hat, just as she was the first time I'd ever met her, making her unrecognizable unless you knew who you were looking at, as I did. It appeared she knew I would be waiting from the way she charged toward us with no hesitation. I sat up straighter, causing Blythe to look at me strangely. "It's Hope Manning," I whispered in her ear.

"I didn't recognize her."

"That's the idea," I said.

Hope was standing in front of us now, taking off her sunglasses. "How is he?"

No greeting, just out with it. I filled her in on what we knew, which she listened to without interruption before settling into the chair opposite us, glancing around as if worried she might be recognized. But no one was paying any attention. The people in this lobby had more on their minds than the exploits of a spoiled movie star, I thought, with some bitterness.

"How long until we know more?" asked Hope.

"The surgeon wasn't sure what he was going to find, so he couldn't give us anything definite," I said.

"Well, I hope he knows what the hell he's doing." She shivered. "My God, how do people live in this constant rain?"

I introduced Hope to my sister, adding that she and Kevan lived in a suburb of Seattle and were able to get here around the same time they'd admitted Ciaran.

"You're the one marrying Kevan, then?" Hope asked.

Blythe nodded.

Hope took off her hat, letting her long hair fall about her shoulders. "Keeping it all in the family, then? Tell me, do you have another sister for Ardan? Maybe a brother for Teagan?"

It had seemed funny when I'd thought the same thing, but somehow, coming from her it did not amuse me. I glanced at my sister. Blythe's face was crinkled like someone had just opened a package of stinky cheese.

Kevan reappeared just then and took over the management of Hope, while Blythe and I went outside to get some fresh air. Standing next to the hospital doors, we took the cool, damp air into our lungs but it did little to lessen the tightness in my chest.

"What an unpleasant person," said Blythe. "What does Ciaran see in her?"

"They go way back." I told her the story of her father, and Ciaran's part in his undoing. "He feels responsible for her."

"Still waters run deep, don't they?" said Blythe.

It was true. The persona Ciaran presented to the world did not portray half the man he was.

"I wonder why Kevan's never mentioned this thing with Hope's family?" Blythe asked.

"Kevan doesn't know. For some reason, their father wanted it kept between them that Ciaran was the one who found the discrepancy."

My sister was quiet for a moment. Biting her bottom lip like she does when she'd trying to figure something out.

"What is it?" I asked.

"I just had an awful thought." She gestured toward the hospital. Hope was sitting next to Kevan, their heads together, talking.

I knew what she was thinking before she said it. She suspected Hope Manning was responsible. I stared at her. It had never occurred to me. She certainly had the financial means to hire people to terrify and murder. But no, Hope's feelings for Ciaran ran the other way. "No, it can't be. She's in love with him."

"Well, the opposite of love is indifference, not hate. Often they go hand in hand," said Blythe.

"Ciaran said that very thing to me this morning," I said. How odd that they would both have said the same thing on the same day. I thought about that concept in terms of Hope and Ciaran. She was the only constant in his adult life. Could she have planned a way to torment him slowly, cause his life to seem always in jeopardy as a way to punish him for the decline of her family? Had today been just one of many attempts on his life in a string of episodes meant to make him paranoid? Or, was today the day she wanted to end it once and for all? Had the other attempts simply failed, or was this a calculated plan to make him suffer for years? I reached into my pocket for the card the cop had given me. Should I call him? What would I say? There was no evidence, obviously.

"Do you think the cops would think I was crazy if I told them our hunch?" I asked.

"It might give them a place to start."

"If Hope's responsible, she would have hired professionals, probably the best in the business. They'll be impossible to trace." I glanced back inside. Kevan and Hope had risen to their feet as a doctor, dressed in surgical clothes, approached. I grabbed Blythe's arm. "It's the doctor."

Holding my breath, we walked back into the waiting room. My legs felt numb, my feet moving of their own accord. The doctor, a compact, lean man in his forties, introduced himself, explaining that he'd been one of the primary surgeons for Ciaran's operation.

His voice was steady and clinical, with no hint of emotion, speaking directly to Kevan. "We identified bleeding around his heart and performed a thoracotomy. This basically means we opened up his chest and were able to stop the life-threatening bleeding. Fortunately, the paramedics on the scene made the decision to send him here. In cases of severe trauma like the one he experienced in the fall, time is of the essence." He paused, taking in an even breath. "There's no head injury, which, given the height of his fall, is extraordinary. The paramedics said he had his goggles on backwards and that they appear to have protected his head from hitting the ice with full force." I sank into a chair, my legs shaking, as the doctor continued, speaking above ambulance sirens that pierced the air. "Both of his legs were broken in multiple places and require surgery, as does his left arm, which appears to have taken the brunt of the fall. The surgical teams are performing these operations now. He's going to have a long recovery, requiring physical therapy after healing, but I believe he's out of danger. Given everything, your brother is a very lucky man."

Kevan's color had returned. He pulled Blythe to him and wrapped his arm around her shoulder. "Thank you, doctor."

My chest expanded as I took a deep breath. He would live. Thank God. A long recovery, but he would live. I looked over at Hope. Her face was unreadable as she typed into her phone. Was she texting the people she'd hired to kill him? Suspicion, like streams of invisible smoke, replaced the relief I'd felt seconds before. If he lived today, would she continue to try and kill him? Was it her? Would she succeed next time?

Hope looked up from her phone, catching my eye for a moment. Her face twitched. Was she flinching under my scrutiny? Did she suspect I suspected her? She turned to the doctor. "When can we see him?"

"We'll keep him sedated for several hours after surgery, to give him time to heal and rest. I wouldn't expect to see him until tomorrow."

"How long will these next surgeries take?" asked Kevan.

"The bones in his left arm were shattered. It'll take the surgeons upwards of six hours to complete. You won't be able to see him until tomorrow morning at the earliest. Even then, he may not be awake, depending on what kind of pain meds are necessary." The doctor, for the first time, had the slightest hint of sympathy in his voice. "You've all been here a long time. Maybe go home. Get some rest, have a meal, change clothes. Someone can call you when he's through surgery, but I don't think you'll be allowed to see him until morning."

After the doctor and Kevan exchanged a few more words about logistics, he left. We were all quiet, except for the sound of Hope texting into her phone. The thought of leaving the hospital seemed incomprehensible to me. I could not leave him here alone. What if something happened and I wasn't here?

"I'm staying," I said.

"Me, too," said Kevan.

Blythe shook her head. "No, that's not how it's going to work. Both of you are coming home with me. We can have something to eat, get some rest tonight, and come back in the morning when he wakes." She touched Kevan's cheek with her fingertips. "Sweetheart, the girls need us to go home so we can assure them that their Uncle Ciaran will be okay. If we stay here, they won't sleep a wink all night. And we're of no use here. He's going to need us tomorrow and for a lot of days to come. We need to be rested and fed."

We both started to protest but my sister put up her hand. "We're going home." She turned toward me, crossing her arms over her chest. "Get up. We're going."

I obeyed, as Blythe addressed Hope. "Miss Manning, would you like to come too? We have an extra room."

Extra room? That was my room. Why would she invite the enemy home with us? Then, it occurred to me. She wanted to talk to her—get her to give us information on whether she was involved or not.

"My sister's a great cook," I said. "And you won't have to stay in some cold hotel."

"Thank you for the offer, but the suite at the Westin is hardly cold," said Hope. "I'm exhausted—I was up all last night playing in Napa. I'd barely closed my eyes when my assistant called to tell me about Ciaran. I took the first flight out of there. All very last-minute."

Kevan hadn't said anything during this entire exchange. I glanced over at him to find him studying Hope's face.

"How *did* you know, Hope, about Ciaran's accident?" The emphasis on the word did. Had the same thing occurred to him? Did he imagine Hope could be involved in all this?

"My assistant saw it on the news. Online, I think."

Was Ciaran famous enough that his skiing accident would be reported on the news?

"On the news?" Kevan's expression made me think of a dark cloud about to unleash hail. A shiver ran through me.

Hope continued, seemingly undeterred by Kevan's expression. "The press think Ciaran and I have been together in Sun Valley all week. I do that sometimes, give false leads to the tabloids so that I can have a few days' peace from the paparazzi. They must have picked up the story from there."

I couldn't recall any press lingering around the lodge that morning. Was she lying? It was easy enough to search from my phone.

"Can we offer you a lift to your hotel?" asked my sister.

"No, I've hired a driver for the day. He's waiting for my call."

Kevan continued to stare at Hope. His left hand clasped and unclasped. Perspiration dotted his forehead.

"Ciaran told me what happened with your family," I said to Hope before turning to Kevan. "Did you know it was Ciaran that figured out what was really happening with the parts?" I asked him.

"No," he said. "My father never told me that."

The vein that ran through the middle of Hope's forehead pulsed. "Isn't that the Lanigan and Manning way?"

"What do you mean?" asked Kevan.

"Secrets and lies. A specialty from both our fathers," said Hope.

"Did you blame Ciaran?" asked Kevan. "For your father's troubles?"

"Of course not. Ciaran's the only man I've ever known, including my own father, who always does the right thing."

"It didn't make you mad, Hope? Mad enough to kill him?" asked Kevan. "Slowly. Over time. Making him paranoid or crazy or both? Maybe you've spent the better part of fifteen years trying to scare him, make him suffer for what he did to your family?"

Hope stared back at him, the vein on her forehead popping. "What're you talking about?"

"Ciaran has felt like someone was trying to kill him," I said. "He wasn't sure if it was imagined or real. Neither did I, until today."

Hope's eyes filled with tears. Two bright spots on either cheek flamed red. "You think I would hurt Ciaran? He's the only real friend I have." She turned her gaze to me. "What would you know about it, anyway? You've been fucking him for a month; I've loved him all my life."

"I'm the one he told of his fears, not you." Even as I said it, I knew how childish it sounded.

"You're the fruit of the month, honey, I can guarantee you that," said Hope. "I'll be with him all his life."

"Truth is, you've got motive," said Kevan. "Doesn't take a cop to see that."

Hope swiped under her eyes where tears had smeared her mascara. "That's completely ridiculous."

"I wonder how many times one of his near-death experiences happened when you were in the same place," said Kevan. "I'm sure the police can track that quite easily."

"It all happened a million years ago," said Hope. "And Ciaran's more than paid me back for whatever supposed harm he did to my family. Who do you think got me to come to Hollywood in the first place? I owe my career to Ciaran. If he hadn't believed in me, I'd still be stuck in Boise, Idaho."

"Who else would do this to him?" asked Kevan. "It's got to be you. I'm sure the police will think this is all highly interesting. We'll get the proof eventually, and you'll pay for what you've done." He stepped close to her, pointing a finger near her face. "If he dies, so help me God, I will make you suffer." His voice choked. Blythe grabbed his arm.

"Kevan, come on. Let's go home," said Blythe.

"You can go to hell," whispered Hope. "All of you. Go to hell." Holding her oversized bag to her chest like a shield, she ran out the hospital doors.

None of us said anything for several long seconds. Glancing around, I noticed that the room had hushed, everyone watching our drama unfold.

CHAPTER 30

LOLA AND CLEMENTINE WERE AT HOME when we arrived, having been picked up from school by a sitter. I paced the front room, checking my cell phone every two minutes, while Blythe took the girls aside to tell them that Ciaran was hurt. Blythe made sandwiches and we all tried to eat something, but no one was hungry. I was about to lose my mind with worry, when the hospital called Kevan. Ciaran was out of surgery but asleep. We could come see him in the morning, unless he took a turn for the worse during the night. I felt like this should make me less worried, but I wouldn't feel better until I could see him, touch him, hear him speak.

I don't know if I slept more than a couple hours that night, waking at dawn to stare at the ceiling in the guest room. Not wanting to disturb anyone, I wandered into the kitchen to make a pot of coffee. Kevan was also awake, staring out the window with a coffee filter in his hand, like he had been about to make coffee but had frozen before he could complete his task.

"Good morning," I said, softly, not wanting to startle him.

He turned to greet me. Dressed in an old pair of jeans and a sweatshirt, his eyes were bloodshot, and he looked as haggard as I felt. "Couldn't sleep?" he asked.

"No. Horrible night."

"Me too," he said.

I motioned for him to give me the coffee filter. "Sit, I'll do it."

He did as I asked, sinking heavily into one of the kitchen table chairs. "I feel like an idiot."

"About what?" I asked.

"That I let this feud between us continue. I've already lost Finn. Shouldn't that have taught me how easily I could lose another person I love?"

"It's not that simple when it comes to family," I said.

Given my own feelings about my mother, I understood that family wounds are the deepest kind of pain, making reconciliation almost impossible. These family disputes become so deeply ingrained in our psyches that we cannot let go, cannot allow forgiveness to conquer resentment. We're unwilling to let go of the stories that run like a never-ending tape, those words hurled in anger that cannot be taken back. Once something is said, they remain like photographs posted on the Internet, only worse, because we retain them behind our eyes, pulling them up without search engines or clever algorithms.

The offenses against my mother pile on top of one another, stacks and stacks of them. The school events she did not come to, all the mornings she was too tired (from a night of sex or drugs) to get out of bed and make us something to eat before school, the very fact that she wanted us to call her Sally instead of mom, (*I'm your friend, Bliss, not some matriarchal archetype*), the boyfriend she caught looking at Blythe in the outdoor shower but did not kick out of the house. How about the outdoor shower itself that ran only cold water? *Perhaps a job, dear Sally, so that we might have hot water?* Oh, yes, it comes back in a flash, like it happened yesterday instead of thirty years ago.

I wonder if perhaps the affronts become a comfort to us, like the clothes in our closets we haven't worn for years? We know it might not particularly serve us to hold onto them, as the dress is outdated, the lacy collar too young for us, the color wrong for our complexions, jeans a size too big or small, but we keep them anyway.

Why can't we let go of these family wounds? I suspect the nature of betrayal, cruelty, or abandonment from those with whom we share the same blood, no matter how we try to forget, feels too big to forgive, because we love them the most. But what if we did let go of injustices, accusations, the ways in which we failed one another? What if we said, *I forgive, I let go, I will move on without ever thinking of it again*?

"He has to be all right, Bliss, or I will never forgive myself for not trying harder," said Kevan.

The coffee maker made spitting noises as the kitchen filled with the pleasant aroma. "He's going to be, Kevan. We're both going to say the things we need to say." I poured coffee in a mug and set it in front of him.

He looked up at me. "What do you want to say to him, Bliss?"

I let out a long sigh. "I have to tell him I love him, and then I have to let him go."

Just then Kevan's phone started buzzing, turning in a circle on the table. He picked it up. "It's a Los Angeles number."

"Hope Manning?"

"Right. Of course." He answered and then was quiet for a moment, obviously listening. "Are you sure?" After he hung up, he put the phone down on the table and looked over at me. "She remembered something and said you would know what she was referring to. Ida Smart, the hairdresser?"

"Moonstone's hairdresser, yes."

"Hope says she remembered who she was, where she knew her from. She remembers her from one of the times she visited Ciaran at college. She said to tell you that she's Willa Fletcher. Hope had a hard time placing her because it had been so long and she was much thinner and older, obviously, than almost twenty years ago."

My heart started pounding hard. "Willa Fletcher? Ida Smart is Willa Fletcher."

"What does that mean?" asked Kevan.

I told him the story Ciaran had told me. "He never heard from her again." Gripping the back of a chair, I swallowed, feeling the few sips of coffee wanting to come up. "Does Hope think Willa is the one behind all this?"

Kevan nodded. "That's exactly what she thinks. She said she remembers how psycho the girl was and that Ciaran didn't really see it until after they'd broken up. She called the authorities, and they're going to bring her in for questioning."

"Could it be? All these years?"

"It's a motive."

"Yes, it is," I agreed.

Kevan's phone rang for the second time. As he listened, his expression changed from worry to relief. "Ciaran's awake. And Bliss, he's asking for you."

* * *

Ciaran's eyes were closed when I entered the room, but as I approached the bed they fluttered open. Both legs were in casts and traction. One arm was covered with a cast from shoulder to fingertips, the other covered just over the forearm. He smiled when he saw me, but his brow furrowed when I started to cry. "Blissful, no crying." His voice sounded weak and blurry, probably from the pain medication. I stood by the bed, careful not to jostle him, and touched my fingertips to his lips.

"Ciaran." I continued to cry.

"Do I look that bad?"

"Yes. Are you in pain?" I asked.

"No, they have me on super drugs." He smiled up at me again. His eyes were glazed and made him appear young and confused. "Did you ski down the mountain all by yourself?"

"No, they had to carry me out of there. I'm never going skiing ever again." I tried a smile but the tears kept coming.

"Now, I said no crying. They've managed to put me back together. I'm going to be fine."

"I was scared, Ciaran. You were so still, and I thought you were lost to me forever."

"I'm tougher than the rest. Now lean down and give me a little kiss."

I did, just brushing my mouth against his chapped lips. He didn't smell like himself, but I didn't care.

"I guess I wasn't crazy after all. Someone really is trying to kill me."

"Ciaran, I have to tell you something. We think we may have a lead on the case."

"A lead?"

I told him of Hope's discovery. "The authorities are questioning Ida, or Willa, right now."

He stared at me, obviously stunned. "Could she have done this, all these years? As vengeance."

"As Kevan said, it's a motive. It's the motive of a deeply disturbed person, but it could be. And Ciaran, if they get her to confess or have enough evidence, she'll be locked up forever. You'll be free."

His eyes shone with tears. I pushed back his thick hair from his forehead. "Bliss, I have to tell you something too." He hesitated, his eyes flickering to the ceiling before coming back to me. "I'm in love with you. I love you."

"What?"

"You're the last item on my bucket list. I want you. I don't want to spend one more day without you. Yesterday, on the slopes, I was certain of it. When I saw you standing up there, scared out of your mind but willing to try this thing for me, I knew you loved me, no matter what we both said about just having fun. I knew I loved you, too, without a doubt, and that if you would have me, however long I have on this earth, I want to spend every day with you by my side. I was going to tell you when you reached me on the side of that mountain and ask if you'd take the risk to love someone like me, who might not be around for long. I wanted to ask you if you were willing to take that chance."

"Ciaran, I love you, too. I would be willing. Of course I would. Anyway, it's no different than anyone else. None of us knows how long we'll have. Loving someone is risking that they could leave you at any moment. One of us will go first and leave the other. That's just the way it is."

"What if it really was Willa all along and she confesses? If it is, I could be free."

"Yes," I said, fighting tears.

"I could live my life like someone who is going to live a long time. I'll decorate the house. And get you to marry me."

I laughed. "Well, let's not get crazy. First we have to get you healthy, and then we can tackle the house."

"And we'll have babies. Lots of babies," he said.

"They have you on some serious drugs."

*　*　*

He fell asleep shortly thereafter. When I stepped into the hallway, Kevan and Blythe were standing by the door to his room. They grinned at me as Blythe held out her arms. I fell into her embrace, my legs still shaking from the heightened emotion of the last hour.

"Babies?" asked Blythe. "Dare I hope?"

"Please tell me you didn't hear all that?"

"Your sister was listening at the door," said Kevan. "It wasn't me."

Blythe shushed him and poked him in the ribs. "The door was open a few inches. It wasn't my fault."

Kevan smiled at me. "I didn't think a woman could tame him. Guess it took a Heywood sister."

"We really were just supposed to be having fun," I said. "I had no intention of taming him."

"Well, fun is supposed to come as natural fallout when you love someone. And taming comes with the territory when a man loves a woman. We're tamed whether we want to be or not," said Kevan.

"You're hardly tamed," said Blythe.

Kevan's phone buzzed from one of his pockets. While he answered it, Blythe hugged me again. "You sure about this?" she asked. "A real commitment takes a lot of work."

I rolled my eyes. "You don't have to worry. I'm sure."

"I'm so happy for you, Sister Sue. Truly," said Blythe.

Kevan had grown still. "All right. Thanks for letting us know. Yes, I'll pass it along." He nodded into the phone. "Maybe tomorrow. He's pretty fragile today. Yeah, okay, thanks."

Still holding his cell phone in his hand, he looked over at us. "That was Hope. She received a call from the Idaho police. They went out to question Ida Smart, Willa, that is, but she was dead. She hung herself. But there was evidence all over her small apartment that she'd been tracking Ciaran for years. They're still sorting through everything, but it's likely they'll be able to piece together the whole story."

"All these years, tracking him, making him paranoid and fearful. What kind of person devotes themselves to that?" I asked.

"I don't know," said Kevan. "But he's out of danger, Bliss. That's all that matters now."

"And can live a normal life," said Blythe, reaching for my hand.

"I need to call Ardan and Teagan. They're waiting to hear if they should get on planes. Thank God they don't have to."

"Why did she kill herself, though?" I asked Blythe after he left. "Why now?"

The answer to that question was answered after many weeks of the police piecing together evidence from over twenty years. Willa Fletcher had devoted her life to hunting Ciaran, planning near-death experiences and using her brother as the hit man, according to the detailed notes in several of her journals. Further details emerged after they brought the brother in for questioning, including that she had planned for the incident on the mountain to be the last one. Neither she nor the brother thought he would live through the fall. Obviously, they didn't realize he's tougher than the rest. In the final note she left in her journal, she said she wanted the evidence easily accessible to the police so that Ciaran's family might suffer, knowing that he'd been hunted and finally killed because he was a bad person who deserved the ultimate punishment—to live knowing that someone wanted you dead and that it was only a matter of time until they succeeded. Her final act, after succeeding in doling out the final punishment, was to end her own life.

CHAPTER 31

THE NEXT AFTERNOON I was sitting near Ciaran's bed, watching him sleep, when Hope appeared in the doorway of the hospital room dressed in jeans and a sweater and holding an enormous Gucci handbag. She dropped the bag at her feet and crossed her arms over her chest when she spotted me.

"You're still here?" she asked.

"Pardon me?"

"I assumed you would've been kicked to the curb by now. How drugged up do they have him?"

Biting the inside of my lip to keep from lashing out, I remained silent. I looked back to Ciaran. He remained asleep, his face peaceful.

"If you don't mind, I'd like to spend some time alone with him." She crossed over to his bed and perched on the side, taking his hand. "I want to be here when he wakes."

"Hope, I'm the one he wants to see when he wakes." I said in a hushed tone, not wanting to wake Ciaran. "He's really not up for visitors."

She stood, crossing her arms over her chest. "I'm not a visitor. I'm his best friend."

"You know what?" I said. "Let's get this out in the open. I understand you have feelings for him. But he and I love one another and plan to make this work." Even to myself it sounded ridiculous. Why was I arguing with this waif like we were in high school?

"I feel sorry for you," she said. "I truly do. Ciaran's not the type to settle down. With you or anyone, but especially not you."

It took some effort not to let my mouth drop open in shock at her words. Instead, I gathered my own purse—Coach, not Gucci—and walked out the door, knowing if I stayed there I would say and do things I regretted. I was ten feet down the hallway when I felt her come up behind me. She yanked at my left arm, pulling me around to face her. She was surprisingly strong for someone so thin.

"You've got a lot of nerve," she said. "Ciaran's mine. He always has been."

"Maybe you should ask him yourself," I said. "He'll set you straight on that. He's never been yours."

She opened her mouth to say something but seemed to think better of it before jerking away and stomping down the hallway toward Ciaran's room. Just as suddenly, she turned back toward me, marching back to where I stood. "You will not have him. I can get any man I want." Her lips trembled, like she might cry.

I softened then. This was a vulnerable woman who loved a man who did not love her in return. It was a horrible way to feel. I had felt it just yesterday. Until I found out he did love me. I needed to remember that and be kind. What would Blythe do, I wondered?

"I know you two go way back," I said, using the gentlest voice I could muster. "But I'm in his life now. You'll have to choose whether or not you can deal with that, because I'm not going anywhere."

She stood there for a long moment with her arms crossed over her middle like her stomach hurt. Finally, she spoke. "If you hurt him, you'll have to answer to me."

"I won't."

"See that you don't." With that, she reached into her bag and pulled out sunglasses. She put them on, slipped the loops of her bag over her slender shoulder and headed down the hall. I watched as she disappeared through the double doors of the hospital wing. I sighed with relief before heading back to sit by Ciaran's bed. I watched him sleep. After about an hour, he opened his eyes and turned his head to look at me. "You're here," he said. "I dreamt you'd be here when I woke, and here you are." He smiled a dreamy smile, his eyes puffy from sleep.

I took his hand. "I'll always be here when you wake."

"Promise?"

"I do."

"If this moment lasted forever, it would not be long enough. Do you remember the last time I said that to you?"

"Yes. The first time I ever sat in a hot tub in the snow."

"Is it too selfish to ask for a lifetime of those moments?" he asked.

"Maybe, but let's do it anyway." I leaned over and kissed both of his cheeks. "Now go back to sleep. I'll be here when you wake."

EPILOGUE

CIARAN WAS IN THE HOSPITAL FOR A MONTH. When his bones were healed enough to have his casts taken off, we went home to Peregrine. Many months of intense physical therapy followed. While Blythe planned her wedding, I helped Ciaran get better, tackling it with the same dedication I had devoted to all the jobs of my life, only this one was fueled by love, not ambition. He was insistent that he be well enough to dance at Blythe and Ciaran's September wedding, pushing himself hard to regain mobility. By the end of August, he was almost back to his old self, with just a slight limp in his left leg that no one but I could see. During his recuperation, Kevan spent many afternoons and evenings with him. I was not privy to the conversations between the brothers, but Ciaran assured me that things were talked about and resolved in the way men do, without much laboring over the details. There were sports to talk about, after all.

Henry and Mrs. Pennington spent the months between Christmas and September travelling together. They arrived just last night to Moonstone's and planned to stay several weeks. I was still hoping they'd adopt me but couldn't get a commitment from them. Moonstone, looking more beautiful than ever, had made quite a bit of progress on getting out of the friend zone, if her car leaving Sam's cottage at six a.m. yesterday morning was any indication.

During those months away from the hectic and stressful work I'd done all my life, in the Idaho air that allowed me to think and breathe, I decided what I wanted to do next. When Ciaran was well enough, we leased a condominium in Seattle and split our time between there and Peregrine, so that I could be close to my sister in addition to starting a new venture. With Ciaran's help, we set up a non-profit organization that provided makeovers and new clothes for men and women in shelters and on the streets who were interested in finding employment and housing. We also offered resume and interview skills. It was in its infancy still, but with my business skills, I knew I could make it work. I had plans to spread it across the country, but for now we were focused on Seattle. To date, we'd given ten women makeovers, most of them from a battered women's shelter. Six of them had secured employment and apartments. The others were on their way. Ciaran had used his contacts to begin the fundraising process and we'd already raised enough money to continue for a year. I was ablaze with passion for my new work, so much so, I had to fight my daily battle against choosing work over relationships. Ciaran insisted I continue to play, even while trying to save the world (his words) and did pretty well keeping me on track. It wasn't as hard knowing I had him to come home to. The ambition that had once plagued me seemed to have been loved away. I no longer cared about proving anything to anyone by how much money or esteem I had. That chip on my shoulder was gone, along with the boy-named-Sue syndrome. Letting go felt better than all that anger and drive, and it opened up enough space to let love inside.

On the day of Blythe's wedding, I woke in Ciaran's bed alone to the smell of fresh coffee. I could hear him downstairs rummaging about in the kitchen. After a minute or two, wearing only a pair of boxers, he came into the bedroom carrying a tray with a kitchen towel covering it. "Good, you're awake," he said. "We have a lot to do today, so I thought we better eat a good breakfast."

He set the tray on my lap and pulled the towel away. There, set into the middle of a peanut butter sandwich, was a diamond engagement ring—a round cut surrounded in tiny diamonds. It was breathtaking. No makeover required.

He went down on one knee beside the bed. "Bliss Heywood, will you marry me?"

I couldn't speak as he slipped the ring on my finger, leaving a trail of peanut butter. "I wanted to ask you on the day your sister is marrying my brother. It just seems right. All these months you've been by my side in sickness makes it abundantly clear what kind of wife you would make. Will you let me give you some years of health now? I promise to make you a peanut butter sandwich whenever you want and to always have strawberry preserves on hand. As a matter of fact, wait—before you give me your answer, I have a few other promises to make you."

He rose and went out into the hallway, returning with a gold box tied in a purple bow. "Open it." Grinning, he sat back on the bed.

I untied the bow and lifted the lid. Inside were jars and jars of strawberry preserves, enough to last at least a year if not more, even given how much I liked them.

"Made in Oregon, like you," he said. "All the sweetest fruit and girls come from there. I promise never to run out. Also, I'll binge watch Netflix shows anytime you want. I'll always have salted-caramel ice cream in the refrigerator. You can spend whatever you want at Nordstrom. I'll try really hard to be neater." He gestured toward the now-spotless dresser. "It's surprisingly nice to have everything tidy. And I'll support this new venture of yours however I can. I'm so proud of you for what you're doing. Anyway, my point is, you don't have to lose yourself just because we're married."

"All right, you've made a good argument. I'll marry you, Ciaran Lanigan." I held up my left hand. "But first you have to lick the peanut butter off my finger." And so, when I said yes to his proposal, we were laughing. Sex with a playboy gets you more than ice cream and tears, after all. Sometimes you get peanut butter and laughter and a new career. If you're really lucky, the playboy turns into the husband and the party moves into the library.